VULCAN RISING

THE ZAUBERI CHRONICLES

J. W. JUDGE

SCARLET OAK PRESS

scarlet oak press

For permissions and information about special discounts for bulk purchases,
contact Scarlet Oak Press at contact@scarletoakpress.com.

ISBN: 978-1-7336655-8-2 (Paperback)

ISBN: 978-1-7336655-9-9 (eBook)

ISBN: 978-1-954974-00-5 (Hard Cover)

Library of Congress Control Number: 2021903254

Published by Scarlet Oak Press (scarletoakpress.com)

For Jack and Caroline.

May we never discourage your imaginations from running wild and free.

Vulcan Rising

THE ZAUBERI CHRONICLES

CHAPTER 1
JOSEPH

JOSEPH GRUNTED as the boy called through the monitor for a second time, "Can I get up?"

He picked up his phone and looked at the time. 5:57am. It was still a little earlier than Thomas was supposed to get up, but telling him to go back to sleep at this point would just create a fuss and yield the same end-result. "Yeah, buddy, come on down."

Joseph returned his attention to his book and waited for the boy to join him on the couch in the living room. Feet thudded to the floor above him as Thomas slid off the bed. The same feet plodded to the stairs, where the sounds crescendoed. Every time. It was as if he were wearing too-big work boots while trying to navigate the stairs. Joseph found it incomprehensible how such a small person made such a racket.

Thomas paused before resuming his descent at a more rapid pace.

Joseph was flipping the page when Thomas came into the room, not saying anything, and sat right up against him. The sectional comfortably seated five, but Thomas glued himself to Joseph's ribs and burrowed in, snuggling so that Joseph had to put his arm around him. Unusual, but okay.

"Did you sleep okay?"

"Yes."

"Not me," Joseph told him. "I had a hard time getting to sleep. Was thinking about a presentation for work."

"Did you stay awake all night long?" he asked.

"Nah. Just woke up off and on."

Several minutes passed with the only sound being that of occasionally turning the pages of Joseph's book. The boy broke the rhythm without looking up.

"Something dark tried to get me on the stairs."

"What?" Joseph wasn't sure he'd heard correctly, or if he had, what it meant.

"When I was coming down the stairs, something black tried to reach out and get me," Thomas repeated.

"You mean you saw a shadow on the wall?" Joseph prodded.

"No."

"Buddy, we've talked about this. The streetlamp shines through the trees and makes shadows."

"No," he said again.

"What do you mean, *no*?"

The boy finally looked up at Joseph. "That's not what it was. It reached out to get me."

"Why did you wait so long to tell me?"

He shrugged.

"Alright, I'll go check it out," Joseph told him.

The boy clung to his shirt as he shifted his weight to get up.

"Bud, I've got to go check it out. You can either stay in here or go with me."

The decision weighed on the boy. Where did the greater fear lie? He watched Thomas summon his courage.

"Okay, let's go," Thomas said.

He was like his mother in that way. Once he made a decision, he committed to it, come hell or high water. Joseph admired that quality, though it was often a source of consternation.

They walked from the living room, through the kitchen, and into the entryway. Joseph grabbed the bannister and turned to check the stairwell. As best he could tell, everything was as it should have been. "Buddy, I don't see anything here. You sure it wasn't the shadows moving?"

"Yes." Just a stoic *yes*.

"Where was it coming from?"

Thomas pointed to the window on the stairwell wall. Joseph had always thought it an odd place for a window. It seemed that it was placed either too high or too low, depending on your vantage point. But never in the right place. Joseph ascended the stairs so he was standing somewhat above the window. He reached down to check the latches. Locked.

Thomas said, "It was coming through the window, but it's not here anymore."

"How do you know?"

Joseph doubted that it had ever been there to begin with.

Thomas shrugged his little shoulders again. "I can feel it."

He was looking at the place in the wall where the thing must have been as he'd come down the stairs. An icy shiver crawled up Joseph's spine.

Thomas turned to look Joseph in the face. "But it'll be back. I can feel that too."

"Alright then." Joseph wasn't sure what else to say. They stood in the entryway a minute longer, looking at … nothing. "There's nothing here, bud. Let's head back to the living room."

Thomas fell in beside him.

"You want me to turn on a show for you?"

"I guess," he said.

"How about that new Avengers show you've been watching?"

"Sure."

"You hungry for some breakfast?"

"Uh-huh."

"What do you want? Eggs, toaster strudel, cereal, something else?"

"I don't know."

Every day, they had the same conversation. So at least the morning was returning to normal. Without having resolved the issue, they settled back onto the sofa. Joseph flipped through the options on the television until he landed on Thomas' show.

When Agatha came through the front door and into the living room, she was still pouring sweat. She turned on the ceiling fan and lay on the floor on her back with her hand towel over her face.

Thomas asked, "How was the run, mommy?"

She raised her arm and gave him a thumb's up.

Thomas waited a bit before telling her, "You're kind of stinky."

Agatha pulled the towel partway down her face so she could leer at him over the top of it. She rolled onto her right side, reached up, and squeezed Thomas' thigh, making him squeal, squirm, and laugh simultaneously.

"Stop, stop," he begged without much conviction.

When she didn't, his leg flung out and kicked Joseph's book, sending it skittering across the floor.

Joseph gave him a scolding look, eliciting a "Sorry," before he too dove into the fray, attacking the boy's ribs. Once Thomas was thoroughly out of breath, his parents ceased their assault on his most ticklish parts.

Agatha announced, "I'm going to take a shower ... because apparently, I'm stinky."

She looked accusingly at Thomas, who covered his mouth and giggled.

Thomas said, "Wait. I want you to make my breakfast first."

"Your daddy can make it while I'm in the shower."

4

"No, I want you to."

Agatha looked to Joseph for help, but he only raised his hands in the air. "I've already been through this and tried. I got nothing."

Agatha looked to Thomas. "What do you want?"

"Honey Nut Cheerios with a banana cut up in it."

"Alright, get to the table."

As Agatha sliced the banana, Joseph called from the living room, "Thomas, tell your mother what you saw this morning."

Maybe pressing the issue in the light of day would help take some of the sting out of his fear. He thought of himself as baking soda and meat tenderizer to a jellyfish sting.

Thomas didn't answer right away. Joseph went into the kitchen and leaned against the door frame. "Go on, buddy. Tell her."

"What did you see?" Agatha prompted.

Thomas looked down at the table. "It was something dark on the stairs. It came through the window."

"Like a bug?"

"No. Big."

"How big? What did it look like?"

"Like a big black lion, but not exactly. And its tail was moving like a snake."

"And what did it do?" she asked.

"It tried to reach out and get me with its claws. So I ran down the stairs and told Daddy. And then it was gone."

Joseph noticed that Agatha had stopped slicing the banana while Thomas told his story, and some of the color had drained from her cheeks that had been flush from her run.

"Well, that sounds scary," Agatha said. "I tell you what. I'll get some fairy dust today and sprinkle it by the window so that thing can't come back in the window."

"Fairy dust?" Thomas asked.

"Yeah. Fairy dust helps keep any bad creatures out. Right, Daddy?"

Joseph responded with a non-committal, "Uh-huh."

Agatha set Thomas' cereal bowl in front of him and said, "I'm off to the shower now."

Joseph followed her out of the room and whispered, "Don't you think it'd be better to tell him it's not real so he won't be scared of it, instead of playing into it?"

"Is that what you did?" She countered.

"Yes."

"And how did that work?"

He turned his lips down in an expression that said, *I'd rather not concede that you're right.* Agatha recognized her victory.

She wiped the remaining sweat off her forehead and patted his cheek with her wet hand. "Good talk," she said, turning to walk away.

Joseph shrugged his shoulder to wipe his face on his shirt. "You're gross. But also, do you need any company?"

Without turning back around, she wagged her finger at him like she was Dikembe Mutombo. "I do not."

CHAPTER 2
JOSEPH

JOSEPH WAS AWAKENED by a strange noise that came from outside. He propped himself up with an elbow, straining to hear what was no longer there to be heard. He had been sleeping so hard and was entirely unable to discern how loud or quiet the noise had been.

"What was that?" he asked.

"Dunno," came Agatha's croaky response.

"Did it sound like an animal?"

"Don't know. I was too asleep."

Joseph swung his legs off the bed and padded over to the window. He peered through the blinds. The moon bathed the ground and trees in soft light. Joseph, having forgotten to look at the clock as he traipsed across the room, judged that it must be very early morning now by the way the half-moon hung above the western sky.

All was still and quiet. No indications that anything was amiss. But as he got ready to return to bed, two figures in dark hoodies and pants emerged from the gap between his house and his neighbor's and walked into the woods behind the houses, disappearing into the darkness.

Moments later, another animal noise. He stared into the tree line but saw nothing. "Alright," he whispered to himself, having decided what to do next.

Joseph walked to his nightstand, pulled open the top drawer, and retrieved his Smith & Wesson .40. It had lain dormant in there a long time in anticipation of a moment like this one. Joseph pulled on a sweatshirt, pants, and a pair of moccasins.

"Going to check on something," he said to Agatha, who had already closed her eyes again.

"Mm-hmm."

With the pistol snugly in his right hand, he crossed the house to the front door, which he opened and closed with his left hand. He reached under the door mat for the key and locked the door behind him.

Joseph stayed pressed against the house as he walked around the front and down the opposite side as the intruders' route. He wished the siding were a darker color to hide his movement, but he couldn't do anything about that now.

He reached the bottom of the driveway and stopped. Waiting. For what? He had no idea. He couldn't very well go stalking into those woods. Joseph realized that he should have grabbed a flashlight or headlamp. Anything that would provide illumination. He patted his pockets. He hadn't even brought his phone.

So he waited. The only movement was his breath emerging from his mouth and dissipating into the night air. A shrill animal scream ripped the silence apart. To Joseph, it sounded like a horse. Or perhaps a donkey. Something in that family. Still, he saw nothing.

Movement. Three figures emerged from the woods. One was much bulkier than the other two and moved awkwardly. As they exited the shadows into the moonlight, Joseph made out that the third man was carrying something, which contributed to his bulk. Whatever it was struggled against him.

The three men moved quickly without running. And they weren't headed in the direction they'd come from.

They were coming toward his side of the house. Joseph had no idea what to do. Whether to do anything. They were closing ground, not a dozen yards from the bottom of the driveway where Joseph had all but made himself a part of the house.

As the darkly clad men came parallel with him, Joseph finally discerned that the third man's burden was a horse. And a young one. A foal. Something was ... wrong with it.

"Halt." Joseph commanded, surprising himself and everyone else. All three men jerked to a stop, turning in the direction of the sound. The foal whinnied and bucked. It arched its head backward as if trying to headbutt its captor.

"Halt?" asked one of the men.

"Yeah. Stop." Joseph found that he had raised his pistol in their direction. He expected his hand to be shaky. While he was nervous about the situation, his hands were steady. Muscle memory and training were funny things when they took over. Even if the skills had been dormant for a few years.

The same voice said, "Okay. We're stopped. Now what?"

Joseph didn't know *now what*. He hadn't had a plan to this point. "I'm gonna need you to leave."

"What do you think we were doing?" said the man carrying the horse.

The first voice had belonged to the other man wearing a hoodie. Those two flanked the man who hadn't spoken yet. A man who had dressed absurdly well for the situation. Black slacks and dress shirt. And a nice pair of Western boots. Not work boots like the other two. He was definitely the head honcho.

The three men stood in a cluster. All three were larger men than Joseph, although he found it difficult to gage the size of the man carrying the foal.

The lead man finally spoke. "Why don't you step out from the shadow and we can sort this out?"

Joseph realized his advantage, however slight. "I'm good. Put down the horse and be on your way."

"Horse?" scoffed the first voice. "That's not a—"

"Shut up," the man in black instructed.

The left-hand man leaned forward as if to set the animal down. The man in black pointed at him, "Don't." And the third man re-uprighted himself. "We will not do that. We're going to take the ... horse and be on our way."

"No. You aren't," Joseph countered. He had no inkling why he cared what happened to this animal. But whatever was happening seemed inherently bad. Evil, possibly.

"Enough of this," said the middle voice. He ordered, "Gary, handle it."

The man on Joseph's right began stalking toward him, reaching into the front pocket of his hoodie.

A deafening bark. A flash of light. Gary fell into a sitting position, holding his belly. The sounds of the night had stopped. Or maybe it was just that Joseph no longer heard them. His vision was interrupted. The imprint of a flame overlay anything that he looked at directly. His peripheral vision showed him that neither of the other two men were moving.

"Now, you're gonna go." Joseph said. "And you'll leave the horse."

Gary had fallen onto his side and was moaning.

Joseph gave further instructions. "Set the horse down. Gently."

The third man squatted down slowly, setting the animal on the concrete. For the first time now that two arms were no longer wrapped around it, Joseph realized that it wasn't a horse. It was ... what was it?

"Y'all, go on now. And take Gary there with you."

No one objected, though the lead mean lingered, his head tilted to the side. He watched Joseph, as if deciding what to make of him. Then he and the third man got on either side of Gary and started trying to get him upright. His human crutches like a football player being helped off the field. Gary's clothes glistened darkly in moonlight. He would have to be all but carried. He moaned a great deal as they jostled him. Eventually, the third man, a hulking figure, picked Gary up and carried him like an infant.

Joseph watched until they limped into the shadows of the trees that canopied the street and beyond his eyesight. Within a minute, taillights ignited. The reverse lights flickered as the driver put the vehicle into gear. The V-8 engine thrummed as it accelerated and carried them into the night.

Joseph heard the front door open and close. Agatha asked, "Honey, is everything okay?"

Joseph remembered the horse-ish thing lying in the driveway behind him. It wouldn't do for her to see that. He shoved the pistol into the waistband at the small of his back and remembered all the times he'd thought movies were ridiculous when they had somebody do that. But he'd never considered that there was nowhere else to put it when you didn't have a holster. He was just glad the barrel wasn't still hot. He jogged around toward the front of the house. His wife was walking his direction as he rounded the corner.

"Yeah, baby. Just ... um ... a ... uh ... fox."

"A fox? I was looking out the back window but never saw anything."

Joseph was relieved. "Yeah. He came around the side."

"Did you get him?" she asked.

"Yeah. Gotta take him back into the woods and get rid of him," Joseph said.

"Now? Tonight?" she asked.

"Got to. He'll attract coyotes and buzzards. Just go back to bed, and I'll be back shortly."

"Alright. Be careful."

"Yep. Will do." Joseph turned around to go the way he'd come.

When he reached the side of the house again, he saw that the horse creature stood looking at him. It was young. Not more than a few weeks old. He just couldn't believe that he was seeing things correctly. Wings. On a horse.

He walked toward the animal slowly. As he got about forty feet away, the foal got nervous. It started looking around a little wildly and shuffling its hooves.

"Whoa, boy," Joseph said, in not more than a whisper. He held out his hands in front of him in what he thought would be a non-threatening gesture. "I'm not going to hurt you. Just want to see if I can help." He walked as he talked. Slowly. The foal seemed to settle a bit.

Joseph approached to just beyond arm's length and stopped. They stood, taking each other in. Maybe the wings were some sort of prank? Some attachment the guys had put on its back. None of this made a good deal of sense. And why was there a horse in the woods?

Whatever the answer, this was clearly a beautiful creature. All white with a pale mane. White wings that folded onto its back. The moonlight gave it an ethereal quality.

Joseph spoke softly to the animal again. "Hey, boy, where did you come from? Is your momma around?"

As he spoke, he stepped forward and raised his left hand to rub its head between the eyes. The foal snorted and shook its head at the approach, but didn't back away. Joseph kept talking and made contact. After a minute, the foal pushed back against his hand. With his right hand, Joseph rubbed its neck.

"That a boy. Nothing to be scared of. Now I'm just going to reach over here to your shoulder. Good boy."

He didn't know whether the talking was helping the animal. It didn't seem to be hurting, though. And oddly, it was helping him. The sound of his voice keeping him grounded in an otherworldly situation. He didn't know whether the foal was in fact a boy. But that also seemed inconsequential in the moment. Joseph continued to scratch and pet its head with his left hand, while migrating his right back to its wings.

"Holy cow," he whispered. "Those are really yours, aren't they? Yep. There. I can feel it coming right up through your hide."

When Joseph started handling its wing, the foal shrugged its shoulders and shuddered. Then it unfolded them. A majestic transformation. Joseph took an involuntary step backwards. It was white as a ream of printer paper. He realized this was probably a dumb analogy, but it's the first thing that came to him. A wingspan greater than the length of its body from head to tail.

"Wow, buddy. That's ... I mean, that's ... wow."

Joseph took to petting its head and neck again, and it tucked its wings away.

"What are you called? Not a unicorn. You don't have a horn." It occurred to Joseph that paying closer attention during literature class would have been helpful about now. "Icarus? No, that's a Greek guy. What did he do? Fly too close to the sun. Hang on. You're a pegasus, aren't you? That's the one with wings, right? Except you're not real. How can you be? I'm just losing my mind or something. Which is fine, I guess."

The pegasus nuzzled him.

"We're gonna need to get you back home."

CHAPTER 3
JOSEPH

JOSEPH REACHED DOWN and around the foal's front and hind quarters, thinking he'd just carry it back into the woods like a big dog. He squatted, lifted, and grunted in quick succession. "Nope. That's not gonna work."

He set the foal back down, its legs scrambling for purchase on the concrete. He couldn't imagine the strength of that hulking third guy to have carried this thing out of the woods. Not just strength though, but balance and agility. The guy had probably been an offensive lineman. Joseph shook his head, trying to rid himself of the distracting tangent. He needed to focus on the problem at hand.

He went back around to the front of the creature and watched it do a quick shiver to resettle its hair and feathers that Joseph had displaced. Joseph told it, "You're a good bit more stout than I'd figured." They both stood there a minute, looking at each other.

"I've got something," he said. "You're not gonna like it, but it'll do. I've got to get something out of the garage." He pointed over his shoulder. "So you don't go anywhere."

The animal flicked an ear forward. Joseph shook his head at himself as he turned, disbelieving that he'd been waiting on some sign of cognition from the horse. Nope, not a horse. A pegasus. Doubt and disbelief hovered around him like a heavy mist.

He walked over to the flower bed and picked up an unconvincing fake rock that held a key to the garage door. He slid open its compartment, retrieved the key, and replaced the rock.

Joseph applied some counter pressure to the door as he opened it, trying to be as quiet as possible. Their bedroom was above this part of the basement garage. If he woke Agatha to this situation, she would … what would she do? What would any reasonable person do? A pool of blood in the driveway. And nearby, a mythical creature that doesn't actually exist. Yeah, it would be fine.

Joseph came out pushing his wheelbarrow. He'd arranged an old blanket on the bottom. The foal had migrated a few steps and was nibbling at some tufts of dormant grass. He picked the animal up, feeling the strain in his lower back, and set it in the wheelbarrow. It filled up the cart entirely.

Joseph shook his head. "You're just about all legs, aren't you?"

He lifted with the handles, glad that he'd spent a little more on the bigger cart that had two off-road wheels on the front. Hauling a couple hundred pounds on one wheel would have been a chore under the best of conditions. But over the uneven terrain and underbrush of the woods? That would have been nigh on impossible. Might still be.

"Alright then," he said mostly to himself. "Nothing for it but to do it."

Then to the foal as he wheeled it across the backyard toward the tree line, "Don't reckon you're gonna show me the way, huh? Maybe we'll know it when we see it. You don't use the same game trail as the deer, do you?"

The foal snorted.

Joseph pushed into the woods, appreciating the ground cover

of pine straw. He'd been in these woods enough during the daytime to know the grade and have a rough idea of the terrain. But never at night that he could recall. He had a sudden recollection of hearing that his cousin had been bitten by a copperhead while walking under an oak tree at night a couple of months ago. Nearly died. So now he had one more thing to worry about. As if there weren't enough going on.

He wished he'd grabbed a headlamp while he was in the garage. That could've been real handy. At least the moon was still out, its light leaking through the foliage.

The woods were louder in the early hour than he would've expected. Crickets and a few early rising birds doing their darnedest to drown out the metallic thud made by the wheelbarrow every time he hit a tree root or a rock.

The forest noises stopped. So did he. A white shadow approached. The foal had spotted it too and whinnied loudly. Its feet were scrabbling against the wheelbarrow as it tried to stand.

Joseph needed to calm it so he could pay attention to what was heading his way. He couldn't make anything out of the shape. It was tall, narrow at the top and bottom, but bulky in its mid-section.

"Whoa, boy," he breathed. "It's alright. Or maybe it's not. I reckon we're about to find out. But you gotta settle down."

The luminescent figure was a few dozen yards away now. The foal wasn't settling. Its whickering becoming desperate. Then the figure responded in kind.

Joseph finally comprehended what he was seeing. He'd not developed any notion of what an adult pegasus looked like. Until about an hour ago, he hadn't thought about them since middle school. But it was certainly taller than he would have expected. A head taller or more than any horse he was accustomed to seeing. The girth he'd had trouble distinguishing was its wings, which were as white as its coat.

The foal kicked the cart, making a deafening sound against

the silence of the forest. Joseph went to stroke its mane, trying to settle it.

"Do not touch him."

Joseph froze, arm suspended out beside him, hovering near the foal. Dumbstruck. After he realized that his mouth was hanging open a bit, he pulled it closed. Even the foal had stilled.

"Say what?"

The pegasus took another step forward. Now a dozen yards away. "Do not touch him. He is royalty."

"Alright." Joseph rubbed his face roughly with hands. "Look, this is all a bit new to me. What with winged horses being kidna—"

"We are not horses. Do not dare to call us that. Servant animals. We are kings and queens, rulers of lands, overseers of the forests. I am Theiona, regent over these lands until Kleron is of age."

Joseph again found himself at a loss. He was going to need counseling after this. "My apologies. No offense intended. I just … well … I didn't know you were a thing, you know. That you were real."

"Yes. I am aware of your ignorance."

"Now, hold on," Joseph was getting a bit cross at the level of condescension being directed at him. The foal whinnied again, redirecting their attention.

Joseph asked, "What do you want to do here?"

"Return the foal to me."

"I don't think he can stand up and get himself out of this wheelbarrow. I'm gonna have to lift him up out of there."

The pegasus made a sound that Joseph interpreted as a grunt of assent. He reached for it without further protest. When he wrapped his arms under its chest and behind its hind legs, he saw in the periphery that the pegasus flinched and turned its head slightly. Joseph set the foal down. It bolted toward its mother and pulled up in front of her. They nuzzled each other. Then she directed Kleron to get behind her.

"Best I can tell, he's not hurt," Joseph said.

"And those who took him?"

"One of them is in a pretty bad way. The other two took him and left."

Theiona nodded.

"Just so we're clear," Joseph said, "I had nothing to do with this."

"I know your role."

"How?" Joseph asked.

"My subjects have reported to me."

"By who?" Joseph held up a hand. "Hang on. What do you mean, *my role*? I'm about to head home, get back to bed, and wake up to tell my wife about a super weird dream I had."

"We require your help." It looked to Joseph that it pained the pegasus to admit this. To ask anything of him.

"What kind of he—," Joseph interrupted himself. "Doesn't matter. I've got a wife and kid. We've got fall baseball. I can't get tied up in this."

"You are involved already."

"No. I returned your foal. Now I've got to go clean up some blood out of the driveway and come up with some explanation for this that my wife will buy. So I'm gonna head back."

"Tell her the truth. She will understand."

Joseph barked an involuntary laugh. "Yeah. No. That's definitely not the solution."

"They are stealing our young," the pegasus said, sounding desperate.

"Whose young?"

"The offspring of those you think are myth and folklore and legend."

"Oh," was the only response Joseph could offer. "Listen, this has been … something. But I've got to get back now. See if I can't get some shut-eye before the sun comes up."

Joseph pivoted his wheelbarrow and returned the way he'd come. He looked back only once as he walked. Theiona and her foal stood watching him retreat. And it was a retreat. He felt the shame of it flush through his cheeks. But whatever was happening wasn't his concern.

He bounced and banged his way back to the clearing of his backyard. When he returned the wheelbarrow to the basement, he came out with one of Thomas' plastic buckets. What its makers had intended for fun would do other work today. He filled it with water from the spigot and dumped it over the pool of blood, to minor effect.

"Dagummit."

He repeated the effort a couple more times, to be sure. It achieved mostly the same result. While some blood crawled toward the drain at the bottom of the driveway, the rest had already coagulated. Joseph returned the bucket to the garage. He screwed the water hose onto the spigot, unspooled a fair bit, attached the sprayer to the end, and walked back out to the stain on the driveway. He rotated the sprayer's nozzle to the jet setting and set about his work. The edges tore away in crimson ribbons. A dam letting loose the river of blood it had held at bay.

"There we go," he said aloud.

After he rewound the hose, Joseph walked into the garage to get a bag of sand. He poured it liberally over the stained concrete. He'd never used sand for this purpose before. But if it would soak up oil, he reasoned that it would soak up blood too.

He took off his moccasins and hosed them down. In bare feet, he trudged across the basement's cold concrete. He laid them down in front of the extra refrigerator. The warm air blowing out would dry them quicker. He pulled off his clothes, one article at a time, and pitched them into the washing machine. The clock on the wall read 4:37.

"Well, no sense pretending to get any more sleep now."

Joseph traipsed to the guest bathroom to take a shower. After he dried himself off, he realized he hadn't bothered to grab any clean clothes. He walked back into the living room wrapped in a towel and found a bin full of folded clothes from where Agatha had been doing laundry the night before.

"Small miracles," he muttered. Of course, this particular miracle paled in comparison to anything else in the last hour or so.

When Agatha entered the kitchen, Joseph was sitting at the table. Both hands cupped around his coffee mug. He never stirred as she made her coffee. She put in her creamer and sugar, sat down perpendicular to him at the table, and asked, "You okay?"

"Hmm?"

"Are you okay?" she repeated.

"Yeah, I'm all right," Joseph answered.

"You never came back to bed," she said.

"Yep."

Had he been looking her way, Joseph would have seen that Agatha was growing visibly frustrated with the direction of the conversation. If the exchange could be called a conversation.

"Why did you not come back to bed?" she asked.

Joseph finally looked up from his cup of coffee and said, "It was already getting morning by the time I finished."

"What did you do with the body?" she asked.

"Took it back far enough into the woods that anything it attracts won't come up toward the house."

"I thought I heard voices outside."

"Yeah, Wesley next door came to check on things."

She said, "Uh-huh. Did I hear a car too?"

Joseph looked a little surprised, having not thought this far into his story. "Uhh ... yeah, I heard that too. It was up the road."

"Okay," she said. "Seems like it took you a while."

"After I got rid of it, I cleaned up the blood off the driveway. Came back, took a shower. And here I am." Joseph was ashamed of telling all these lies, but what was the alternative? Tell her the truth? He wasn't quite sure he believed it yet himself.

"Alright," she said, bookending the conversation. "You want any eggs or bacon before you go in to work?"

"If you're making some for Thomas, I'll have some too, but don't make it just for me."

"Okay, let me finish my coffee, and I'll get it started."

CHAPTER 4
JOSEPH

THOMAS SCREAMED. A scream of terror and of pain. Joseph jumped out of the bed and ran to the stairs. He took them two at a time, and Agatha followed right behind him. By the time they got to Thomas' room, the scream had devolved into wailing and sobbing.

When Joseph rounded the corner, he saw that Thomas stood in the middle of his bed. In his Batman pajamas. His arms crossed over his chest, clutching himself.

Joseph grabbed him up and held him like an infant. Agatha squeezed in close with them and began patting his leg. When she touched him, the screaming began again. Joseph had a hard time making out his words, but Thomas was reaching toward his leg.

Joseph laid him back on the bed, and pulled up the leg of his pajama bottoms. Agatha hurried across the room and turned on the lamp. Her back was still turned when Joseph found something inexplicable.

"What the hell?"

She scurried back across the room to see blisters and gashes on the boy's leg. Three of the marks ran parallel to each other from his calf to his ankle. The blisters and redness around them made the shape of an elongated hand. Maybe a claw.

Joseph looked at her with fear and questions in his eyes. She offered no answers. Thomas continued to moan in pain.

Agatha gave instructions. "Go get the ointment from our bathroom and an ace bandage. We'll wrap it up, and you can take him to the hospital."

Joseph rushed out of the room to get the supplies.

By the time he returned, Thomas had calmed, though he was still crying. Agatha was sitting on the bed with him, stroking his hair and soothing him, singing softly. She retrieved the items from Joseph and told him to hold on to Thomas. Father and son watched as she applied the Neosporin and wrapped his leg in the bandage.

Joseph asked, "Do you think we should call an ambulance?"

She answered, "No, it's not so bad as that. Just take him up to Children's Hospital."

Joseph cradled the boy again, carrying him down the stairs. Before he opened the garage door, Agatha asked, "Joe, do you think you should put on some clothes first?"

Instinctively, he looked down. All he had on was boxer shorts. He flushed. "Guess I'd better."

"And don't forget your keys," she added.

At the emergency room, Joseph left his car in the U-shaped driveway. He unlatched Thomas from his car seat and carried him inside to the admissions desk. The clerk smiled and asked, "Is he hurt or sick?"

This struck Joseph as odd, but he said, "He's got some burns and cuts."

"Alright," she said. "How did it happen?"

Joseph answered with uncertainty, "I don't know."

The smiling clerk seemed unfazed. "No problem. Go set him

down, and I'll have some paperwork for you to fill out. We'll call you back when someone is ready to see him."

Again, Joseph did as instructed. As he filled out the paperwork, he came to a section asking how the incident happened. For the first time, he asked Thomas what had happened.

In a quiet and trembling voice, the boy said, "It was back."

"What was back?"

"It. The black thing. The black thing was back. From the stairs." His voice was all the quieter as he said it.

"Buddy, the black thing isn't real. I told you that. It's just a nightmare."

"It's not a nightmare," Thomas answered, looking him directly in the eye. "I saw it. I felt it."

The boy just pointed at his leg.

Joseph didn't have an answer for that and looked away. "I don't know what you saw or what you felt. But we can't tell them that. They're gonna think we're nuts. I'll figure out something to write down ... I guess."

Joseph finished scratching out his answers and turned the paperwork in to the front desk. Then they waited. Joseph wrapped his arm over the boy, who rested against his chest.

A young woman approached. "Are you Mr. Walls?" she asked.

Joseph answered, "I am."

She gestured to an otherwise empty waiting room. "Figured I had pretty good odds of getting that right."

He offered a grim smile. The nurse said, "We've got a place ready for y'all. If you'll follow me."

Joseph picked Thomas up again and got in line behind the nurse.

When they entered the exam room, Joseph set Thomas on the bed.

The nurse said, "My name is Jenny. I'm going to check out your leg. Can you stick it out here for me?"

She looked like she was barely old enough to be his babysitter, much less his nurse. She started unwrapping the bandage. Thomas winced and tried to pull his leg back in.

Jenny talked to him gently. "It's alright. I'm almost done with this part. Did your momma wrap this for you?"

"Yes," Thomas answered.

"She did a great job."

After she had fully removed the bandage and inspected everything, she said, "Oh my! What got ahold of you?"

Joseph jumped in with an answer, knowing that he needed to give an explanation before Thomas had a chance to tell her whatever it was he had dreamt up.

"We don't rightly know. He started hollering in the middle of the night. Must've got scraped up in the woods and started having a reaction later."

Thomas shook his head. "Huh-uh. I told you it was that black thing that came to get me. The one from before."

The nurse looked at Joseph, then at Thomas. "Tell me about the black thing. Was it a dog? Sit up and let me check under your shirt."

"Not a dog, really. Bigger. Like a lion. And it was in my room."

As Thomas answered, she searched his torso, arms, and legs for any other signs of trauma. Raising and lowering his arms. Pulling up the pants legs on his pajama bottoms.

"Was it a coyote?"

"No. If it was a coyote, I could've talked to it."

The nurse wasn't tending to him anymore. Joseph could see that she was doing her best to figure out what the kid was talking about.

"Okay, so something black tore up your legs, but how did you get those burns?"

"It did that too."

"How?"

Thomas' eyes started welling up. His lip quivered. Joseph put his hand on the boy's shoulder. "It's alright, buddy. Just tell her."

The boy tried to recompose himself. The nurse squatted down right beside him.

"When it grabbed my leg and started trying to pull me, that's when I screamed. It kept tugging until it heard Daddy. Then it went away."

"Where did it go?"

"I don't know. Away."

"But how did it get out?" she asked.

Thomas shrugged.

The nurse looked to Joseph, who shrugged as well.

"I think he got into some poison oak or something. I don't know."

The nurse appeared to be skeptical. And for good reason, Joseph thought.

"Thomas, I'm going to have your daddy step out of the room for a minute. I've just got a couple more questions for you."

Joseph's face reddened. "The hell I am," he hissed.

Thomas covered his mouth and pointed, "Daddy, you said hell. You're not supposed to say that."

Joseph forced a smile down at the boy. "You're right, bud. I shouldn't have said that."

"Mr. Walls, please. Make this easy. I have a couple of questions I have to ask him. You can wait right outside the door."

Joseph understood the implication. He was leaving the room one way or another. It was a matter of whether he was going to make a fuss about it.

"Bud, I'm gonna be right there in the hallway. You answer Miss Jenny's questions."

"Alright, Daddy."

Joseph let himself out, and the door closed behind him. He crossed his arms and leaned against the wall. He realized how tired he was as his shoulders slumped. A couple straight nights of uninterrupted sleep would be really nice.

He wasn't standing there for more than a minute or two before the nurse popped back out.

"Well, what'd he say? That we're awful and hit him? Or burn him with cigarettes?"

"I'm not accusing you of anything. But I have to ask the questions."

"Well?"

"He gave me the same story again."

"He's got a bit of an imagination." Joseph pushed himself off the wall and stood upright. "Look, he told us the same thing. I don't know what happened. I just woke up to him hollering."

"Any animals in the house?"

"A dog. But not one that could or did do this," gesturing back toward the room.

"Did he come into contact with any open flame?"

"No."

"Any chemicals?"

"Only the regular cleaning stuff. But those are under the kitchen sink or in the hall closet. He hadn't been into them. He was in bed."

"What about earlier in the day?"

"I mean, I wasn't home all day, but my wife didn't say anything."

The nurse made notes on the tablet as they talked.

"What happens next?" he asked.

"We'll go back in there, and I'll clean out those cuts real good. The nurse practitioner will come by, check him out, probably ask some of the same questions. She'll probably prescribe an antibiotic for him. If he needs anything for the pain, he can take children's ibuprofen or Tylenol."

"Is he going to need stitches?"

"No, they're not deep enough for that. They'll heal on their own. But he may wind up with a set of scars."

"Yeah, it's a shame he doesn't have a better story to go with it."

"I don't know," the nurse flashed a smile. "Some creepy black thing trying to drag him out of bed is a pretty good story."

"Ha!" Joseph barked a laugh despite the situation. "I reckon so."

When they re-entered the room, Thomas fidgeted with the sheets and wore his most earnest expression. "Daddy, do I have to go to school tomorrow?"

Joseph looked at his watch. "Tomorrow is today now, so I guess you probably don't."

"Cool." Now he was all smiles. "Do you have to go to work?"

"Yep. I still have work."

The nurse said, "Thomas, I've got to get a good look at those cuts and make sure they're clean. It's going to sting a bit, okay?"

"Okay," he answered quietly.

"Why don't you tell me about your favorite TV show?"

Thomas started telling her about his favorite Avengers and the bad guys they faced. Joseph tuned out the conversation and allowed himself to wonder what exactly was happening.

CHAPTER 5

AGATHA

AGATHA SHUT her car door and looked south. Vulcan was there on his pedestal, overlooking the city. Watching. It had been a long time since she'd been in this realm. Or at the very least, it had felt like a long time. She was a different person now. A softer person. Living a normal life. Or imitating it as best she could.

And now, she was being dragged back.

She had no doubt that Vulcan had something to do with it. He always had something to do with it. For a hundred and fifty years, his particular brand of venom had rained down on this city.

But why this? Why now? Everything had been more or less dormant for the better part of a decade.

And Thomas was just enamored with that statue.

Mommy, Vulcan is the Roman god of fire.

Mommy, Vulcan is the tallest cast iron statue in the world. Never mind that he has no idea of what cast iron is.

Mommy, the Vulcan statue is 56 feet big.

It was hard to tolerate when she'd spent fifteen years fighting him and his ilk, trying to keep him from subjugating her people. Or exterminating them.

But that was a problem for another day. Right now, she had a more pressing issue to attend to. She turned to the building's entrance and took an anticipatory breath. The persona she was slipping into felt like the real her again. Like pulling on her favorite pair of well-worn jeans.

Agatha stepped off the elevator and brushed past the receptionist, who called after her, "Can I help you?"

Agatha answered, "No," as she strode toward double doors at the back of the floor of offices and cubicles.

There was a weak, "Ma'am, you can't ..." that either trailed off or decided on another course of action.

In her desk outside his office, the Warden's assistant delivered an even more gratifying response. No words. Just a sharp intake of breath. Agatha flung the doors open with a magnificent crash.

"Agatha," the Warden greeted her with a scowl as she entered. "Only you would have the temerity to force your way into my chambers like this. A phone call would have sufficed. Or perhaps you might even have scheduled an appointment."

His voice dripped with polite contempt. But she ignored it altogether.

"I would've expected you'd have fixed those doors by now."

He had recovered his composure somewhat. "They are fixed," he said. "Or at least, they're fixed as to most people."

A smirk showed itself at one corner of her mouth.

The Warden gestured to a chair, "Would you care to take a seat?"

When Agatha plopped down, she found that the chair was lower than it should have been. She had forgotten that the chairs he kept for guests sat lower than his own chair so he could leer down at them and make himself seem a more imposing figure.

"I'm not here to catch up on old times."

"You don't say. How long *has* it been?" he wondered.

"A lifetime?"

The Warden frowned. "That's not nice. Not nice at all."

Agatha's smirk worked itself into a grin. "Nice never worked very well for me."

"Your sister was always much nicer," he said.

The grin disappeared now. "And look what that got her."

"Geez, Agatha, do you have no heart?"

She leaned in, invading the space above his desk, causing the Warden to push backward in his oversized, executive chair. "Oh, I have a heart. It's dark and full of memories. Would you like to hear some of them?"

The Warden tried to recompose himself. He pulled at the bottom of his waistcoat and straightened his tie. "No, I don't think that would … uh … benefit either of us. And it may deviate from the purpose of your visit. Which is what, exactly? Because I recall us having an agreement."

Agatha crossed her arms over her chest. "We *did* have an agreement."

The Warden put on a confused expression. "Do we not now?"

"I don't know. Do we?"

"Stop answering questions with questions." The Warden was growing weary of the exchange. "I don't have time for this nonsense. Either get on with what you're here for or get out."

Agatha gestured to the door. "We've pretty well established that I'll come and go as I see fit. As for our agreement, it was really simple. All you had to do was leave me and mine alone. But you couldn't. And so I'm here to provide some clarification."

"I did. I have," he protested. "I have no idea what you're on about."

Agatha watched him, measuring his words, his demeanor.

"My boy is in the hospital right now with burns and claw marks on his legs. Your cat was in my house."

Now it was the Warden's turn to evaluate her. "My cat, as you call him, has been nowhere. I have him chained up. Still."

"How sure are you about that?" Agatha asked.

"Quite," he answered. He grabbed the top of the monitor on his desk as if to swivel it. "Would you like to see?"

"No, I don't need to see it." Something was different about that situation than she had expected, but she couldn't place it. "Are there others like it?"

"Of course, there are others," he said.

Agatha specified, "Are there others *here?*"

"Ah. As for that, I do not know. I'm not aware of any."

Agatha wandered over to the outer wall of the office and walked her fingers across the spines of the books shelved there on dark-stained built-ins. The entire office projecting a position of authority. She turned to face him again.

"Listen to me. I'm living out a quiet, blue-collar existence in the suburbs. I'm keeping my end of the bargain. But things are happening. Things not of my doing—"

"Nor of mine," the Warden interjected.

"We'll see if that bears out. You'll recall that you have taken quite enough from me. You'd be surprised how little provocation I require from you to help you get your comeuppance."

"Still quibbling over a couple of unterlegen from twenty years ago, I see."

Agatha's face flushed with anger. "Careful. You'll not use that word around me. And you'll absolutely not refer to my friends as such."

"Regardless, you'll recall having some culpability for that, I suspect."

That still stung. Agatha felt her heart racing. She flexed her hands instinctively. The Warden had glanced down at her hands too. Rather than do something regrettable, Agatha swiveled and started toward the door. "I've got to get home before Joseph."

"Where does he think you are right now?"

"Home, fretting over my son like a good mother," she said.

"And what's he think happened to the boy?" the Warden asked.

"He'll think whatever the doctor tells him to think. Probably some sort of reaction to something. An allergy. I don't know. He's trusting like that."

"You haven't told him? How much does he know?" the Warden asked.

"I told you. A quiet life in the suburbs."

"And the boy? Is he—"

Agatha changed direction back toward the desk. "Don't ask about the boy. Never ask about the boy."

The Warden raised his hands, feigning surrender. "Just curious. That's all."

Agatha held up a finger and made a circling motion. "I'll burn it down. All of it."

"Noted," said the Warden, trying to sound as if his eyes hadn't widened in fear at her gesture.

She headed back toward the doors that were hanging slightly askew and called over her shoulder, "Want me to fix these for you before I go?"

"Thanks. I can handle it."

Agatha paused with a hand on the frame. "You need better security. Can't have just anybody barging in here like this."

"My security is fine, thank you. And to be fair, you're not just anybody, are you?"

"No. No, I am not." That quick grin again. "Remember that. And tell whoever needs to hear it, whoever it is you're answering to — because let's face it, we both know that you're not running this show yourself — to remember that as well."

The Warden acted affronted. "I am the warden of this entire region, Agatha. I answer to no one."

Agatha crossed her arms and cocked her head. Her loathing and contempt on full display.

The Warden continued to defend himself. "But even if there were someone who I collaborated with—"

"Ha! Collaborated. That's giving yourself a lot of credit."

He picked up where he had left off, "—it would be for the benefit of our people. He has ideas, Agatha. We have allowed these unterlegen to relegate us to a lower class for centuries. We live in fear and are subjugated because of it. He can lead us back to greatness. To ruling like we once did. We can avenge the inquisitions and assume our rightful place."

"At what cost?"

"Cost? To whom? These usurpers should understand their place in the order. We can lead the ascendance, taking back what is ours by right."

She had never seen him so passionate. It was scary that someone in power was propagating these ideas. This was going to be a problem, eventually. But she'd have to tend to that another time.

Agatha shook her head. "I don't have time for this right now. I'm only here for one reason. Someone is messing with my boy. Don't let that slurry of bad ideas that's percolating in your head cause you to forget what I said."

She spun on her heel and walked out.

CHAPTER 6
JOSEPH

"DADDY! DADDY!"

Joseph scrunched his eyes to read the clock from across the room. 3:40am. He fumbled for the monitor beside him, punched the button, and asked, "What do you need?"

"Can I come to your bed?" came the boy's request.

"No," Agatha whispered to him.

He relayed the message. "No, buddy. It's too early. Go back to sleep."

"I'm scared," he complained.

"There's nothing to be scared of. Just go back to sleep."

"Yes, there is." It was defiant. A statement of fact.

Thomas whimpered. Joseph was fighting a losing battle and only drawing out its inevitable conclusion by fighting it. "Be up there in a minute."

With a grunt, he shoved off the covers and sat up. The cold air struck him like it had been a bucket of water. A cold spell had hit, and he'd forgotten to turn on the heater. But at least the power bill would be down next month. He pulled on a pair of sweatpants. As he padded down the hallway toward the stairs, he paused to punch a couple of buttons on the thermostat to activate the heater.

Joseph quietly pushed open the door to Thomas' room and knelt down beside his bed.

"What's wrong?"

"I don't want to be alone anymore."

Joseph's dad-heart broke a little when he heard that. "Okay, buddy. Scooch over. I'll lay down beside you for a couple minutes. Let me have some of those covers."

They nestled in, and within a few minutes, the boy fell asleep again. Joseph didn't. He'd always found it impossible to sleep with another person touching him. He shuddered in movie scenes when couples slept all wrapped around each other. Are there actually monsters who sleep like that?

Thomas snored gently. Joseph had finished his work here. As he began the slow process of extracting himself from the bed without waking the boy, Thomas jerked and sat up. "Something fell on my legs!"

"What?"

"Something fell on my legs."

Joseph ran his hand over the bedcovers, hoping it wasn't another water leak like last time. But it wasn't even raining out.

"There's nothing here," he determined.

The boy argued, "Uh-huh. Look at the leaves."

Joseph strained his eyes in the dark, assisted by the dim glow of the Captain America night light. He scoured the middle of the bed where the boy had curled his legs up. There were no leaves.

"There's nothing here. That's just the bedspread."

Rather than conceding that his imagination was running wild, Thomas said, "It's an animal. He's curled up by my feet. And he's heavy."

Joseph's frustration level was escalating. "Bud, there is nothing here."

"He says he's a giant panda."

"What?" Joseph asked. A question he was tiring of repeating.

"The animal. He says he's a giant panda," the boy replied.

"So he just told you—"

"Daddy, you're interrupting him," Thomas whined at him.

Joseph's already thin patience was now translucent.

"He's not really a giant, like in *Jack and the Beanstalk*. He's just called a giant panda."

"Yeah, I know what a giant panda is."

"He wants to know if we have any bamboo."

"No, we don't have any bamboo. He can walk himself up the road and get some. There's a whole pile of it growing in the empty lot."

"Ning thinks maybe you aren't being a good host. What's a host?"

Joseph sighed. "Somebody who has guests in their house. Ning?"

"That's his name."

"You came up with that pretty quick."

"I didn't come up with it. That's what he told me. He says he's here to keep me company so I won't be alone anymore. And to protect me."

"Protect you? From what?"

"You know," Thomas answered timidly.

"Geez, Thomas. I can't deal with this tonight."

Even in the dark, he saw the boy's eyes well up and heard the whimper he was trying to hold back. Joseph was at a total loss.

"Okay. I'm sorry." Joseph reached down and wiped away the couple of tears that had spilled. "I'm sorry, bud. I was a little rough there. I'll lay here for a few more minutes until you go back to sleep." He patted the boy's pillow. "Lay back down now."

The boy said, his voice still sounding constricted, "I don't need you now. You can go back to your bed."

The unexpected turn confused Joseph. "You sure?"

"Yes. Ning said he'd stay until morning."

There was far too much creativity cycling through the boy's brain for it to only be 4:00am. And there was no use trying to make sense of any of it. Joseph worried that he was going to be the weird kid in his class. He might still get another hour of sleep if he headed down now.

"You sure you're good now?"

"I'm good."

"Alright then," said Joseph and patted the boy on the hip.

"Watch out for Ning. You almost hit his nose."

"Right. Sorry."

Joseph pushed himself out of the boy's bed and headed back toward his room. He wasn't sure what was happening, but was relieved that he could try to get some more sleep. When he climbed back into bed, Agatha asked, "Everything okay?"

In the dark, she couldn't see the peculiar expression on his face.

"I guess?"

"What does that mean?" she asked, pushing herself up onto an elbow.

"Well, he said he was scared and didn't want to be alone anymore, but now apparently there's a panda in the bed with him so everything is okay. But there's nothing in the bed other than that boy. Oh, and the panda can talk."

"Okay."

There was silence for a few minutes.

"Things are getting kind of weird around here," Joseph observed.

"I know," Agatha said.

"That's ... not the response I was expecting."

"I know," she said.

"I think we need to talk in the morning."

"I know," she said.

Sleep didn't come easily for Joseph after that. There was too much strangeness going on. When the alarm started fussing at him at 5:00, he felt like he had barely closed his eyes again.

CHAPTER 7

AGATHA

AFTER SEEING the boy off to school, Agatha grabbed a cup of coffee and sat down at the kitchen table across from Joseph.

"Well?" he said

"Well, what?"

"Well, what the heck is happening around here?"

"Why don't you start with telling me what really happened outside the other night?"

She had caught him off guard, and it showed all over his face. He tried to recover. "What do you mean the other night? There was a coyote. I told you that."

"Joseph. Look at me." He looked up from his coffee mug. "Do you think I'm a moron?"

"No, ma'am, I do not."

"Do you think I didn't look outside when that pistol fired?"

"Well, I had—"

"Besides, it was a fox. Or do I misremember that?"

These were not questions that required answers from him, but he couldn't help but keep trying to provide them. "No, you're right. It was a fox." This felt an awful lot like being called to the principal's office.

"Of course, I'm right. And do you think I didn't see three

men out there with one of them laying on the ground and an animal in the driveway?"

"I, uh—"

"Do you think I didn't notice the sand in the driveway to soak up the blood?"

"That might've been from the coyote," he said.

"Fox. It wasn't." Agatha said flatly.

"Then, no, I expect you saw all those things."

"So why don't you tell me what happened?"

"It's kinda hard to explain," Joseph fidgeted with some crumbs on the table, like a child caught in mischief.

"Try me. I've got time."

"Not really sure where to start. I'm not even really sure what happened."

"How about I tell you something that maybe will make it a little easier for you to tell me?"

"Okay."

"This is going to be a little hard for you to hear," she warned.

She had surprised him again. "What does that mean?"

"That means there's something about me I haven't told you."

"Oh boy. Alright. Go for it, I guess."

"I am … well, we don't really have the right word for it."

"What do you mean *we* don't have a word for it?" Joseph asked.

"In English. We don't have the right word for it in English," Agatha explained.

"Are you meaning to tell me you speak another language? I thought it was gonna be way different from that by the way you were carrying on."

"I do. But that's not what I'm trying to tell you."

"Oh."

"I'm … you could say I'm a witch."

Joseph gawked at her.

"Did you hear me?" she asked.

"I don't rightly know."

"I said I'm a witch," she repeated.

"Yep. I heard you then." Joseph took a deep breath and exhaled. "I need a cigarette."

"You don't smoke."

"I *didn't* smoke. I do now."

"You don't even have any cigarettes."

"I will have when I get back from the store. Then I'm gonna have a smoke."

Joseph got up from the table, snagged his keys off the wall and went down to the basement. The garage door raised and lowered. She drank her coffee and flipped through the news feed on her phone. She'd always wondered what this moment would be like. When this secret would see the light. It was bound to eventually. She'd even had the conversation with him dozens of times in her head. Each time it took a different direction. None of them had involved Joseph going for a pack of smokes during the middle of it, though. That was a new wrinkle.

About fifteen minutes later, the garage door raised again. Joseph's truck door opened and closed. Shortly after that, she heard a good deal of coughing. She laughed. The whole thing was absurd. Agatha took her coffee mug to the sink, rinsed it, and loaded it into the dishwasher.

When she got outside, Agatha asked, "How's the smoking going?"

"I think it's gonna take some getting used to."

"You want to pick a different vice?"

"Nah. I'll stick with this for now."

He took another drag and coughed some more. "So do you do spells and potions and whatnot?"

"No, I'm not that kind of witch."

"There are different kinds of witches?"

"Yes," she answered.

Leaning against the house, Joseph looked at her sideways. Until now, he'd been staring off into the tree line. She knew he was trying to wrap his mind around this new revelation. "Are you a good witch?"

"Like, am I good at being a witch? Yeah, I guess I am."

"No," Joseph shook his head. "Are you a good witch, like Glinda the Good Witch?"

"Oh. Well, I guess it depends whose side you're on."

"There are sides?"

"Oh yes," she said, "there are most definitely sides."

"Then I reckon I'm on your side."

"In that case, you'll find that I'm a good witch."

"Alright," Joseph said. Several minutes of silence followed. Agatha let him have them. She imagined this was tough to process. She'd grown up with it, immersed in it, and there had still been things that made her blink with disbelief.

"You said there were several kinds of witches?"

"Yes."

"What kind of witch are you?"

"A zauberin. It means, like, sorceress or enchantress. I can talk to animals."

"Like, you can talk to the dog?"

"I could. I don't. He's an idiot."

"That confirms my suspicion." He looked at his half-smoked cigarette before grinding it under his boot. Joseph nodded and smiled for the first time all morning, "I'm gonna need something stronger."

"You'd better get on to work."

"Yep." He walked back into the garage and opened the door to his truck. He turned back toward Agatha. "Seems kinda weird to be going to work after this."

"It'll be fine. Nothing's changed." Joseph laughed an unexpected laugh. Agatha smiled, and he pulled the door closed. After he started the truck, she knocked on the window.

When it had stopped lowering, she said, "Tonight, you can tell me what happened the other night."

"Oh, yeah," he said, having forgotten he still had his tale to tell.

"Have a good day. Good luck with your presentation."

"You too. Or, yeah. You know."

He raised the window, shaking his head at himself, and started backing out.

CHAPTER 8

AGATHA

FROM ACROSS THE HOUSE, Elle yelled, "Agatha, your boyfriend is at the door!"

Agatha hated her for that. She jumped up from her bed and hurried to the door before Elle could inflict further embarrassment. The girls passed each other in the hallway. When Elle made kissy noises, Agatha stuck her nose up, trying to take the high ground. Ms. Nancy had threatened to ring Agatha's neck if she didn't control her anger. Five years in, and that's what they were still struggling with.

She opened the front door. Will stood there with a long piece of grass hanging out of his mouth like he was some cowboy. Or what he thought a cowboy might do.

"Hey," she said.

"Hey, what are up to?"

"*Not* doing chores," she answered.

"Want to go for a hike?"

"Where at?"

"The trail behind the tennis courts. It goes to an old pump house, and runs along the creek for a bit."

She shrugged and looked down to assess what she was wearing — jean shorts so faded that the blue had about run out of them and a white Van Halen shirt she'd lifted from Elle's clean laundry pile. She'd be pissed if it got ruined. "Okay." Then turning back in to the house, "Elle, I'm going out."

"Don't care," was the response from the back of the house.

"Y'all are so sweet to each other," Will said.

"Whatever. What's in the backpack?"

"Water. Snacks. Sandwiches. Compass. Knife. The usual."

"Geez, how long are you planning to be gone?"

Now it was Will's turn to shrug.

It was the thing about him that most amused her. He was always over-prepared. For every situation. Meanwhile, she couldn't count the number of times she'd been told that if her head wasn't screwed on, she'd forget it too.

They walked the couple of blocks to the park with Will talking the whole time about baseball and Michael Jordan on the Barons and how they had to go see him. Agatha responded where expected, but the conversation didn't really require much input from her. Will could talk all day about anything. About nothing.

When they got to the tennis courts, Will took the lead. They walked along the outside of the chain-link fence on the edge of the concrete and tried to avoid overgrown weeds and fire ant mounds.

Once they got around to the back of the fence, Agatha asked, "Now where?"

There was no obvious path for them to follow.

Will pointed toward a pond that looked more like a swamp.

"That's not a trail."

"It's a trail. It's just covered up a bit."

Will slung his backpack around to the front and started rummaging through it. He handed her an aerosol can. Bug spray.

"Here, we're going to need this."

Agatha rolled her eyes at him. He smiled. And she began

forming a cloud of repellent around herself. She handed the can back to him, and he put it back in his bag.

"You're not going to use it?"

"No. I rubbed myself down with a dryer sheet and stuck one in my hat. Heard that works."

He lifted his hat off his head to show her.

"You're an idiot," she laughed. "You're going to get malaria from the hoards of mosquitoes that feast on you."

"Nah. It's gonna work. You'll see." Will slapped his neck. "Maybe."

They started down the remnants of a footpath that may once have been a trail. Looking ahead, she just made out a building recessed in the shadows of a canopy of trees at the far end of the pond. The layer of algae and bugs that blanketed the water looked like prime grounds for snakes and alligators.

The path took them around the pond's edge, alongside the cattails. The details of the pump house emerged. Shuttered windows. A partially collapsed roof. A mill wheel that probably hadn't turned in the last half century.

"I'm not going in that place," Agatha called to Will up ahead of her.

"Yeah, me either. I hear it's haunted."

"It's not haunted. You just made that up."

"Maybe, maybe not. But you're too chicken to find out," he teased.

"I'm not chicken. And I'm not falling for that."

He whirled around and raised his arms in a gesture that said, *If you say so.* He always tried to shame her into things they were both otherwise too scared to do. It usually worked. A dare was a hard thing to turn down.

The path carried them right to the door of the pump house before it meandered off into the woods.

"Is this really what we came out here for, to go in this rundown pile of crap?"

"No. It's a bonus. But if you're too scared to go in, it's fine. I mean, you are a girl, so ..."

She turned and walked up to the door. It was more ornate than she'd expected. The years had worn away the finer details, but there was a landscape carved into its surface. She ran her fingers over the cascading hills and trees, a house in the foreground. She reached down to the brass door handle and turned it. The latch clacked. She pushed the door open.

One deep breath and Agatha stepped inside before she could convince herself to do otherwise. It wasn't as dark as she'd expected. The collapsed roof allowed in light that filtered through the foliage above it, giving everything a greenish hue. She saw the source of the collapse, a giant limb from one of the ancient trees. Large enough of itself to have been a tree. The pump house was a single room. Other than the dirt and debris that had accumulated on the rotting floorboards, it was empty.

She said over her shoulder, "Nothing here, you big wuss."

Will peaked his head in before the rest of him emerged. He walked up beside her. "Well, that's disappointing."

They stood there a minute longer until Will announced, "Alright, let's go. There's something I want to show you."

They headed down the path and into the woods, leaving the decidedly unhaunted pump house behind them. The burbling sounds of the creek to their right.

After a while, Agatha asked, "So where are we going?"

"You'll have to wait and see."

"It better not be something dumb."

Will shrugged, "Maybe it is and maybe it's not. But it's not that far, and you can judge for yourself."

She really hoped he was right. It was getting to be stifling hot. She'd just about kill to go lay in the creek for a bit. But her mother had told her, "You're becoming a woman now. No more swimming with the boys unless you have a swimsuit," which she didn't.

Will announced, "We're here."

"We're where?"

"This is what I wanted to show you."

"A bunch of vines?" Agatha was grumpy because she was hot, and her skepticism was showing.

"No, not just a bunch of vines. Come check out these flowers. They're like something from an alien planet."

Agatha walked over to where Will had squatted. In front of him was a bizarre flower. Its purple petals were laid wide open. And there was a set of what she could only think of as rigid strings with an ornate purple and white design that became red in the center, where it gave way to a green tower topped by something akin to green lobster eyes.

Agatha wanted to still be ornery, but couldn't help but be curious.

"What is it?"

"A passion fruit flower. Want to know its scientific name?"

"Not really." She was curious, but not that curious.

She saw the dejected expression on Will's face, even though he was trying to hide it. He loved sharing information. It's just that he always had so much of it.

"Go ahead. Tell me. I know you're dying to."

"*Passiflora incarnata.*"

"So we came all this way and I'm pouring sweat to see a flower? Even if it is a pretty weird one?"

Will reached into the vines with both hands. He had to turn his face to keep it from getting buried in the foliage. He rummaged around, sweeping his hands through the tangle of vines.

Agatha stood waiting. Arms crossed, hip cocked to the side.

"Will, do you know any other girls who would put up with this?"

He twitched his nose and blew some air out, trying to get a bug away from his face.

"Oh, I'm sorry. Did you want to go hang out with the girls? Maybe go to the mall later? Try out some new makeup together?"

Agatha made a sound as if she were gagging.

"Yeah, that's what I thought." Will's eyes brightened. "Here! Got it."

He pulled his hands out of the tangle of vines. In each was a purple something the size of a baseball and shape of an egg.

"What the heck is that?" Agatha asked.

"Passion fruit."

"And I guess you're going to want me to eat that?"

Will set the passion fruit down in front of him. "Hand me my backpack."

Agatha reached down, grabbed the bag, and handed it over. Will dug out his knife and started slicing one of the purple alien-looking eggs.

He handed her one half and held back the other for himself.

Agatha took what he offered and looked down at it. It was teeming with a yellow and black mass. The light gleaming off of it made it look like it was squirming.

"I'm not touching that."

Will scooped out the interior of his half of the passion fruit with his hand, stuffed it into his mouth, and garbled, "Try it. It's so good."

Agatha really wished she had a spoon. She didn't want to get all sticky.

"Fine. Whatever." And she followed suit.

After they'd both cleared out their seeds, Will said, "You can eat that white meat part too."

"Meat?"

"Yeah, that's what you call that part of the fruit. We learned that in Mr. Walker's class. Where were you?"

She shrugged her apparent indifference. But she kind of hated that Will always knew more than her.

Will quartered his half and handed the knife to her. He started gnawing the white meat off the rind.

Agatha laughed. "You look like a mouse."

He made a rude gesture and said, "Get to it, Fievel."

She did. And it was so much better and sweeter than she'd expected. She sat down beside him on the edge of the trail.

They ate the other one and foraged for more. Until they'd each eaten three and were both sticky messes.

Agatha stood up and started walking away.

"Where are you going?"

She pointed toward the creek as she walked. Will hopped up and followed on her heels. At the worn rocks on the edge of the creek, Agatha flipped off her sneakers and stepped into the water. At its deepest, it came to just below her knees. She bent at the waist and started rinsing her hands and arms, then her face. The summer sun had warmed the water to a tolerable level, but since a canopy of trees overhung the creek, it wasn't overly warm.

Will started out rinsing his hands and forearms, but the situation quickly devolved into him splashing Agatha. When she looked up, glaring at him, he said, "What? I'm trying to help."

A full-scale water fight erupted.

Agatha was in the midst of throwing water at Will when she froze. She held up her hands to Will in a halting gesture. She transitioned her right hand to point behind Will.

"I'm not falling for that."

He continued splashing.

As loud as she could whisper, "Will. Bear."

Will stood at the creek's edge. "Still not falling for it."

Their noise had both attracted the bear and prevented them from hearing him sooner.

Before Agatha delivered a second warning, the bear which had been on all fours swiped at Will, tearing across his lower back. Will yelled in pain and surprise, and spun around. As he did, the bear reared up on its hind legs and bellowed, his claws out and teeth on display. Will fell backwards into the creek and recovered enough to prop himself up with his elbows. But he had otherwise frozen in fear. The bear towered over him.

Agatha crept toward him, careful not to make any sudden movements as the bear continued to apprise them. She was terrified. She put a hand on Will's shoulder as she approached from behind him. He shrieked and jerked away.

The bear began to rage again. It took a step into the water toward them. Agatha stood up from where she had been squatting at Will's shoulder. The bear stood more than a foot taller than her. Its sable fur glistened. Its musky smell strong. It woofed and grumbled at Agatha.

She stared directly into its eyes.

Will scooted further back from the creek's edge so he was beside Agatha. "What are you doing?"

Agatha didn't respond. The bear had quieted somewhat as it and Agatha continued to stare at each other.

Will whispered again, "What are you doing?"

"Trying to talk to him."

"You're what?"

Agatha was no longer paying him any mind, but whatever had been transpiring between her and the bear had shattered with her shift of concentration. It shook its head and dropped back to all fours, pacing the bank between them and the trail.

"Where's your knife?"

He nodded toward the trail, "With my backpack."

When the bear made a last huff and turned up the trail, Agatha's shoulders sagged in relief.

The reprieve was short-lived. Several yards up the path, the bear whirled and began bellowing again. She realized now that it had only been giving itself more room to attack. It hadn't been a retreat, but a tactical decision.

The bear began its charge. Despite the panic Agatha was

feeling, her demeanor remained calm. She raised her arms. She registered that behind her Will was yelling something.

She pressed the heels of her hands together. Her open palms directed at the bear. A comet rocketed out of her hands. The light from it blinding. It struck the bear in the chest, but not squarely because of the angle. Flames splashed across its shoulders and belly. The animal shrieked as the flame burned through its fur and down to the flesh.

The bear made a hard right, crashing through the undergrowth and setting small fires as it went. Its noises were terrible and primal. Fear and pain. The stench of its burned hair and skin and fat was inescapable.

Agatha suddenly leaned over, hands on her knees. She retched a couple of times, and threw up into the creek. When she finished, she straightened and wiped her mouth on her shirtsleeve. She turned to check on Will and found that he was staring at her, mouth hanging open.

"Are you okay?" She walked toward to him with a hand out to help him up.

He scurried backward through the water in a crab walk.

She was shocked. But in any other frame of mind, she wouldn't have been. When she thought about it later, a part of her understood. But it didn't alleviate the pain.

"What ... what was that?" he asked in a tone that was more accusation than question.

Agatha didn't have a response prepared. She couldn't very well tell him and betray everything. She had already broken her word. Not that she had many options. What should she have done, let it maul them? She had done what was necessary.

She shrugged.

Will looked incredulous, but he finally got up.

Agatha tried to turn him by the shoulder. "Let me see your back."

Will jerked away.

"Don't touch me. I mean, what the hell, Agatha?"

She was hurt and ashamed. She'd never been ashamed of what she was before. But she'd never had to face it in the context of someone who was ... other. She turned away so he wouldn't see her eyes well up.

Agatha walked back to Will's pack and tossed in their belongings. Once he'd caught up to her, she handed the pack over to him without another word. They walked home in silence.

Will walked with her up to her front door, and said, "Goodbye."

He had never said *goodbye* before. It was always *catch you later* or *see you tomorrow, or* something else equally innocuous. But never *goodbye.*

Agatha could only bring herself to nod her head. She reached for the door handle and turned back to Will. She cleared her constricted throat. "You can never tell anyone."

"I know."

They watched each other for an extraordinarily long time. Agatha pushed the door open and stepped into the house. She made it to her room and shut the door before the sobbing began.

CHAPTER 9
JOSEPH

JOSEPH SHUFFLED down the stairs after putting Thomas to bed. Agatha was sitting on the bed in a long tee shirt that was thin with age. She had legs that Joseph didn't want to look away from. He remembered an expression his grandmother used to use, "Legs up to her hind end." It had always struck him that it kind of described everybody, but whatever. He didn't really want to be thinking of his grandmother right now.

"So you wanna ...?"

Without ever looking up from her book, she said, "Ask for what you want, Joseph. Don't act like a shy, sixteen-year-old."

"Come on," he complained. "Why do you do this?"

"Because it makes you uncomfortable."

"That's dumb," he argued.

She shrugged her shoulders. "Suit yourself."

Joseph flung himself down onto the bed and grunted. "What do you want me to say, 'Do you want to have intercourse with me?'"

"Yes."

"Yes, you want to? Or yes, that's what you want me to say?" he asked hopefully.

"Why not both?"

"Great!" He sat forward and started tugging at his shirt."

Agatha tutted at him. "Not so fast, cowboy. Aren't you forgetting something?"

He hadn't forgotten. He'd just hoped she had. But he knew better than that. "Hell's bells, Agatha. There's a word for what you're doing. Actually, I'm pretty sure it's two words. But regardless, it's not nice."

She pulled her feet in and let the shirt tail fall further up her legs as her knees bent. "I don't have the slightest idea what you're talking about."

He rubbed his palms against his face. "I'm gonna have to take a cold shower before we talk."

"Well, the quicker you get to talking, the sooner you can — what was it you said? — have intercourse with me."

"You're killing me. Where do you want me to start?"

"How about with you leaving the house?"

He told her every detail he could recall about the three guys exiting the woods with the foal. Their exchange in the driveway. Shooting the one and them leaving. Him loading up the colt into the wheelbarrow and pushing it through the woods. And about the talking horse.

Agatha interrupted, "Wait. Did you call the pegasus a horse?"

"I mean, I … not exactly. But I kind of implied it. Maybe referred to the baby as a horse with wings."

"How did that go?" she asked.

"Not well."

Agatha laughed. "I expect not."

"Hold on," he said. "So you know there are pegasus out there?"

"Yes."

"And that they talk?"

"Yes."

Joseph's eyes widened with the potential of a revelation.

"Does that mean I'm ... uh ... magical ... because I can talk to them?"

She laughed again. "No, dummy. They can talk, just like you and I can."

"Oh. So I'm not magical?"

"No."

"Oh," he said again, both relieved and possibly disappointed. He wasn't quite sure. In fact, he was not sure of a good many things anymore. "How do you know?"

"Because you don't know the super secret handshake," she said.

He raised an eyebrow at her.

"There's no handshake, but you're not magical."

He sat quietly for a couple of minutes. She waited, knowing what was coming next.

"Are there more things you haven't told me?"

"Yes."

"Alright. Well, I have secrets too," he said in pretend petulance.

"No, you don't," she said definitively.

"How do you know?"

"I can read your mind."

Joseph's eyes got wide again, and his head swung toward her. She erupted in laughter. And he pounced on her, ending this chapter of the conversation.

The lights had been off for a while and the house quiet when Joseph asked, "You still awake?"

"Uh-huh."

"I still have some questions," he said.

"That's to be expected, I guess."

"I just kind of realized I don't know all that much about you from before we met."

Agatha said, "That's not a question."

He sighed at her. "Let's start with this. Is there more to you being a witch — should I call you something other than a witch?"

"Witch is fine for now."

"Okay," Joseph started over, "Is there more to you being a witch than just being able to talk to animals."

"Much more."

"Would you care to be more specific?" he asked.

Agatha rolled from her back onto her stomach and propped herself up on her elbows. Joseph pushed himself to a sitting position, leaning back against the headboard. Then he reached and turned on the lamp. He wanted to see her when she told him whatever she was about to say. Through her squint, Agatha said, "I'm kind of a badass," and flushed brightly.

"A badass, huh?"

She had buried her face in her hands to hide her combination of shyness and apprehension at the admission. It muffled her response, "Kind of."

"That's not very specific," Joseph said. "But I can work with it. Can I give us some context here?"

Agatha nodded. "That might be helpful."

"I was a soldier."

"Uh-huh."

"Served tours in Afghanistan and Iraq."

"Uh-huh."

"And survived a helicopter crash."

"Yeah, I recall you having a hitch in your giddy-up still when we met."

"Okay," he said, "So when you say, 'I'm kind of a badass,' what does that mean?"

"It means those things are kind of cool, but have you ever fought a demon?"

Joseph dramatically covered his face with his pillow, reached over and turned off the light, then slid down into the bed.

"You done?" Agatha asked, having not moved.

"Every question leads to about six dozen more. Yeah, I'm done. This is a much longer conversation than I expected. I mean, I'm not gonna be able to sleep, but I have to try."

She was a little concerned. "Did I scare you?"

That first episode of introducing her abilities to someone had left scars that had never quite healed.

"On the contrary," he said, "next time weird noises are coming from outside, I'm sending you out to cast spells at them or whatever."

"I don't do spells," she said.

"Oh."

She leaned in and whispered to him, "I do fire."

CHAPTER 10

AGATHA

JOSEPH CAME out of their room in jeans and a sweatshirt. A Remington Model 700 over his shoulder.

"Where are you going?" Agatha asked.

"Back out to the woods."

Thomas popped his head up from his bowl of cereal. "Daddy, are you going hunting?"

"Not really. Taking it just in case."

"In case what?" the boy asked.

"I've been hearing some coyotes howling during the night."

"Can I go with you?"

"Not this time."

Thomas returned to his cereal and his cartoons, having exhausted his line of questions.

Agatha said, "You won't find what you're looking for."

"You're probably right."

"But you're going anyway?"

"I am."

"Know how long you'll be?"

"Until I get some things sorted out."

She smirked. "Did you take some water and snacks? Sounds like you may be awhile."

He reached around and patted the backpack he was carrying, then headed out the back door.

Agatha returned to folding the towels she'd been working on. She'd been worrying over Joseph. He was a grounded man, who'd had thrust upon him that mythical creatures are not imaginary, his son can talk to animals, and his wife was a witch. Not that she enjoyed referring to herself as a witch. Too many ridiculous connotations. And it didn't really reflect her skill set. But one thing at a time.

She reloaded the basket with the folded towels and picked it up to deliver them to the master bathroom. As she walked through the kitchen, she asked Thomas, "You need anything else to eat?"

"Huh-uh."

"Excuse me?" she prompted.

"I mean, no ma'am."

"Pause your tablet for a second."

Thomas touched the screen.

"You want to go on that hike?"

"Yeah!"

"Okay. Run upstairs and brush your teeth. Put on a bright shirt. We don't want to sneak up on Daddy. And get your duck boots on. The ground's going to be wet still."

Agatha followed her own instructions. She grabbed a backpack with some bottles of water and snacks, uncertain how long they'd be. They reconvened at the back door.

"You ready?"

He nodded. "Where are we going?"

"I don't yet know. I think we'll discover it as we go. Right now we're just going for a walk in the woods."

The morning was crisp. The earliest signs of winter were showing, or at least what passed for winter in the South. The mornings were cooler anyway. The only sure sign of the seasonal change was the arrival of conference championship games in college football. While she was uncertain how long their excursion would last, she was pretty sure they'd all be home in time for the 2:30 SEC game on CBS.

They walked for a while, Agatha helping Thomas down the steeper grades. "Let's go to the creek and follow it for a bit."

Thomas pointed, "Daddy knocked that tree down."

Agatha saw the mess of wood pulp that Thomas was indicating. "He just knocked it down with his hands?"

"No. He said it was eat up with termites. So he kicked it really hard, and it fell down and busted everywhere. It was really funny."

"Sounds like it."

They made their way to the creek and hung a right. "Do you know where the creek goes if you keep following it?"

"Yep, Daddy told me. The Cahaba River, where we go fishing."

"That's great. I didn't know you knew that."

"Daddy tells me lots of things."

"Yeah. He's a good daddy, isn't he?"

Thomas nodded as he jumped over fallen trees, taking the path of greatest resistance.

Agatha sat down and patted the rock beside her. "Thomas, come sit with me."

He skipped from one rock to the next and plopped down beside her.

"Snack?" she asked.

"I'm not hungry."

"I want to talk to you about something."

Thomas' expression transitioned to the same one worn by all children upon hearing those words. Guarded concern.

"The other night, when Daddy came up to your room, and you told him there was a panda—"

"A giant panda," Thomas corrected.

"A giant panda on your bed with you, and Daddy couldn't see it—"

Thomas interjected to defend himself, "I wasn't lying."

"I don't think you were lying."

"Oh. Okay."

"Did the panda talk to you?" Agatha asked.

"He said he was there to make me feel better and keep me safe."

"Did you hear him with your ears? Was he talking out loud?"

"Huh-uh. It was like … with my heart."

"Is that how you talked to him too?"

Thomas nodded.

"Has he come back?"

"He comes after y'all put me to bed. He likes to curl up against my feet."

"What do you call him?"

"Ning. That's what he said his name is. Are we done talking yet?"

"Not yet. Is there anything else you can do that other kids can't?"

Thomas became a statue.

"You're not in trouble."

Agatha tried waiting him out. But he persisted in avoiding her eyes and not responding to the question. He fidgeted with some pebbles between his feet.

"Do you want me to show what I can do?"

Now Thomas looked at her, eagerness in his eyes. Agatha smiled at him. "Okay. Watch my hands."

She cupped her hands and held them between the two of them so that Thomas could see. Agatha stilled herself, and after a few seconds a ball of fire the size of a golf ball formed and hovered above her hands.

"Wow," Thomas whispered.

Agatha smiled at the joy and wonder on his face. She didn't

know if this was the right time to tell him these things. But she also didn't know if there was such a thing as the right time. She'd been about his age when she'd become aware of her abilities. And then only because during a temper tantrum, she'd nearly burned the house down. So maybe sooner was better. Or not. Who knew? Though it seemed like outside circumstances were dictating the timing of Thomas' education.

"Your turn, Thomas."

His look pled with her not to require him to show what he could do. Agatha hunched down to be eye level with him. In something barely north of a whisper, she instructed, "Show me."

Thomas stood up. He walked a few steps away to the carcass of a fallen tree. He reached down and with both hands scooped up the rich, dark soil resting next to it. He brought it back to his mother and sat down beside her. For a minute, he did nothing but sit there with his hands on his lap.

"Go ahead," she prompted.

Thomas raised his arms a few inches from their resting position on his legs. He stared at them, as did Agatha. They watched as plants sprouted from the soil. Leaves emerged on the stalks and unfurled themselves. In a matter of seconds, the plants went from fledgling to flowering.

Thomas looked up to his mother. Her eyes glistened with tears as she said to him, "You are a miracle." Agatha leaned forward and kissed his forehead. "Have you shown anyone else you can do this?"

Thomas shook his head.

"How long have you known?"

He shrugged.

"You must not show anyone else. Only me and Daddy. Do you understand?"

Thomas' cheeks flushed, and he nodded. His eyes shone with tears.

"You aren't in trouble, baby boy."

"I'm not a baby," he argued in a thick voice.

"Of course not. Would you like to know what you are?"

He nodded again.

"You are a schopfer, a creator. I have never met someone before who can do what you can."

Thomas' cheeks remained flushed, but from embarrassment at the praise.

"I can do other things too," he said.

He stood up to return the soil and plants to the ground where he'd gathered it. He squatted down and replaced the earth, tamping it gently to keep the vegetation stable and upright. He then stepped over to a small dogwood tree that was naked and dead. He set his feet and placed his palms on its trunk. After a moment, the bark appeared healthy. The shift was subtle as it moved outward from his hands. Agatha was certain she wouldn't have noticed it if she hadn't been watching so intently. Buds appeared on its branches, then flowered. Within a minute, leaves adorned the tree. Whatever blight had killed it was but a dark memory for the tree.

Thomas returned to her and sat down. She hugged him tightly to her.

"I'm kind of hungry," he said. "What snacks did you bring?"

Agatha handed him the pack. As much as Thomas' abilities awed her, she also feared for him. If anyone knew ... or perhaps they already did.

"Are you cold, Mommy?"

She realized she was trembling.

"No, baby, I'm okay. Finish your snack and let's see if we can't find your daddy."

With a mouthful of small chocolate chip cookies, Thomas announced that he was done. They resumed walking along the creek bank. She walked. Thomas hopped, jumped, ran, fell, and walked in no particular succession.

Up ahead she saw an orange shirt. Joseph was standing still, his rifle raised. She let go of a shrill whistle. Joseph looked over to her and gestured for her to be quiet.

"Thomas, come here," she called quietly. "Your daddy's up ahead. He sees something, so we need to be quiet as a church mouse. You see him?"

Thomas nodded.

"Okay, quiet as you can then."

Agatha smiled to herself as Thomas tromped ahead of her. Despite his best efforts, he was as subtle as a herd of armadillos. Once the boy reached his father, Joseph tucked him up under his right arm and pointed with his left. Agatha placed a hand on Joseph's back and watched over his left shoulder. An enormous buck was grazing. She'd never seen such an elegant rack. He'd somehow survived many hunting seasons.

Agatha leaned into Joseph, "I want to show you something."

She brushed past Joseph, moving toward the buck.

Joseph whispered in protest, "You're going to scare him off."

"He knows we're here. He's not scared."

She approached slowly but with confidence. The buck stopped his grazing. He raised his head up to its full height. Proud and majestic. Agatha stopped when she was an arm's length away. She bowed her head in deference. The buck appeared to return the gesture. The two looked directly at each other for a couple of long minutes.

Agatha turned to Joseph and Thomas. "You may approach."

As the guys started walking, Agatha heard a snort and abruptly turned her head back toward the buck.

"Joseph, leave your rifle."

He did as instructed, and they joined Agatha.

She said, "Show your respect. He is the Elder."

Thomas bowed willingly. Joseph more reluctantly.

"Can I pet him?" Thomas asked.

"You may not," she answered. "He is wild and free, and will not abide it."

She returned her attention fully to the buck. After a minute, she addressed Joseph, "He knows the Pegasus you are seeking. You will not find her."

"I never sai—"

Joseph didn't finish his sentence. Agatha was looking at him with the expression that is universal among married couples when both of them know the other is acting like a moron.

"Fine. Why not?" he asked.

"She wills herself not to be found."

Joseph countered, "Those guys the other night found her."

"They had ... help that you do not have."

"What does that—" Joseph flicked his head in the boy's direction.

"Thomas," Agatha chastised in a commanding tone.

While they had been speaking, the boy had approached the deer. He raised his hand slowly. It lowered its head, and he placed his hand on the flat area between its eyes.

"He said it's okay."

"You shouldn't have asked. It was impertinent."

"I didn't," the boy answered.

"Okay, come back to me now."

Thomas' hand lingered before he complied.

"It's time for us to go," she said, looking at Joseph. "Ready?"

"Yeah, I reckon so."

CHAPTER 11

AGATHA

THOMAS RACED AHEAD of his parents, pulling at vines and branches, pretending to be Tarzan. Joseph and Agatha had walked quietly for a time when Joseph asked, "So, like, Hogwarts — is that a real thing?"

Agatha cocked her head. "Are you asking me if Hogwarts School of Witchcraft and Wizardry is an actual place?"

"Well, no, not Hogwarts exactly. But is there a school for witches and ..."

She watched him fumble for a minute, trying to figure out the right word, before filling in the gap for him.

"Warlocks."

"Right, okay. Is there a school where y'all go to learn about ... everything?"

"No. No school," she said. "We use apprenticeships."

"Nice. Very old school. No pun intended."

Agatha shook her head at him.

Joseph said, "You know, some wives humor their husbands and laugh at their jokes. Even the bad ones."

"Oh, is that what you want — a girl that fawns over you and bats her eyes and tells you how funny you are?" Agatha leaned toward him and pretended to fan her face. In her best Scarlett

O'Hara impression, she said, "Oh, Joe, I do declare, you are just the funniest man I ever met."

"Alright, knock it off. You're right. I don't want that."

"Good, because it's not happening. I won't go pretending things are funny for the next fifty years 'til I'm an old woman putting you in the ground."

"Hang on now," Joseph interjected. "How come I'm the one dying first here?"

Agatha shrugged, "Statistics."

"Eh. Statistics are just numbers. You can make 'em say whatever you want."

"Maybe," she replied. "But there's a bunch of them saying you're going to kick it before I do."

"Alright, whatever. Back to this apprenticeship thing. How does it work?"

Agatha held her mother's hand as they waited for the door to be answered. When the door handle turned, she buried her face in Gertrude's skirt. It smelled of lavender and something else she could never identify that was uniquely her mother's. She closed her eyes as tightly as she could.

"Good morning, Gertrude. How's everyone doing?"

The voice didn't sound like a witch's voice. It wasn't ugly and craggy. Still, she didn't dare look.

"We are all well. Thank you. And we're so glad that you're able to take on Agatha."

At the mention of her name, Agatha clutched the fabric tighter.

"Miss Agatha, how are you today?" came the stranger's voice again. She knew she ought to respond. She couldn't.

"Agatha, honey," her mother squatted down beside her. Agatha pushed herself into her mother's shoulder, "let's not be rude now. This is Ms. Nancy, and she's going to be your special teacher. Can you you look up and say hello?"

Agatha shook her head against her mother.

More firmly this time, Gertrude said, "Agatha, look up and speak to Ms. Nancy."

Slowly, she peeked out. Despite knowing that her mother was a zauberin and having some notion that she might be as well, her only other associations with witches were from Scooby Doo and *The Wizard of Oz*. She was expecting the usual warty crone in all black. Her surprise at Ms. Nancy's appearance must have shown on her face.

Ms. Nancy smiled and held out her hand, "When you can perform glamors, dear, you can always appear to have yourself together."

Agatha nodded. She didn't understand the words entirely, but was pretty sure she got the idea. She shook Ms. Nancy's hand.

"Now, we are well introduced," said Gertrude. "After school this year, the bus will drop you off here at Ms. Nancy's house for ... tutoring."

"What kind of tutoring?" Agatha asked.

Nancy suggested, "Shall we go inside and get out of this miserable heat?"

They gathered around her kitchen table.

"Ms. Nancy teaches gifted students and shows them how to use their abilities."

Agatha protested. "I'm already smarter than the other first graders. I don't need a tutor."

"Yes, well," Gertrude said, "we're not talking about that kind of gif—"

"May I?" interrupted Nancy.

Gertrude nodded.

"Agatha, look at me. You are a *zauberin*."

"I'm n—"

"You are. Do you know what that means?"

"I'm a witch?"

"You are so much more than a witch, Agatha. You are a sorceress, an enchantress. You have powers that are amazing and terrifying."

Agatha was both proud and embarrassed. She didn't want to be different. She had never thought of herself as these things before.

Nancy asked her, "Can you do things that other kids can't?"

Agatha nodded.

"Tell me," Ms. Nancy instructed.

Agatha looked at her mother for guidance. Gertrude nodded at her.

"I can make fire."

"Show me," Ms. Nancy said.

"I don't think—"

"Show me."

Agatha held her hands out in front of her, cupped as if she were holding water in them. She looked into them intently for several seconds before the room erupted into a blinding orange flash. Gertrude shrieked with surprise. Nancy squealed and motioned with her hands, extinguishing the blaze. Everyone sat still for a minute, silent.

Agatha was sure she was about to get kicked out of her apprenticeship before it even started.

"Well," announced Nancy, "that was … something."

She paused as she looked around at her scorched walls and ceiling and the light fixture above the table whose metal and glass were molten distortions. "I'll be honest. I was expecting … less."

Agatha had shrunk to about half her size. Her posture reflected her disposition. "I'm sorry. I'm so sorry. I was nervous."

"Sorry?" Nancy said, now seeing the effect of her words on the girl. "There is nothing to be sorry for. This," she said, gesturing around the room, "this is nothing. A minor inconvenience. I expect we will endure much worse during your training."

"You're still going to teach me?" Agatha was surprised.

"Look at me very closely. I wouldn't not teach you."

Agatha's spine straightened, and her pride began the work of recollecting itself.

Ms. Nancy continued, "I was expecting a spark. Perhaps the smallest flame. Most children, we have to coax their gifts out of them. Give them room to breathe and grow. Like the most delicate of flowers. But not you. Our work together will be containment, constraint. Lest you set the whole world ablaze. In some ways, this is much more difficult. Are you prone to losing your temper?"

Gertrude snorted, trying to stifle a laugh. "Her sister is terrified of her."

Agatha flushed brightly.

"We will work on that as well. You must control your entire self."

Ms. Nancy looked squarely at Agatha.

"Agatha, there is one other thing and you will have to promise me to abide by it. Or we will not go forward. Do you understand?"

Agatha nodded.

"You must never use your abilities around the other children. Ever. Under any circumstances. The results would be devastating. Are you with me?"

"Yes," Agatha said.

"Now promise me."

"I promise that I won't do that around other kids. Ever. Under any circumstances."

"Good. Now when does school start?" Nancy asked.

Gertrude said, "They start on Monday."

"Very well. After school, you will come here. You may come

straight in. You don't have to knock. And we will start getting your abilities in hand. So to speak."

"The fireball thing, how does it work?" Joseph asked.

Now Agatha was the one fumbling. She'd never had to describe how she did it before.

"It's not exactly science, but the best I can tell, I can summon energy — like, a lot of energy — and it builds up, and then I can discharge it like a fireball or a stream of fire, or whatever the situation calls for."

"That's awesome."

"Yeah. It is."

Joseph grinned at her and shook his head, adopting a smug expression that said he knew the answer to his next question. "You didn't do it, did you?"

"Didn't do what?"

"You promised not to use your magic in front of ... uhh ... regular people."

"Regular people?"

"I mean, I don't know. I'm trying to think of a non-offensive way to say it."

Agatha was going to enjoy taking this opportunity to needle him over his word choice. And he would endure it, because what else was he going to do?

"So you went with calling yourself *regular*, which would presumably make me *irregular*, as the right way to phrase that?"

Joseph held up his palms by his shoulders in a universal expression of *I don't know*. "Look, in *Harry Potter*, they call non-magical folk muggles. Do you have a thing like that?"

"Back to *Harry Potter*, are we?" she asked.

"It's really my only reference point."

"Honestly, our abilities are more like comic book superpowers than what you're thinking of. But no, we don't have a term for muggles. Or at least, there is a term, but it's ugly and you won't hear it from me. Mostly, we have names for ourselves, and the types of abilities we have."

"Like what?"

"There are healers. Folks like me who can manipulate energy or matter. And there are people who specialize in chemistry and hexes and stuff."

"So what's the word for us commoners?" he insisted.

"I don't know why you want to know, but whatever. It's unterlegen. It means like inherently inferior or beneath us. But it's the context and connotation that makes it more vicious, and that's not something I can really explain."

Joseph was undeterred and let it roll right off him. She admired that quality in him.

"I'm right though, huh? You used your powers in front of other kids."

"You don't know everything," she protested.

Joseph couldn't hide his gloating, or at least didn't want to. Now it was his turn.

"Actually, it happened twice." Agatha's mood darkened even as she said it. "And the second time, I got summoned by the Zauberat."

"I don't know what that means. But that's definitely a story I need to hear."

"No. You don't."

A couple of minutes passed as they watched Thomas try to cross the creek and stay moderately dry. The water that sloshed out of his boots with each step gave away that fun had been a higher priority than warmth. Agatha wouldn't have expected anything to the contrary. Watching him helped keep her in the present and let her disentangle herself from the quagmire of memories that pulled at her.

Joseph said, "I guess that's why they call it the Magic City."

This elicited an extraordinary eye roll from Agatha.

With as much innocence in his voice as he could muster, Joseph asked, "What?"

"Here's what. First, that was another terrible joke. Like, one of your all-time worst. As in, nominated for the hall of shame of jokes. Second of all, what we've been talking about is exactly why it's called the Magic City."

"Oh, please," he said. "You actually think that, do you?"

She stopped walking and crossed her arms over her chest. "I guess you're going to explain what you think is the real reason to me?"

"I mean, it seems kind of necessary. People started calling it the Magic City in the 1870s when the city just kind of popped up overnight after they put in the railroad."

"Joseph, look at me."

He did.

"Nothing is an accident."

"What does that mean?" he asked.

"Neither of these things excludes the other from being true."

Joseph sighed. "I just can't with this. Not everything is a thing. It's just a dumb nickname."

They both paused, not really wanting to get into whatever this was going to be.

Joseph sighed and asked. "If I rescind my joke, can we go back to normal, like it was before this conversation? Heck, like it was before those guys tried to steal that horse?"

"Pegasus. And there is no normal. There is only what you know now that you didn't know then. If you choose to ignore it now, to be willfully ignorant of it, that doesn't mean it will go away. But it does mean you'll be acting like a coward."

That had come out a good bit harsher than she'd intended. She imagined that his blood was simmering at that comment. His face reddened and she could see his jaw muscles working. She raised a hand up to stop his response before it started.

"I'm not calling you a coward. I believe you have too much inner strength and goodness to walk away from this."

"Whatever this is, I didn't ask for it."

She shrugged. "Yet, here we are."

There were several more minutes, long minutes, of silence while they each tried to figure out how to proceed. She knew Joseph would need to process this, to allow his worldview to shift and broaden. She was mildly surprised he hadn't shut down the conversation already.

"You know this is kind of a lot, right?"

"I do."

"What happened to Thomas, was that ... I don't know ... on purpose?"

He was connecting dots. That would make things easier.

"I don't know."

"But you think it was?"

Agatha nodded her head. "I think that's a possibility."

"So what now?" Joseph asked.

"Nothing ... yet."

"You just told me that someone may have attacked our kid. But you don't know if we should do something."

"I'm working on it. And as best I can tell, you still only half-believe what I'm saying because your brain hasn't caught up to the growing evidence around you that there's a world around you that until very recently, you didn't know existed. So, no, there's nothing we should do. There are people who handle these things. And I'm not one of them anymore."

"But—"

"Stop. You have all this newly acquired information, so you think you need to act on it. I appreciate about you that you're a fixer. But you're not in a position to fix anything here. Besides, we don't even know to a certainty that there's anything that needs fixing."

"What about Thomas?"

"What about him?"

"He thinks he can talk to animals."

"He *can* talk to animals. You saw it for yourself. Besides, he agrees with me that Waffles is a moron. I told him it can be our secret for now. Just the three of us."

"Okay."

"Okay? No more questions?"

"I have some thinking to do. I'll be back with more, I expect."

"I expect you will."

CHAPTER 12
JOSEPH

JOSEPH POKED Thomas in the ribs to get his attention. The boy squidged down to protect his ticklish parts. Joseph said, "Pause your show for a sec."

Thomas hit the button on the remote and the Ninja Turtles halted their assault on Splinter and company.

Even though he already knew what the answer would be, Joseph asked Thomas, "You want to go fishing or hiking?"

Sometimes it was just fun to hear the answer.

"You don't have work today?"

"Nope. Sunday, remember?"

"Oh, yeah."

"So, fishing or hiking?" Joseph asked again.

"Umm … since we went hiking yesterday, fishing!"

"From the shore? Or do you want to take the canoe?"

"Canoe."

"I had a feeling that would be the case. Go get dressed. The park opens at 7:00, and we want to be there when it does."

"So we can get to the good spots before anybody else?"

"That's right. Now go on, and I'll make you some eggs."

Thomas bounded back down the stairs a couple minutes

later, wearing an Avengers sweatshirt along with pants that didn't match.

"Did you put your pajamas in the hamper?"

Thomas let out an exasperated groan.

"On your way back up, stop and ask your mother if she wants any breakfast."

Joseph thought this was pretty clever. He didn't want to have to tell the boy to change clothes, but knew Agatha wouldn't stand for the pairing. When he heard Thomas whining that those were his favorite shirt and favorite pants, he knew it'd had the intended affect.

By the time they'd finished breakfast and cleaned up the dishes, it was 6:30. "Alright, bud. You ready to head out?"

"Do you still have to get the stuff ready?"

"Nope. Truck's already loaded, and the canoe's in the back."

"How'd you know that's what I was going to pick?"

"Just had a hunch."

"Did you get my life jacket? I have to wear it in the boat, remember?"

"I did. Tell your mother bye and let's get rolling."

Thomas went over to where Agatha was still sitting with her cup of coffee at the table. Thomas hugged her around the waist, and she moved aside his haystack hair to kiss him on the forehead.

"You couldn't have brushed that mess?" she asked Joseph.

"He's gonna have a hat on. Besides, the fish don't care what his hair looks like."

She rolled her eyes. "What time will y'all be back?"

"Dunno. Depends on the fish. Probably around lunch."

"Send me pictures," she instructed before he shut the door.

They got off the highway to take the back entrance to the park. The quiet little road took them to the attendant's booth. Joseph drove up and rolled his window down. The park attendant covered her mouth with her arm to hide a yawn.

"Sorry about that," she said. "Welcome to Oak Mountain State Park. Y'all are early this morning. I barely just got here."

Joseph smirked, "Well, early birds and worms and all that."

"Alright, how many are you?"

"One adult, one child."

"Seven dollars."

Joseph pulled three bills out of his wallet and handed them across.

He asked, "Is either lake catching better than the other?"

"I hear Lunker has been of late. But there ain't no accounting for it. It's basically the same water."

Joseph tipped his cap to her. "Thank you, ma'am. Have a good one."

"You too."

He pulled through and took a left at the Y-shaped intersection. They followed the park road for a half-mile until the lake opened made the gravel exit to the left and swung around so he could back the truck down to the boat launch.

As Joseph put the truck in park, he told Thomas, "I'm just going to yank the canoe out, then park the truck in that lot over there."

Thomas was already unbuckling his seatbelt.

"Can I go ahead and get out?"

Joseph had vague memories of the anticipation and excitement he knew Thomas was experiencing. Of course, he hadn't even had a seatbelt to contend with back then, much less a car seat. It's a miracle they'd survived childhood at all.

"Yeah, bud, you can get out."

Thomas slid out as soon as Joseph opened his door.

They went around to the back of the truck, where Joseph loosened, then unlatched the ratchet strap that had secured the canoe. He gave a tug on the boat and kept on pulling as it came

with him. Joseph set the nose on the ground before he pulled
the tail end off the tailgate. Finally, he retrieved the back end of
the boat and set it on the ground.

"Let's go park the truck. Then we can go."

"Can I stay here with the boat while you park?"

Joseph considered it. "That's fine. Get your life jacket on so
you'll be ready."

He knew Agatha wouldn't have made the same decision. Her
risk tolerance was a bit lower when it came to the boy. After
parking the truck, he snatched his waterproof box off the
passenger seat and filled it with his keys, wallet, and phone.

When he got back to the canoe, Thomas was already seated
on clasped. Ready to go. Joseph gave the boat a shove. The
canoe made a combination of noises as it scraped across the
rocks and into the water. Joseph pushed until the last moment
that he could leap in without getting his feet wet. The boat
rocked fiercely from left to right. Thomas' eyes got wide at the
prospect of them capsizing. Joseph sat as quickly as he could,
and the canoe steadied itself. The fishing tackle and rods
remained secured.

Thomas said, "I thought we were going to tump over."

"That was a little closer call than I'd have cared for. Ready?"

Thomas nodded.

The sun was so low in the sky that it hadn't yet topped the
hills. A thin mist blanketed the lake. The whole scene was pretty
as a painting. Thanks to an abnormally warm fall, most of the
foliage was still in the midst of its autumnal turn.

Joseph thought it all looked almost magical. Then he almost
laughed, realizing the turn in meaning that word had taken for
him in the last week. He tried to redirect his thoughts elsewhere, wanting to escape all of it for a morning.

"We're headed over to that slough across the way there."

Thomas looked to see where Joseph was pointing.

Joseph provided some additional instruction. "We'll have to

be careful not to cast too far, or we'll wind up in those trees or the seaweed."

Thomas squinted at him. "How come they call it seaweed if it grows in the lake."

"Couldn't tell you. Just the way it is."

Joseph could tell he hadn't satisfied the boy's curiosity with that response. But Thomas let it go. He suspected he was going to run out of answers long before Thomas ran out of questions. Just as well, though. He was a smart boy, and Joseph was only a passably smart adult. He took after his momma in that way.

Joseph pulled them up to within forty feet of the grass bed they were aiming at.

"Alright, I'm putting a crankbait on your line and a jig on mine, and we'll see what they're biting at this morning."

Thomas was positively bouncing in his seat as he waited for Joseph to finish tying the knot and trim off the excess line.

Joseph handed the rod up to Thomas. "Give 'em hell, son."

"You're not supposed to say that," Thomas corrected as he cast his line, landing the first cast well short of the grass.

"I know, but it's what my daddy always used to tell me."

"Who was your daddy?"

"Reel slower. You're not racing the fish back to the boat. Gotta give them time to see if they're interested in what you got. You never got to meet my daddy. He passed a long time ago."

Joseph made his first cast, landing the jig just into the grass. Maybe the hungry bass would think it was a big, plump beetle that fell into the water.

"What's it mean — he passed?"

"It means ... uhh ... he died."

Thomas cast a littler further this time. It was always trickier sitting in a canoe than standing on the shore.

"Then why didn't you just say that?"

"Don't know, bud. Sometimes we just say things in a way that sounds nicer."

Joseph watched the gears turn in the boy's brain as he mulled over this new information.

Thomas seemed to reach a conclusion. "But he's still dead, no matter how you say it."

Joseph laughed at the lack of subtlety. "You're right about that."

"Why are you laughing? I wasn't making a joke."

"I know you weren't. It just struck me funny. We'll give this spot a couple more minutes before I paddle up toward that old tree."

"Was he a good daddy?" Thomas asked.

Joseph cast, trying to decide how to answer. Listening to the sound of his rod whip the air, followed by the small splash of his lure. The light lapping of water against the hull as it rocked slightly.

"He did the best he knew how."

"What does that mean?"

This wasn't going to be the quiet, relaxing morning he'd hoped for.

"It means he had a hard life. Saw a bunch of bad things. He probably wasn't a very good dad, but I think he did the best he could."

"Are you a good dad?"

Joseph's eyes misted over a little. That was unexpected. He took a second and cleared his throat, "I try to be. But that's something you'll have to decide for yourself one day."

Thomas didn't hesitate. "I think you are. You're a good dad."

"Thanks, bud."

Joseph's line suddenly went taught, and the rod bent. He gave a quick jerk to set the hook and started reeling. He could tell from the resistance it wasn't a big one, but it was a fighter.

"Can I do it?" Thomas asked.

"Sure. Set your rod down."

Joseph handed his rod over to the boy. "Keep reeling. Don't let it get slack, or he'll try to come off of there."

Thomas kept reeling. The rod flexed and bent. But the spot in the water where the line broke the surface tension kept drawing closer. Once Thomas reeled it up to the boat, Joseph grabbed the gunwale with his right hand to counterbalance himself as he reached with the left to pull the fish up out of the water. A nice little smallmouth bass.

Thomas was beaming.

Joseph disentangled its mouth from the hook and handed it up to Thomas. "Grab it by the lip like I've showed you. We got to take a picture to send mommy."

Joseph snagged his phone out of the waterproof box. He took a couple of pictures. "Now give it a kiss."

"Gross!"

"It's for good luck."

Thomas was skeptical, but did it anyway. Joseph took a couple more pictures before Thomas wiped his mouth on his shirtsleeve.

"Put him back in the water now. Hold him there for a second before you let him go to let him recover."

Thomas did as instructed. When he sat upright again, Thomas asked, "So who caught it?"

"Whoever reels it in gets credit for it."

"So I caught the first fish?"

"Yep." Joseph was sure he'd never seen the boy more proud of himself. And in that moment, with soft, golden light breaking over his face, Joseph was also sure there wasn't a more beautiful sight.

CHAPTER 13

JOSEPH

"I kind of want to go hiking instead," Thomas said.

"You do? We haven't been out here all that long."

Thomas shrugged. "I don't think the fish are hungry anymore."

"That's fine. If you're sure that's what you want."

"I'm sure."

Joseph reeled his line in and placed his rod in the holder. "Hand me your rod."

Thomas did. Joseph secured it, closed up the tackle box, and started paddling them in to shore. He gave a couple of hard strokes as they closed in on the ground beside the boat launch. The canoe scrubbed the grass and mud as it made land.

"Alright, bud, hop out. Make it a good jump so you don't wind up in the mud."

Thomas stepped on the bow of the canoe and leapt as far as he could, easily clearing the water. Joseph followed suit, and dragged the boat ashore.

After loading up the boat into the truck bed, Joseph said, "Strap in so we can head down to the hiking trails."

"Do I have to wear my seatbelt?"

"It's a couple miles down the road, so I guess you'd better."

"I'm excited about hiking. What are we going to see?"

"Depends. You want to hike around the lake and walk across the dam? Or go to a waterfall?"

As he talked, Joseph headed south on the park road to the trailheads.

"I've never seen a waterfall before."

"Well, that settles it. We're headed to a waterfall."

Thomas actually clapped with excitement. "Does it have a name?"

"Yep. It's called Peav— What the..."

A man stepped into the roadway and stopped, feet planted shoulder-width apart. He wore a black button-down shirt, black pants, and polished black boots.

Joseph slowed the truck as it approached the man.

He didn't move.

Joseph stopped.

For a long minute, there was nothing except the two men staring at each other.

It wasn't until the man in black cocked his head just so that Joseph recognized him from the driveway episode. But before he any more than registered it, the man raised his arms out beside him, palms up, fingers splayed, as if he were trying to lift something. Joseph saw his muscles straining until his view of the man got cut off. The asphalt and earth between the truck and the man rose like a wave. Joseph shoved the truck into reverse, but his rearview mirror showed him there was nowhere to go. A wave of roadway rose behind them as well.

With a thunderous crash, the swells smashed down onto the nose and bed of the truck. Joseph raised his arms to cover his face. He felt the truck buckle, then rebound into the air. It rolled as it rose up. Joseph witnessed the destruction below him. A pit had opened up from the force of the impact.

As the truck arced back down, Joseph turned his head to look over his right shoulder at Thomas in the back on the passenger side. The color had left his face, and he gripped the harness of his car seat with both hands. A derailed roller coaster would draw the same reaction.

The truck smashed into the ruined earth. Rocks and dirt reaching through the shattered window toward Joseph. The last sound that reached him was metal wrenching and torquing against the ground.

Blackness mutated into fuzzy gray.

Joseph's ears rang.

His first identifiable sensation was being sick. His stomach convulsed and heaved, which caused terrible pain. He groaned.

He found that he lay on his side. No, that wasn't right. His face was pressed against the ground. And his left shoulder. But he was suspended.

Shapes emerged through the gray.

Joseph reached with his right hand and grasped his seatbelt. Still buckled.

Other parts of his body started registering pain. Left arm and shoulder, both legs. Face. Not just his face. His head was on the verge of ripping itself apart.

If there were any sounds, the ringing that contributed to the pain in his head masked them.

Joseph saw movement in his periphery. A person hovering in the passenger window. Her mouth moved. She waved to get his attention. Joseph heard only ringing.

Fear and adrenaline shot through his body as the thought of Thomas permeated the fog. He tried to look into the back. Couldn't. He shouted for the boy. If Thomas responded, he didn't hear it.

The seatbelt wouldn't unlatch. Too much pressure. Joseph thrashed, trying to free himself. Pain poured into his body with the movement. It didn't matter. He used his left arm to push away from the ground. A fresh wave of pain and sickness.

He took enough pressure off the seatbelt for it to unlatch. With the release, Joseph slumped to the ground. Sliding onto his back and looking up.

The woman in the window was talking to him. The car seat was empty. Maybe she'd already gotten Thomas out.

The ringing in his head was lessening. He heard the woman's voice, but not her words.

He held out his right hand, signaling for her to stop talking. She did.

"The boy? Did you get the boy? Out of the back?"

Even talking hurt. Pain in his chest that hadn't identified itself until now.

"It's just you," she answered.

"No. In the backseat. My son."

The woman slid to her left, shaking her head. "There's no one else in the truck."

Panic replaced all other inputs. Every other sensation.

Joseph drew in his legs and leveraged himself into a sitting position. He wrangled himself upright by pulling on the steering wheel with his left hand and reached up to the center console with his right. He leaned across his seat to look into the back of the cab. Empty.

The car seat harness was unlatched and dangling.

He climbed up and through the front passenger window. The woman was trying to help him, but was accomplishing little.

"Stop," he directed.

She retreated and slid over, perching on the front tire. He pulled himself on the door panel and extracted his legs.

Joseph yelled for Thomas as loudly as he could manage. Repeatedly.

Nothing.

"You didn't see a boy?"

Joseph recognized her as the attendant from the booth at the park entrance.

She shook her head.

"What about another man? Did you see anyone else?"

"Nobody. You're the only one I seen."

Joseph's mind was running away with itself.

"Looks like a sinkhole just opened up right under you," she said.

Joseph shook his head as he looked around, trying to figure a way down from the truck. "There was a man who did this."

"Sir?"

"There was a — nothing." There was no way to explain to this woman what he'd witnessed, which seemed to be the running theme of the last couple days. "How'd you get down?"

The park attendant transitioned to her stomach and slid down from the hood to the ground. Joseph followed.

He raised his hands and began yelling for Thomas again.

"I've called for a paramedic and the police."

That reminded Joseph of Agatha. He needed to call her. But what to tell her?

"Think he might've wondered off?"

Joseph considered it. "He couldn't have gotten out of his car seat by himself, I don't think."

He needed to talk to Agatha. He grabbed his phone out of his pocket. Somehow it had survived the crash.

"Hey," Agatha greeted him. "I didn't expect to hear from you yet. Everything okay?"

"No. Something happened."

She inhaled sharply on the other end.

"What happened? Is Thomas okay?"

Joseph wasn't sure exactly how to answer. "No. I don't know. He's gone."

"What?"

There was a rising hysteria in her voice. The sickening sensation he'd had since regaining consciousness became more acute. He pulled the phone away from his face. He hunched over and threw up into the grass at his feet.

"Joseph? Are you okay?"

"I banged my head pretty good. Everything's still a little wobbly."

He could tell that she was trying to keep it together. He heard the rattle of keys on her end.

"Are you still at Oak Mountain?"

"Yeah."

"Tell me what happened." Her voice changed. She was switching from panic to planning. That was good, because he wasn't thinking straight yet.

He described as best he could what he had seen.

Agatha said nothing.

"You still there?" he asked.

Her phone had switched to bluetooth while he was recounting events.

"Yes. Give me a minute."

He waited.

"Who's there with you?"

"Just the park attendant. Guess she heard the commotion. But she called 911. I can hear the sirens."

"Does she know Thomas was with you?"

"I mean, she hasn't seen him or nothing. But I told her he was missing, and I've been hollering for him."

"You need to convince her you were confused. No one was with you," Agatha said.

"What? Why?"

"What are you going to tell the police when they get there? That some guy made the earth rise up and brought it crashing down on your truck?"

"Oh. Yeah. I guess—"

"Do you know how much more complicated this gets if a

kid's missing. Every layer of police. Amber alerts. All of it. And there's nothing they can do. This is not within their capacity to handle."

"Yeah, I—"

"So you have to tell her it was just you."

"Well, I paid for the two of us when I came in."

"No. You didn't. Just you. She misremembers that."

Joseph hesitated, "Alright. I'll do what I can."

"You have to. Say as little as you can to the police. I'm about fifteen minutes out. As long as there's not a train stopped on the tracks."

"Okay."

"Joseph," a tenderness in her voice that wasn't there a minute ago, "are you okay?"

"I'm pretty banged up. But I don't think anything's broken."

"Alright, I'll be there quick as I can."

She hung up.

Joseph walked back over to the park attendant who stood at the edge of the crater.

She looked at him and said, "I never seen anything like it. A sinkhole just *whomp* swallowing up the earth like that."

"Yeah. Hey, I was confused about my boy earlier. What with hitting my head and all. He's with his grandparents."

"Sir?" She looked at him with uncertainty. Skepticism.

"I just talked to my wife." He patted the phone in his pocket. "The boy is fine."

"Well, who was in the truck with you when you came into the park?"

"Huh? What d'you mean?"

"You paid for an adult and a child."

"No, you're mistaken. It was just me. Five bucks."

The attendant was shaking her head. "I don't think that's right."

Joseph felt guilty about what he was doing. This poor lady

had done nothing to warrant being lied to and confused. But Agatha was right. The alternatives limited their options in a way that wasn't tenable.

"Ma'am, I know I've got a goose-egg here, but don't you think I'd recall if I had someone else in my truck with me when I got here?"

He could tell she didn't quite agree with him, but she couldn't argue with his logic.

"Yeah, I 'spect you would," she conceded.

There was an uncomfortable silence between them as they watched the ambulance make the curve and approach the scene. He needed to redirect the conversation, while trying not to freak out about Thomas missing. Once Agatha got here, he could have his come apart.

"No police?" he asked.

"They don't have jurisdiction here."

"So who fills out a report if there's, you know," he gestured toward his vehicle that appeared to be in the process of being ingested by the earth, "an accident?"

She looked at him for a long second before answering. "You're looking at her."

"Ah."

Well, that certainly didn't bode well for him. At least he was in good hands with the insurance company. Or so they said anyway.

The paramedics parked and hopped out. He endured an exam and a strong recommendation that he go get checked out at Shelby Baptist. He declined to be transported by ambulance but said he'd have his wife take him, though he had no intention to follow through.

Agatha arrived on the heels of the tow truck. She rushed to him from her car. She hugged him tightly, and quietly asked, "Thomas?"

Joseph shook his head.

"We need to get out of here," Agatha said.

"And go where?"

"Get our boy back."

Joseph nodded, and they broke their embrace. As they walked past the tow truck driver who was getting a set of chains from his truck, Joseph asked, "You got a card?"

The driver reached into his shirt pocket and handed one over.

"Appreciate it. I'll call you later."

They got in the car with Agatha driving. Joseph felt his chest constricting with anxiety. He started breathing in heavy gasps. The shock had worn off. The adrenaline had dissipated. Reality was setting in.

"Hey," Agatha admonished, authority in her voice, "get yourself together. We have things to do. I need you for this."

Joseph nodded. He slowed his breathing, trying to regain his composure. At least physically. Mentally, he was still a bit frayed. And emotionally ... well, he just needed to compartmentalize that for now. It had been a few years, but he'd done it before.

"You know who took him?" Joseph asked.

"Not exactly. But I know where to start."

"And?"

"I'm still working on the plan. How's your head?"

"Still attached. I think it'll be fine."

CHAPTER 14
JOSEPH

JOSEPH HAD NEVER SEEN Agatha the tactician before. There was so much she hadn't revealed to him about herself. Throughout the day, she'd been withdrawn and ill-tempered. She was working out a plan in her head, whereas his head was still somewhat fuzzy.

"Alright," Agatha announced, coming to a decision. "We're joint going to ask a few questions of somebody, but he's not going to be happy to see me again."

The look of worry that he'd been wearing for most of the past ten hours changed to one of uncertainty. "Should I bring a gun?"

"What? Of course you should bring a gun. Bring all the guns."

He shrugged. "I didn't know if it would work."

"Joseph, they're zauberi, sorcerers, not bulletproof."

Joseph opened the safe in his closet and pulled out a black duffle that he started loading up with weaponry. "Oh. Okay. What are you bringing?"

"Me. I'm bringing me. I am the weapon."

"You don't need to bring a wand or something?"

"I don't have a wand. That's not a thing. Sticks aren't magic.

People are."

"Fine. Where are we going?"

"Downtown Birmingham. I'll tell you more on the way. I'm driving. Got everything we need?"

Joseph raised up the elongated duffle bag. "Hope so. If it takes more than this, it's going to be more than we could handle, anyway."

Once in the garage, he lowered the bag into the trunk and hurried around to the passenger side. Agatha seated herself behind the steering wheel and started pulling her hair up into a ponytail. He knew what the gesture meant, even if she did it subconsciously now. Things were about to get real. The first time he'd noticed was when she went into labor with Thomas. Now he recognized it as her tell. She was getting ready.

By the time they got onto the interstate headed north, Agatha still hadn't told him their destination. Hadn't said much of anything. He barely recognized her. The physical features were the same. But her entire demeanor had transformed from the meek woman he'd known for years to something ... formidable. The metamorphosis hadn't been sudden. He realized now that the evolution had begun the night she'd told him she was a witch. Not a witch — a zauberin. But it wasn't even her who had changed, just his understanding of who she is.

Agatha saw him watching her. "What?"

"I ... uhh ... nothing. Where are we going?"

"The Pythian Temple."

"What the heck is that?"

"A building downtown. You know where the Lyric Theatre is?" Agatha asked without waiting for affirmation. "It's across the street."

"Why there?"

"That's where the Warden is. He'll know what's happening. The black thing that burned Thomas' leg belongs to him."

"You didn't think to mention this sooner?"

"You'll recall that at the time, you didn't even know I was a zauberin. So it probably would have been an awkward conversation."

"Yeah, so that reminds me of a question that nagged at me — why didn't you go to the hospital that night?"

"I visited the Warden."

"I don't know who that is."

"He's like the governor of all zauberi, the magical folk, in this region."

"So, what, you just popped in unannounced to visit the governor in the middle of the night?"

"I didn't make an appointment, if that's what you mean. He and I have a history. And I needed to make sure he wasn't messing with my family. We came to an understanding."

"Don't miss your exit." Joseph prompted. She steered hard to the right and took the 3rd Avenue North exit.

"So what's the plan here?" he asked.

"We're going to have another chat."

"Looks a lot more like we're prepared for an invasion, rather than a conversation."

"I've found that a show of force sometimes encourages cooperation."

"I can get behind that."

They parked beside the Lyric Theatre. The streets were empty. Steam seeped up from the manhole covers. And there was an overwhelming smell of trash that was overdue to be picked up.

"Where's the temple?"

Agatha pointed diagonally across the street.

"That's just an office building."

She shined her flashlight on its facade above the ground floor: Pythian Temple of Alabama.

"And you think Thomas is in there?"

"No, but I think the people who will know are in there."

Joseph walked back to the car where Agatha had already popped the trunk. He pulled his duffle bag out and said, "I'll wait until we get inside the building to get anything out. Don't want to be any more obvious than I already feel."

They walked across the street to the entrance of the Pythian Temple. Joseph got that same feeling he had before missions during his deployments. And similar to what he experienced while playing sports in high school, although the stakes were less then. Every time, he wanted to find somewhere to be sick. The anxiety peaking a few minutes before tipoff or kickoff. But as soon as the ball was in play, he was cool and ready to go. Years of subsequent experience had taught him that as soon as they breached this front door, his training would kick in and his heart would decelerate.

"Are there cameras?" he asked.

"Don't know. But they'll be expecting me."

"How's that?"

"I was pretty clear about things the last time I was here."

"Where are we going once we get in?"

"The basement. There'll be an elevator on the right. We'll go beyond it to an unmarked door at the back of the hallway on the left."

He turned his head and asked, "The basement?"

"Yeah. Can I explain it later?"

Joseph nodded. They stood on either side of the front door. He asked, "Is it going to be locked?"

Agatha, standing closest to the handle, reached over and tugged on it gently. The door began to swing open. She pushed it all the way to where Joseph could grab and fully open it so it wouldn't impede his entrance. They both rushed in to an unoccupied entryway. A bare hallway stretched out in front of them. A stairwell leading to the second floor to their left. And an empty reception desk and standard waiting room chairs to their right.

"Is this normal?" Joseph asked.

"So far."

Joseph set his duffle bag on the floor and pulled out two AR-15's. He handed one up to Agatha. She shook her head.

"I need to keep my hands free."

Joseph wore a confused expression.

"You'll see soon enough," she assured him.

He set the rifle back in the bag and took out a belted holster. He secured it around his waist and snugged his Smith & Wesson into place.

"What did you have me bring all this gear for?"

"Just in case."

"In case what?"

Agatha crouched beside him. "Don't know yet. Alright, down the hallway. Elevator is on the right. Beyond that, the door to the basement is on the left."

"Got it."

They proceeded down the hallway, inspecting every cranny and shadow. When they got to the basement door, Agatha flung it open, Joseph pushed past her, swiveling to his left to clear the stairwell. Empty. Agatha followed him in.

She whispered. "There's another door at the bottom. It'll open to a set of cubicles."

Joseph raised an eyebrow at her.

"What? Witches have to do paperwork too."

He shrugged. They made their way down the stairs and stopped at the bottom. Joseph pressed his back to the crash bar, closest to the latch side. He took a deep breath and pushed it open, following the arc of the door, his AR-15 sweeping the room along with him.

The cubicles were empty of people. Papers lay strewn across the floor.

Joseph whispered, "Still normal?"

Agatha shook her head.

He led them past the cubicles, toward a hallway. He peered beyond the outside cubicle wall. Right, then left. Nothing. The elevator and a reception area were to the left. From what Agatha had said, this place should have been buzzing with the life of nocturnal office hours. He was sensing they were the only ones here.

Joseph made a left turn, keeping his shoulder against the wall as he crouch-walked. A pillar at the end of the wall partially obstructed his view but provided some cover. He paused as Agatha sidled up to him. He pushed himself into the open, side-stepping his way to the elevator wall and sweeping across the reception area. Still no signs of life. Everything looked a little disheveled.

"Clear."

Agatha's demeanor changed as she emerged from behind the pillar. She went from cautious and hyper-alert to angry. Joseph raised his rifle as Agatha brushed past him. She strode down the hallway to a set of double doors. The offices they passed were empty. Chairs and papers askew. Power lights for monitors still on, but none of them attached to a computer.

Agatha kicked open the double doors and stepped in as they crashed against the wall. She roared in rage and frustration. Joseph had never seen such raw energy and emotion from her before. She was always so composed. But you take the cub, and you have to deal with mama bear.

Joseph lowered his rifle. There were no threats here. The office they were in was more ornate than anything else they'd seen. Dark wood paneled the walls. One of those big executive chairs. Paintings adorning the walls. This was the Warden's office. Had to be. Only the head honcho got to have a space like this.

"Get back."

The first words Agatha had spoken in a couple of minutes. Joseph looked at her. But she wasn't present with him anymore.

She was physically in the same room, but that's about as far as it went. He positioned himself by the doorway.

Agatha stepped to the center of the room. She folded her hands together as if she were holding a butterfly.

Joseph saw a glow emerge from the seams of her fingers. As it intensified, Agatha slowly pulled her hands apart. A fiery sphere levitated between them, growing as the distance between her hands increased. Then the sphere elongated and split like the cells he recalled seeing replicate in science class. But that was nothing compared to his.

Agatha held one sphere in each hand. And with a sudden flick of her wrists, she became a flamethrower. It happened so quickly that Joseph couldn't identify what had happened. He raised his left arm to shield himself from the intensity of the light and heat.

The Warden's desk erupted in flame. Then his chair and the books on the shelves behind it. The walls themselves started to burn. Agatha poured flame over every surface of the room, as she backed toward the doorway, where Joseph stood dumbstruck.

He turned and began walking toward the stairwell they'd used before. The fire alarm blared. Seconds later, the sprinkler heads spewed water. But they were no match for the inferno Agatha was creating. She walked backwards across the length of the building, setting fire to everything within reach of her flames. By the time they reached the stairwell, the combination of heat, smoke, and steam were becoming intolerable.

He bounded up the steps and peeked over his shoulder as Agatha stood, taking in her handiwork. Then she began her ascent as well.

He popped the trunk of the car with his key fob as they ran to the vehicle. Smoke was already pouring out of the lower parts of the building. He tossed in his bag and slammed the lid as he hurried to the driver's door. He could already hear sirens before he closed the door.

Joseph shoved the gear shifter into drive and headed north on 18th St. He crossed three lanes and made a left onto 4th Ave. As he turned, he checked his rear-view mirror. No lights or sirens behind them yet. No pedestrians or bystanders on the sidewalks. They should be okay. Should be able to get to the interstate and head south with no problems.

Driving through downtown, he realized it'd been a bit since either of them had spoken. What was there to say? What he had just witnessed was truly unbelievable. In the most literal sense of the word.

He sneaked a glance at Agatha under the auspices of checking his side-view mirror. She looked haggard. Maybe that was too strong a word. But worn down. He didn't know if it was the use of her powers. Or the magnitude of the loss they were attempting to avoid coping with. Or more likely, some combination of the two.

After they'd been on the interstate for a few minutes, Joseph ventured to break the ice.

"So ... you do fire?"

Agatha didn't respond. Didn't avert her gaze from where she was looking out the window. Didn't so much as acknowledge him.

She didn't say anything the rest of the drive.

CHAPTER 15
JOSEPH

JOSEPH PULLED the car into the garage, killed the ignition, and closed the garage door from within the car. They sat in an unbroken silence. Dejected. The satisfaction that destroying the Pythian Temple elicited had already fled. Their venture had yielded no actionable results. They had no idea where Thomas was or who had him. Or at least, he had no idea. "What now?"

She answered in a coarse whisper, "I don't know yet. I don't have any answers right now."

He considered that before speaking again. "Look, I know it's not fair for me to be relying on you like this right now. I'm just totally out of my depth here. These aren't the bad guys I'm used to. I mean, if we were in Afghanistan, I'd know what to do. But this? This is totally foreign to me."

She didn't say anything in response. But he watched Agatha's face brighten. "I know what we need to do. We've gotta go see Oberhaupt."

"Who or what is that?"

"He was my commanding officer."

"What did you call him?"

"Oberhaupt. It means, like, chief or chieftain."

"What are y'all — a band of wild Indians?"

"Ignoring for a minute that that was totally racially insensitive — yes. We used guerrilla tactics, like the Apaches. And like George Washington for that matter."

Joseph let go of the steering wheel and raised both hands above his head. "I surrender on all fronts."

The moment of levity somehow made the situation all the worse. Even the overhead light on the garage door opener compounded the gloom by going out. Another silence descended on them.

It was interrupted by the growling of his belly. He felt bad about being hungry. It seemed somehow irreverent. "I know we're not supposed to be thinking about food in this moment, but I'm starving. I haven't eaten anything since we lit out this morning. Let's go in and I'll scramble up some eggs and make toast. You want any?"

Agatha nodded and pulled on the handle of her car door.

"Hang on," he said. "I just want to tell you — this is kind of weird to even say — you were incredible tonight. Not like 'oh, that was cool,' but like really and truly incredible. I never knew something like that was even possible."

Even in the dim light, he could see her blush. Not out of embarrassment, but out of pride. Out of being recognized for something that truly set her apart. When he was growing up in church, that's what the believers were called — set apart, sanctified. And that's how he'd begun to think of Agatha. And Thomas, too.

"Are we going to get him back?" she asked.

"Come hell or high water, we're getting that boy back." It was more bravado than confidence, but he knew they both needed to hear it.

He set their plates on the table. The empty chair almost unbearable.

"Come here," Agatha beckoned him. "Does your head still hurt?"

"A fair bit."

"Kneel down in front of me."

Joseph did as he was told.

"I was never much of a heilerin, but I can do what amounts to first aid."

She placed her hands gently on the sides of his head. Fingers splayed behind his ears. Thumbs just above his eyebrows. He closed his eyes, not knowing what to expect. The last thing he'd seen from those hands was them burn a building to the ground. He felt her apply pressure. Then a sensation like the pain and fogginess he'd had since the accident being pulled out of the front of his head, to the edges, and dissipating entirely. The pressure lessened.

When he opened his eyes, she was sitting there in front of him, hands in her lap, watching him. "You're not going to spit out black flies or something like that guy in *The Green Mile*, are you?"

She pushed him backward with her bare foot. "You're an idiot. Don't think I won't give you another concussion."

Joseph grinned. He pushed himself up off the floor and sat down at the table, the grin vanishing when he saw Thomas' empty chair again.

They ate quietly for a bit. The only sounds were those of food being chewed. Joseph's mind raced to come up with something to talk about, so he had something else to listen to.

He remembered a question that had been gnawing at him. "How come everything sounds like some variation of German?"

"Everything *what* is in German?"

"All the names for the magical stuff. It's all in German."

He enjoyed being the one to surprise her about something for a turn.

"How did you know it was German?"

"After my helicopter crash, I spent some time at the American military hospital in Germany. It sounds different."

"It's where we're from. My people. What do you know about the Black Forest?"

That one stumped him. He took another bite and pointed his fork in Agatha's direction as an answer came to him.

"Chocolate and ham."

"Unbelievable. Maybe I didn't miss anything by dropping out of school."

"You never told me that before."

She shrugged and looked back down at her plate. While he was usually pretty obtuse, even he could see there was more to this story.

"It never came up."

"Right. Kind of like you having superpowers and fighting demons never came up. So how do we get in touch with Ober ... your CO?"

"I'll text him." She grabbed her phone from beside her plate, punched a series of buttons, and returned the phone to the table.

Joseph was looking at her incredulously.

"What?"

"You just text him?"

Agatha's was dumbfounded. "What did you think we did?"

"I don't know. I hadn't thought about it, but I would've thought—"

"Don't even come at me with owls. I will knock you right out of your chair."

Joseph put on his most offended expression. "I am affronted that you would think I would say something so juvenile as that."

She smiled at him, a weary smile. But it still counted.

"It's past midnight, so I don't know that he'll get back to me right away."

"Alright, I'm gonna go take a shower. I smell like a campfire."

. . .

Joseph had no more than rinsed the soap out of his hair, when Agatha knocked on the bathroom door.

"Hurry up. We're going to meet him."

"Now?"

"Yes, now."

"Alright, give me like three minutes."

It was just as well, he figured. He wasn't going to catch any sleep, anyway. Might as well be doing something.

He came out of the bathroom with his towel wrapped around this waist. Agatha had changed clothes — jeans, a dark sweater, and boots. Now wasn't the time to think about how much he liked her in jeans. But he did anyway. He just had the sense not to say anything about it.

Agatha told him, "You're going to want your duck boots."

"We expecting to get wet?"

"Yes."

"Okay. Want to tell me where we're going?"

"The Pizitz Building."

"You're not gonna burn it down too, are you?"

"I don't plan to."

"Well, that's reassuring. You know that Pizitz is only like a block-and-a-half from where we were earlier, right?"

"I do."

"You don't think that's going to be a problem?"

"I don't."

"Okay."

Agatha said, "Let's take your truck just in case, though."

"Can't."

She looked momentarily confused. "Oh, right. We'll park and walk a bit then."

"I don't think the Pizitz is open right now."

"We aren't going in the front entrance. And Oberhaupt gave me the code to the keypad."

Joseph nodded, satisfied for now. Or at least satisfied enough not to continue this game of twenty questions. He couldn't tell if she was being intentionally mysterious or just didn't want to talk anymore.

"Ready?" she asked.

Joseph tossed his hands up. "I guess, although you haven't really given me any expectation of what I should be ready for."

"Should just be a nice, informative conversation."

"In the immortal words of Ron Burgundy, 'I don't believe you.'"

CHAPTER 16

JOSEPH

JOSEPH OPENED the car door and pointed with his thumb, "Wonder what all that commotion is over there?"

"Shut up."

"Looks like there was a building fire."

"Uh-huh."

"I still think we could've parked in the building's parking deck," he said, as they started walking the block toward the west side of the Pizitz Building.

"Too many cameras."

"There's going to be cameras, regardless."

"Sure but if anyone goes back looking at camera footage — and they won't have any reason to — it'll be a lot harder to identify two random folks than if they had our license plate to trace back to us."

"You act like someone who's had to consider these things before."

Agatha winked at him. "And you act like someone who hasn't."

When they got to the building, they took a right through the courtyard. Agatha took the opportunity to spit on a replica of

Vulcan with the inscription, "Your Friendly Neighborhood Vulcan".

"What was that about?"

"I'll tell you once we're inside."

They took a left into the alley where they bypassed a service entrance and approached a door that said Exit Only. Agatha punched in a set of numbers on the keypad, and the magnetic lock disengaged. They entered at the landing of a stairwell.

"What floor?" he asked.

"Down."

"What is it with y'all and basements?"

"Not a basement this time."

They descended two flights of stairs and met a blank cinder-block wall. Best he could tell, they were stairs that led to nowhere. But he watched Agatha place her hand on the wall. And suddenly there was an entrance. Nothing had opened. There wasn't a door. It wasn't even like the wall had disappeared. It's just that now there was an entrance where he hadn't seen one before.

More than an entrance, it was a portal. With runes inscribed in it. And carvings of mythical creatures. He ran his hands over them. The building had been constructed in the 1920s, but this was somehow older. He knew Agatha was watching. He had so many questions. This time, though, he would just swallow them for now.

They crossed the threshold and entered a shallow cavern. The light from the entrance fell off quickly, so Joseph didn't immediately have any impression of its length or width. But the smell and general ambiance were familiar to him and brought back a rush of memories of going to Ruby Falls as a kid. The nostalgia combined with the aura of the place nearly overwhelmed him.

"This is a sacred place," she whispered.

He nodded.

Only then did he realize that he both heard and smelled water. Not the musty tang of standing water. This was fresh, clean.

"Where are we?" he asked.

"You know the underground river that runs under Birmingham?"

"The mythical one that no one's ever found?"

"Uh-huh."

"I see. Guess we should have brought some headlamps."

Agatha held her right hand up above her head. She formed an orb of magma that ascended to the cavern's ceiling and went ahead of them. Joseph could see now that this was a tunnel that opened up into a broader space.

The walls were adorned with several evolutions of artwork. As they walked, he saw what he recognized as primitive cave art depicting battles between man and beast, which gave way to much more elaborate work with colors and incredible detail. There were the same runes that appeared on the entrance.

The tunnel was a steady descent toward the mouth of the cave. Agatha's light preceded them. As it entered the cave ahead of them, it floated upward, expanding itself and bathing the place in an ethereal orange glow.

"Wow."

"Still wish you'd brought headlamps?" she asked.

"Definitely not. Would've felt ... inappropriate. That's not the word. Incongruent? I don't know. But out of place for sure."

"I know what you mean. Come on. We're going to follow the river a bit."

They splashed down into the ankle-deep water. Under the orange light of Agatha's fire, it looked more akin to a lava flow.

"How far are we going?" Joseph asked as he sloshed through the water, trying different kinds of steps to figure out which one caused the least resistance and splashing.

Agatha asked, "You know how Einstein's theory of relativity says that time isn't a constant?"

"No. No, I know nothing about that. But you already knew that."

She smirked, "You're right. But to answer your question, I don't know. It changes."

"The entrance to wherever it is we're going changes? Then how will you know when we get there?"

"I'll know it when I see it."

Joseph shook his head. "You know, there's a word to describe you."

"Oooh, this should be good. Let me hear it."

"Coy."

"Ah. Well ... that's probably true. I was expecting far worse."

"Not after I've seen what you can do. I'm all 'yes ma'am' and 'no, ma'am' from here on out."

She beamed, which was its own form of magic. "That's a good boy."

They walked for a while. Distance was impossible to determine. All the while, the molten orb cast flickering and roving shadows on the cavern's features. The only sounds being that of the running water and their walking. Agatha was much more graceful. Joseph had started with large steps that made him look like a giant trying to squash villagers, but had settled on more of a gliding stride that kept his feet in the water.

Joseph couldn't help but broach a subject he was more than a little curious about. "Is this a good time for me to ask about you spitting on Vulcan's statue?"

"As good as any, I guess. But I think you're going to find some of it hard to believe."

"Oh, I'll be the judge of that." Joseph said, thinking he'd be hard pressed to be surprised by anything at this point.

"Let's start with this: Vulcan is real, and he's behind everything that's happening. With Thomas. The Warden. Everything."

Joseph stopped in his tracks. The water flowed around him. "Well. That was kind of a lot."

Agatha stopped too. "Told you."

"So what do you mean when you say he's real?"

"I mean he's as real as you and me. And he is evil and twisted. And extraordinarily powerful."

"How is that even possible?"

"There are deep and ancient things you know nothing about, Joseph. He has been here a long time. He has taken many forms and been called many things. But this has been his home for centuries, when it was still nothing but wilderness. And people like me have been waging war against him, to keep him at bay. No one has ever known why he chose this place, but I have a feeling we are on the verge of it now."

"Okay. Let's start with some basics, like, where is he?"

"He's exactly where you think he is."

"A pedestal on top of Red Mountain?"

"Okay, well, maybe not exactly. But close enough. He and his cronies have made their lair within the old, sealed mine shafts that burrow into Red Mountain."

"So when you say you've fought him, what do you mean by that?" Joseph asked.

"What do you mean when you say you've been to war? It's the same thing. Different enemy. Different weapons."

She started walking again. Joseph followed.

"So what happened? Did y'all win?"

"There is no winning. But we didn't lose. We forced him underground, so to speak."

"Now who's delivering the bad jokes?"

Agatha shrugged without turning around. "He has needed time to rebuild, restock, reinforce. It's been a few years now since anyone's heard from him. But with everything that's happening, I expect he's making another play at something now. As for what it is, I have no idea."

"I just want to be clear that we're talking about Vulcan, the Roman god of fire and forge."

"Yes and no. Don't think of him as a god. You might as well think of me as a goddess if that were the case. There are no gods, at least not in that sense. The Greeks and Romans called us that because they didn't have other words for it. And over time, they ascribed to us powers that we do not have, like immortality. Before them, the ancient civilizations called us angels and demons. In the Dark Ages, we became sorcerers and witches. But the reverence was lost, and there was only fear. Persecution drove us underground. And now we are all but forgotten. Legends. We are called superheroes and relegated to cartoons and comic books.

"We are not any more or less powerful now than we ever were. We just operate behind a veil of disbelief. A veil that we ourselves propagate, because it allows us to be left alone and insulate ourselves.

"But there are those like Vulcan who are discontent with the status quo. Who would have us resurrect ourselves to the positions of power and dominion that we once held. It is not reasonable or rational, or even plausible. The world has changed. But his lust for power and control drives him toward that end. So we have to assume that whatever he is attempting to achieve right now, Thomas is a part of that. I don't know why or how. But it's the only conclusion I can draw."

Joseph chewed on that for a minute, "If he's not immortal, how is it that he's been alive for a couple thousand years?"

"Extraordinary long life is one of his abilities. In addition to controlling fire at a much greater magnitude than I can achieve. But he is not immortal or invincible. He can be killed. Somehow. And I intend to find out."

Before Joseph could pummel her with additional questions, Agatha announced, "Here we are."

Joseph had never been praised for his observational skills, and they failed him again here. "We're where?"

"It's actually not your fault this time. You are not capable of finding it. Otherwise, anybody could just stumble upon places they've got no business finding."

"Makes sense."

They exited the river to the bank. Joseph followed Agatha's lead in walking toward the unremarkable cavern wall. As they approached, there was inexplicably a portal where there hadn't been a moment ago. But unlike the previous iteration he'd seen, this one was opaque. There was no seeing through to the other side. Only an inky blackness that shrouded it.

Agatha stepped into it and was swallowed. He took a breath and did likewise. He emerged into what he immediately guessed to be an underground bunker.

"Welcome, Kommandantin. We have been expecting your arrival."

Joseph heard the speaker before seeing her. He had expected a military uniform, not skinny jeans and a gray t-shirt.

"Call me Agatha, please. It's been some time since I have worn that title."

"As you wish then."

Agatha directed her thumb at Joseph, "This is my husband, Joseph."

Gray shirt nodded to him.

"Follow me. I'll take you to Oberhaupt."

She led them down a gray corridor that was entirely without decoration. Joseph recognized it as having a distinctly military flavor about it. They passed a command center where people sat engrossed in their computers. This sort of blew his mind. He'd figured that people who had magic literally at their fingertips wouldn't be reliant on the same technology as the rest of humanity.

The trio came to a nondescript door midway down the corridor. Their escort knocked, and they heard a thunderous, "Come in."

"Oh, right," Agatha turned to Joseph. "I forgot to tell you — he's a giant."

When Joseph rounded the corner, his mouth fell open. Agatha might have prepared him before this for the colossus behind the desk. Everyone who had ever been described as "a mountain of a man" before was wrongly identified. Joseph knew now how David felt when facing Goliath.

"Agatha!" he bellowed. "Aren't you a sight for sore eyes?"

"I'm surprised you're glad to see me."

He waved her off. "Sit, sit."

"In that case, sir, it's good to see you again."

"Don't start sir'ing me now." He looked to Joseph, "Fifteen years of being the most impertinent zauberin I ever knew, and now she wants to go changing the rules."

Joseph was gawking at him with a peculiar expression, trying to figure something out. "You remind me of somebody, and I can't quite place it."

Agatha and Oberhaupt shared a look and rolled their eyes in amusement.

The giant said, "Can I spoil it for you so you don't derail this meeting in ten minutes when you figure it out?"

"Sure," Joseph said, a little disappointed that Oberhaupt was about to solve the mystery for him.

"Michael Clarke Duncan."

"Yes! You're like a super-sized Michael Clarke Duncan! That's amazing!"

"You good now?" Agatha asked.

Joseph sat back in his chair like a burden had been removed from his shoulders. "Yeah, I'm good. Sorry."

Now it was Oberhaupt's turn. "And who are — oh, I know who you are. You're the one who stole our Agatha from us."

Joseph became as confused as he'd been at any point in the last several days. "Umm … I don't … what?"

Oberhaupt's eyes brightened, and he returned to Agatha. "He doesn't know? You didn't tell him?"

She replied flatly, "No."

"Well, now," he said with a toothy grin. "Isn't that interesting."

Joseph said, "Guys, I gotta admit, I'm a little out of the loop here."

"Later." Agatha's face blazed with an embarrassment that had curdled into anger. She turned to their escort, "You, you're dismissed."

The girl received an affirming nod from the giant and left the room, closing the door behind her.

"That's you," he said to Agatha, referring to the departed escort. "Or not you, but near enough."

"I very much doubt that. But it doesn't matter. Now that we've got the niceties and meddling out of the way, you know why we're here? You've still got your mice scrabbling through every cranny they can find, I'm sure."

Oberhaupt considered how he wanted to respond. "I do. Now it's my turn to ask a question. The Warden's office — was that your doing?"

"You know it was," Agatha answered.

"Not very subtle."

"I believe a lack of subtlety was always one of your gripes with me. Besides, I warned him."

The giant nodded.

Joseph was a child listening to the adults talk. He understood the words they were speaking. But there was so much history and subtext behind everything that he couldn't quite put everything together. He was missing some pieces to the puzzle. The corner pieces.

"You think he took your boy," Oberhaupt posited.

"You think he didn't?"

"I don't know one way or another. But I suspect you're probably right. And if I had to guess further, I'd say that Vulcan is likely involved too, and has established some hold over the Warden that I don't yet understand. He has a way of doing that."

Agatha asked, "But why Thomas? And why in such a public space?"

"Vulcan is becoming bold, reckless. He is not content to operate in the margins any longer. His patience is waning."

"And Thomas?"

"Thomas is one of many young who have been taken. He is searching for something. Let me ask you, does Thomas have your abilities?"

Agatha didn't answer.

The giant attempted to wait her out, but her non-response wasn't a delay. She had no intent to answer the question.

"Agatha, what you know may be a key ... to many things."

"He can speak with animals."

"And?"

"And nothing."

Oberhaupt wagged his gargantuan finger at her. "That is a falsehood. But it is answer enough."

Joseph blurted out, "You'll have to teach me that."

"Give it time. She has tells. It is perhaps the only subtle thing about her."

Joseph grinned at how uncomfortable Agatha was with being spoken about in third person while she was in the room.

"Where is he being kept?" She asked.

"Don't know. There are two questions that remain unanswered — where and why?"

"Who else have they taken?"

"I cannot give names," Oberhaupt said. "But between the zauberi and the Mythicals, maybe a couple dozen."

Joseph pounced on his opportunity to contribute something meaningful to the conversation. "We know about the pegasus. I kind of had a run-in with the guys who were taking it."

"Ahh. Well, isn't that a tidy coincidence? She mentioned that an irreverent low-born — her words, not mine," as he raised his hands innocently to the insult, "had laid hands on the foal."

"She could have been more appreciative. I, uh, also shot one of the guys."

Oberhaupt dismissed this last statement, "Haven't we all."

Agatha snapped her fingers at the two of them. "Focus. We need to put a plan together."

The giant's eyes blazed with a ferocity that Joseph hadn't seen yet. Something she'd said triggered an adverse reaction.

"No. *We* don't. Agatha, you chose not to be a part of this any longer. You don't get to reinsert yourself just because it now aligns with your interests."

Joseph watched her shrink under the scolding. Her own fire and irreverence quenched.

Oberhaupt continued, "We will decide the best course and act upon it. Then we will inform you of the result. But let me be clear, you will not be involved and you will not have any input."

By the time he had finished, all the color had drained from Agatha's face. Joseph didn't know exactly what she'd expected when she came here. But it wasn't this.

"And one more thing — do not interfere."

She stood. Joseph took his cue and did likewise. She stormed out of the room.

"We'll show ourselves out," Joseph offered.

Joseph caught up to her in the corridor.

She instructed, "Do not say a word until we're out of here."

He had no idea how they were going to find their way out.

Every branch off the main corridor looked exactly alike. Maybe they should have left some breadcrumbs.

Agatha took an abrupt right. He swung wide to make the turn.

In what he still thought of as a miracle, the blank wall at the end of the hallway became an exit without appearing to have done anything. Before entering the opacity, he looked over his shoulder and found that their escort was trailing them, making sure they found their way out.

CHAPTER 17

AGATHA

AGATHA HAD NEVER CONSIDERED Joseph to be particularly chatty, but now that they were back in the underground river on the return trip, he wouldn't shut up. It was as if he thought that if he allowed for some silence, it would remain intact indefinitely.

"That was a good idea," he said. "I really thought they were going to help us."

She didn't have a response for that. She didn't really know what she had expected.

The upstream return trek required a bit more effort and had an altogether different air about itself. Where before there had been hope, despondence replaced it. Even the light that Agatha cast had a gloomier hue.

"How long will it take them to tell us what happens?"

Agatha stopped and whirled around so abruptly that Joseph ran into her before bringing himself to a clumsy stop.

"What do you think is about to happen next? Because if you think I'm about to go home and sit on my hands while I wait for the Gevalti practice squad to put together a rescue op for my son, you couldn't be more wrong."

As her anger swelled, so did the size and brightness of the light-giving orb.

"Ags, I—"

"Don't interrupt me." Fierce tears streamed down her face now. But despite her instruction, she didn't follow up with anything else. She wasn't sure what to say. She needed some time.

"Agatha, I might have been provoking you slightly there. I needed to know where your head was at. Listen, I already told you, I'm in for whatever it is we have to do to get our boy back."

She nodded.

"Even if that means disobeying direct orders from a giant," he added.

"I don't take orders from him anymore."

"It kind of sounds like you were never very good at following orders in the first place."

The corners of her lips turned up, and she wiped her face with her palms. "I know you find that hard to believe."

"Yes, absolutely," he agreed. "It came as a total surprise to me."

She punched him lightly in the chest, and her smirk turned into a smile. Until Joseph started asking his next question.

"What did Oberhaupt mean back there? About me?"

"What do you mean?" She knew full well what he meant.

"Don't. You know what I'm talking about. Did you quit this life because of me?"

Agatha had tried to bury this. Not to think about having given up something she loved for something she may come to love. It still hurt. "Because of you, yes. But not for you. Not in the way that you're asking."

Oh, no.

She checked again. Two lines. She read the box again just to make sure she was right about what it meant. Two lines meant positive. Positive meant pregnant.

No. No. No.

She dropped the stick onto the floor between her feet. Elbows on her knees, face in her hands.

Alright, get yourself together.

"You alright in there?" Came the thunderous inquiry.

"Yeah, yeah. Hold your horses." He could be exasperating.

Agatha stood up and pulled her jeans back on. She grabbed the test off the floor and shoved it into her back pocket, making sure that it didn't poke out the top. There were few things capable of making this worse, but that would be one of them.

After washing her hands, she opened the door to find the giant leaning against the wall. "Hangovers get harder to shake off as you get older."

"Is that your way of telling me how bad I look right now? And why are you hanging out by the girls' bathroom?"

"The Warden wants to have a chat with us."

"What'd you do this time?"

"Me? It's not my shenanigans that normally get us summoned to the principal's office. If you were maybe just a tiny bit more compliant..."

"Whatever. You know what, it's not a hangover. Something's not sitting well with my stomach. I'm going home to either be sick all day or sleep this off."

She left him standing there in the corridor. She couldn't deal with whatever banal thing the Warden wanted to fuss at them about.

By the time she got into her car and started driving to her apartment, Agatha knew she didn't want to be alone right now. She changed course and headed east of the city. Home.

She had thought the drive would help settle her down. It didn't. By the time she pulled into her mother's gravel driveway, she was a bit of a mess. If she'd been wearing mascara, her face would've been a black smear.

Gertrude opened the screen door and met her on the front stoop. Seeing Agatha's splotchy face, she asked, "What's wrong, baby girl?"

Agatha leaned in for a hug and let herself have a good cry.

"Let's go in and you can tell me what happened."

It had been a long time since Agatha had been in such a state.

Gertrude draped her arm over Agatha's shoulders and led her to the couch. They sat with Gertrude's arm still wrapped around her daughter. Agatha tucked her feet up under her and suddenly felt as lost and helpless as the sixteen-year-old version of herself had once been.

"Alright, sister, tell me what's going on."

Agatha reached around to her back pocket and handed the pregnancy test over to her mother.

"Oh, I see. So this wasn't planned then?"

Agatha shook her head.

"The guy you've been seeing for a while?"

She nodded.

"Have you told him yet?"

Agatha finally had her breathing under control. "No," she croaked, "I just found out before I came here."

"Ah. Do you like him?"

"I mean, yeah. We've been dating for like a year."

Gertrude asked, "So what's he going to do when you tell him?"

"*If* I tell him, he'll ask me to marry him."

"So what's the problem?"

Agatha sat up. "He doesn't know."

"Doesn't know what?"

"Anything. He doesn't really know anything about me. What I am."

"Oh. Let me think a minute."

Agatha watched her working through the scenarios.

Gertrude said, "I will tell you what I see as your options, but I will not tell you what I think you should do. Can you accept that?"

Agatha nodded.

"Fine. The way I see it is, you have three options. You can not tell — what's his name again?"

"Joseph."

"One. You can not tell Joseph and raise this baby on your own. Not on your own, exactly. I'm always here. Two. You can tell Joseph and get married and start a new life, leaving this one behind."

Agatha tried to interject. Gertrude held up a finger.

"Behind. Entirely. You understand better than most why that must be."

Agatha's throat constricted, and tears flushed to her eyes again.

"And third?" she croaked.

"You can decide not to keep the child and act like this never happened."

"You disapprove of that?"

"I already said that I will not give you my opinion. I raised you as an independent woman. Only you can choose your path. But once you have chosen, there is no turning back. No waffling. No second guessing. That is not a luxury you have."

"I understand."

Gertrude hugged her tight.

"I'm so sorry, baby girl."

"What do you have to be sorry for?"

"That so much has landed on you so young. I wish that I could have protected you from some of it."

"If wishes were fishes, right?"

They shared a troubled laugh.

CHAPTER 18

JOSEPH

AFTER RETURNING from the underground river, Joseph decided to forego a second shower within … what? A few hours. Hours that passed like years. Though he wondered what kind of bacteria and microbes he might be bringing back with him from that cavern. He needed sleep. He'd been awake for twenty-four hours or so now.

But sleep did not come easily. Thomas was still missing. It looked like no one was going to help them. Apparently, he had derailed Agatha's life and now he wondered if she resented him for it. All these trains of thought converged onto one set of tracks. And rather than the stress of everything bleeding off, it swelled.

Somehow Joseph nodded off anyway. But what sleep he found was fitful and stunted. Long before he felt rested, he got fed up with both the effort it was taking to sleep and his concern that he would awaken Agatha. He turned his phone face-up to check the time. Still a couple of hours until daylight.

He shifted out of the bed and shuffled over to the closet, where he grabbed some not-quite-dirty jeans off the floor and pulled a flannel shirt off the hanger. He wasn't sure why, but he felt a strong compulsion to take a walk in the woods behind the house, where this had all started.

He scribbled out a note for Agatha: *Going for a walk. Back in a bit. - J*

As quietly as he could manage, Joseph opened the door to the garage. He put his clothes on and grabbed a pair of his yard-work socks, the ones that Agatha had told him he couldn't wash with the rest of the laundry because they littered the other clothes with grass clippings. Finally, he laced up his boots and grabbed a coat and hat, and stepped out into the crisp pre-dawn morning. There wasn't any frost on the ground, but they were overdue for it.

Joseph took the same path that had led him to Theiona. The dry leaves crunched and crackled under his boots. He smelled the decay. In a weird way, it was refreshing. Or maybe just grounding. While he didn't have a plan, he found himself walking toward the creek. It was always the same for him. Given an option when hiking or walking, he always chose the path that led him alongside water.

He heard the creek long before he saw it. The sound of water carried through the forest, cutting through the quiet of the early hour. The nocturnal creatures had headed off to bed in anticipation of the sunrise. And the diurnal animals hadn't yet awakened to see what the day held for them. He coveted this rare and lonely hour of true solitude.

At the creek, Joseph sat down on a flat boulder. He crossed his legs and sat quietly for a minute, before burying his face in his hands and weeping. It was too much. It was all too much. His chest was so tight that he could hardly breathe. His heart pounded against his ribs. He was hopeless, powerless.

"You are not alone."

Joseph about jumped out of his skin when he heard the voice. He tried to gather himself into a defensive posture while he cleared his eyes and peered into the grayness that surrounded him.

She stood there in her magnificence, as impressive as she had been the first time.

"You ought not sneak up on a fellow like that," he chastised.

The pegasus answered, "I did not sneak. You were making too much of a commotion to hear me."

He couldn't tell if she was mocking him or stating it matter-of-factly.

"They took my boy."

"I know," she said.

"How?"

"I know a good many things. The woodland animals report to their stewards. It is my business to know. I have a vested interest in these things. You may recall that they came after my young before coming for yours."

"How could I forget? It was the spark that set all this off."

"Only for you."

He found it frustrating how everything she said was shrouded in mystery and raised more questions than answers.

"I don't know what that means."

"You are new to this arena. Many of us have been contending with these forces since long before your revelation. This is just the newest tactic in a centuries-long struggle."

"But why kidnapping our young?"

"While I do not yet know the answer, I can tell you that Vulcan is not hasty or foolhardy. He will have a reason. Just as you have a reason for being willing to be involved now, when you were unwilling the last time we spoke, when you believed it was only my offspring at stake."

"Look, I don't know what to tell you. You went from non-existent to asking for help within a matter of about fifteen minutes. It was a lot to come to terms with."

"Have you considered that if you had acted sooner, you could have prevented this? That your son could be safe at home in his bed now, rather than Vulcan's captive?"

Joseph's face flushed with heat. His anger bubbled to the surface. "That's not fair."

"Your concept of fair is of no consequence."

"Maybe. But your hypotheticals aren't particularly helpful either."

There was an awkward moment between them before the pegasus admitted, "They have succeeded in taking my foal."

"What? Why did you wait until now to tell me?"

"We were discussing other matters."

"This is *the* matter. Geez. Talk about burying the lede. How did it happen?"

"There was a struggle, but they overcame me." Theiona turned to the side stiffly and with obvious pain.

He hadn't seen her approach, and so hadn't seen how she must have been walking. There was a gash on her right side. It had mostly stopped bleeding now. But of greater concern was her ribcage. Where it should have been convex, it was … damaged. Deformed.

"Holy cow! We need to get you to…"

Joseph stopped mid-sentence. He was going to say *get you to a vet*. But that wasn't really an option.

Theiona nodded her head. "My choices are very limited."

Joseph stood up from his perch on the boulder. "I'll go get Agatha. She fixed my concussion."

"Very kind of you. But I'm afraid my wounds are beyond Agatha's abilities in this area. Don't worry for me. There are others I can seek. However, we have graver concerns."

Joseph agreed. "We do."

"I have something of an idea. Do you know Volk's Cave in Smoke Rise?"

"Smoke Rise," Joseph thought aloud, "Up in Blount County?"

"Yes, there is a cave there. It is of some renown. Do you think you can find it?"

"I mean, I guess? I'll fire up the ole Google machine."

The pegasus tilted her head. "What is a google machine?"

"Nothing. Nevermind. I can find it."

"Good. You and Agatha meet us there at sunset."

"Us?"

"The others like us, whose offspring have been taken."

"Yeah. Okay." Joseph half turned to leave before stopping himself. "Hang on. There's like fifty miles of forest between here and Smoke Rise. How are you going to get there by tonight?"

Theiona said nothing, but unfurled her wings. Joseph was smitten with how extraordinary a creature she was.

"Right. Forgot about that. Adios, then. See you tonight."

CHAPTER 19
AGATHA

THE INK WAS HARDLY dry on Joseph's note when Agatha picked it up to read it. She couldn't lie there any longer trying to rest while her baby was in the hands of a monster.

There was a knock at the door. Not a polite knock either. A rattling-the-door-in-its-frame kind of knock. The dog barked and made some growling noises. But it was a coward and wouldn't go any further toward the sound than the doorway of the bedroom.

Her first thought was that Joseph was back and had forgotten a key. But that seemed unlikely. He's the one who'd put spare keys around the house.

Agatha walked to the front door and placed her left hand on the handle. She briefly considered that she was wearing just a pajama top and underwear. With her right, she could feel the energy swirling about it, heating up in anticipation of being set ablaze. She flung the door open. No one and nothing was there.

The knock thundered again while she stood peering out. It came from the back of the house.

Agatha closed and locked the front door. She made her way to the other end of the house, turning on a couple of lamps as she walked. The gray light filtering through the half window in the back door revealed a broad, muscular torso. Anger rippled through her. She unlocked the back door and unlatched the door handle enough that it opened a few inches. Agatha turned and began walking away.

The door creaked as the giant pushed it open and ducked in. "Such hospitality," he said, entering the house.

Over her shoulder, Agatha said, "If I'm gonna have company, I have to put on a bra and pants."

"Don't get all gussied up just for me."

She returned clothed and found him in the living room. He seemed to occupy most of the room. She was glad that whoever had built the house had opted for the extra expense of ten-foot ceilings. As it was, he already hunched and had to be mindful of the fan.

"Well?" she prompted.

"I did not like how our meeting ended."

"You're telling me."

"Agatha, I am your friend."

"You sure have a peculiar way of showing it. Or is it one of those things where the enemy of my enemy is my friend?"

Oberhaupt sighed. "We are not enemies. Were never enemies. Even when you abandoned me. I am your oldest friend, perhaps your only friend."

Her anger was rising. "You are my oldest friend only because you killed the rest of them."

She was being unfair, but she didn't particularly care in this moment.

"I had nothing to do with that," he defended himself.

"So you've always said. But you certainly took advantage of the opportunity it presented, conscripting me into the Gevalti."

"I didn't ... you made a choice. And as I recall, you fairly enjoyed your time."

"You turned me into a killer," she said as she unleashed years of pent up anger and frustration.

"I turned you into a warrior. I gave you the opportunity to put your unique skills to their highest and best use. And you were extraordinary. But then you quit. Without a word to me. You abandoned your brotherhood."

Agatha clenched her jaw.

He held up a hand. "I know why you did it. And I'm not here to discuss how you went about it. I'm here to say what I couldn't earlier."

Agatha crossed her arms over her chest and shifted her weight onto one hip, adopting the same posture that she had nearly twenty years ago upon first meeting the giant.

"I'm all ears," she said in a tone laced with venom.

"The Gevalti has been compromised."

Her expression softened. "What do you mean?"

"Vulcan has infiltrated our ranks." His upright posture sagged. The Gevalti was his life's work. She understood the pain it must cause him to admit this. "I do not yet know who or even how many."

"I see."

"If I had been more inviting or brought you into the fold, you would have been in graver danger still. The boy too."

She nodded, understanding. "What about the other way around? Do you have people on the inside of Vulcan's ops?"

"We're working on it. It's sticky."

Agatha asked, "Do you know the specifics of Thomas' abduction?"

"No."

As she told him what happened, his face grew more troubled.

When she finished, Oberhaupt said, "I know of only one person with the ability to control and move earth like that."

"Well, that's an understatement. You practically raised him."

"And you fought alongside him for a time."

"What will you do?" she asked

"What I always do. Watch, listen. Gather intelligence about who is with me and who is not. And when the time comes, I will crush them. For breaking my trust. For siding with Vulcan. We are in a precarious position right now. Vulcan is gaining power and influence. But he is searching for something too."

"Well, let's not be all mysterious about it. What's he looking for?"

"I don't know yet. But it has something to do with the young ones he's taking. Does Thomas have any gifts? Something extraordinary?"

"You already asked me that."

"It is not unlikely that you would have held back then."

"Just to recap the situation and make sure I understand. The Gevalti has been infiltrated. Vulcan is scouring the earth for something. You come here asking me for the second time about my son's gifts. Tell me why I shouldn't think you're with him."

Oberhaupt's ruddy complexion darkened. He took a step toward Agatha. She didn't budge.

"You have forgotten yourself," he said. "Vulcan has taken everything from me. I would sooner die."

Agatha's heart was racing. It hurt to do what she was doing, but she didn't know now who to trust or how to test it.

She shrugged her shoulders indifferently. "Acting all angry and indignant is exactly how I would expect someone to act if they were pretending they hadn't turned their loyalties."

"You are impossible," he said, brushing past her and knocking her backwards with the impact.

"Leaving so soon?" she mocked.

He stopped before exiting the living room. "You cannot do this alone. It is always the same with you — trying to push people out. If you want the boy back alive, you will need help. I have been through the fires with you. And I will go again. But I will not stand here and have you disrespect me."

Her defiance began wilting as the weight of everything

landed on her. She was tired. "But how do I know I can still trust you?"

"You don't. All you can have is faith and see how far that carries you."

"It's been six years. So much has happened. The boy is everything to me."

"I know. But I will not talk you into believing I am with you. You must decide for yourself. And when you do, you know how to find me. But be discreet and assume that everything you do is being watched."

With that, he walked out of the living room, out the back door, and into the yard.

She had so much more to say. But she did not chase him. It could wait. Would have to wait.

Joseph emerged from the woods as Oberhaupt exited the house. He quickened his pace to intercept the giant as he strode across the yard.

"Fancy meeting you here," Joseph said, trying to sound casual. But his glance toward the house signaled his concern.

"Everything is fine."

They stopped a dozen feet from each other.

Joseph made a quick, nervous laughing sound. "Yeah, Agatha can take care of herself ... so I've discovered. But everything is decidedly not fine."

Oberhaupt nodded his head in concession. He looked toward the east, where the gray sky was showing the faintest hints of color.

"I'd rather not be here when day breaks. I'm rather hard to conceal."

Joseph tipped his cap to the giant. "Until next time, I guess."

He hurried to the back door and into the house to check on

Agatha. He heard water running and followed the sound to their bathroom, where Agatha was washing her face.

As she patted her face dry with a towel, Agatha asked, "How much of the forest did you bring in with you on those boots?"

Joseph looked over his shoulder, following his path. "A fair bit."

He never ceased to confound her with his limited ability to focus on only one thing at a time. There were times she thought that the room could burn down around him without him noticing if he had locked in on a particular task. Meanwhile, she was juggling knives and cooking dinner at the same time.

"So I see you've started having other fellas over when I step out for a bit."

She threw the towel at him without bothering to answer or look his direction.

"What did he want?"

"To tell us Vulcan has compromised his unit but that we can trust him."

"Can we?" Joseph asked.

"I think so," she answered. "I can't imagine what Vulcan would have to tempt or coerce him with. And everyone that he cares about is long since gone."

"Except you."

Agatha didn't answer that. Didn't know how to answer it. So she changed the subject.

"Tell me — how was your morning constitutional?"

"Well, I had my own visitor," Joseph said. "Theiona's foal has been taken."

"I had a feeling they wouldn't stop with just the one attempt."

"She's in pretty rough shape." He put his hand to his ribs, indicating the area of damage. "Must've put up a hell of a fight."

"What does she need from us?"

"Wants us to meet her at some cave up in Smoke Rise."

Agatha grunted.

"You know it?" he asked.

"Volk's cave."

"Yeah, that's it. Is there something special about it?"

Agatha nodded. "It is a gathering place. Has been since the First People were here. While there, the congregees can do each other no harm. It is a haven where many treaties and alliances have been forged."

"She wants us to be there at sunset."

"Who else?"

"Others who've had their children kidnapped."

Agatha warned, "Just a heads up. You're likely to see some things you've never seen before."

CHAPTER 20

THOMAS

THOMAS CALLED for Ning in a whisper. Within a matter of seconds, the giant panda appeared within his cell. The white parts of him seemed almost to glow in the relative darkness. The only light that radiated into the room came from caged bulbs strung intermittently along the top of the corridor.

"Hello, young master."

"Ning, I'm scared."

"With good reason, I suppose. Looks like you're in some sort of dungeon."

"They said it's a mine. We're inside a mountain."

"Ah, yes. That makes sense. It's a bit vacuous down here, wouldn't you say?"

Thomas regarded him without responding for a minute. When Ning turned back around, Thomas said, "I don't know what that means."

"How old are you?" Ning asked.

"Six and a half."

"No, I suppose you don't."

"Ning, you aren't being very helpful."

"What is it you require, young master?"

"Can you get me out of here?"

"Well, no. That, I cannot do. Or won't? Or maybe shouldn't? Regardless, no. That is a bridge too far, as they say."

Thomas began crying. He did not attempt to hide it or thwart it. He was not ashamed of it. He was angry and scared, and trying to be as brave as he could. He raised his voice, "What can you do?"

"It depends on what you ask."

Thomas tried to stop himself from crying so he could think. He wiped his face on his blanket. Ning sat down beside Thomas and started munching absently on a bamboo shoot that he had pulled from seemingly nowhere.

"Do you have to do what I say?"

"No. But I can only do what you say. But there are ... limitations. Some things, I cannot interfere with. Or shouldn't. Or won't. The lines get a little hazy."

Thomas found himself confused by Ning's explanations. As he was trying to work it out, his belly started growling. They had brought him food since he'd been down here, but he'd refused to eat it, so they took it away. Now he regretted that.

"Can you bring me some food? I'm hungry."

"What would you li— no, don't tell me. It doesn't matter. I cannot change your physical circumstance."

"Will you go check on him, then? They brought him in after I got here. He's scared too."

Ning looked past Thomas and followed the direction he was pointing. There was an animal huddled in the corner of another cell several feet away. With an exaggerated harrumph, Ning got to his feet and waddled directly through the cell bars and over to the other cell, where he sat down near the animal's head.

Thomas reached out and touched the metal cage that housed him to test whether he could put his hand through them like Ning had done. But he was firmly encased.

He watched Ning's conversation with the animal, but couldn't hear anything. He noticed that his bottom hurt. The pallet they'd given him didn't have much padding. It was still warmer than lying on the stone floor, though.

Ning came back and lay on the ground, wriggling around, scratching his back. Having satiated himself, he rolled over onto the pallet and nestled in.

Thomas used his foot to nudge the panda. "Ning? What did y'all talk about?"

"Of course. Silly me. As you can see, he is a pegasus."

Ning caught Thomas' blank expression.

"You don't know what a pegasus is?"

Thomas shook his head.

"Well, then. A pegasus is like a horse — but don't tell them that; they get testy on that subject — but it has wings and can talk. They are royalty. They are also quite uppity, if you ask me."

"Are they like unicorns?"

"Oh, no. No. No. Pegasus are intelligent and intuitive. Unicorns are … well, they are … not that."

Thomas asked, "Why is he here?"

"You *are* full of questions. He doesn't know any more than you do."

"But I bet you do."

"I have suspicions, but I know nothing to a certainty. That is not my assignment."

Before Thomas could inquire further, there was a loud clanging in the distance. When they heard voices and footsteps echoing down the corridor, Ning said, "I must go now."

Then he winked out of the cell.

A moment later, Ning popped his head back in. "Young master, you must tell them nothing." Then he withdrew his head and was gone again.

Thomas looked over to the pegasus, who appeared to be shivering slightly but otherwise did not move. Thomas stayed still as two men walked in their direction, although he could not yet make out their words.

They stopped outside his cell, appraising him.

One man dressed in a suit and had a neat appearance that did not fit the environment. The other was monstrously large, such that he dwarfed the other man. He seemed to be a part of the mountain itself.

"Who are you?" the larger man asked.

Thomas gathered every bit of courage that was in his tiny body. He stood up and answered, "Thomas David Walls."

Vulcan said, "Well, Thomas David Walls, I know who you are, and I know your mother."

Thomas wasn't sure what response he wanted, so he said, "Me too."

Vulcan's laugh rolled like thunder.

"Are you Goliath?"

"No. I am Vulcan."

"You don't look like Vulcan. He has a really big bottom."

Vulcan laughed again and his amusement twinkled in his eyes.

"I like you, Thomas Walls."

"Did you know David cut off Goliath's head?"

Vulcan's expression changed from one of mirth to a wry grin. "Are you David?"

"He was older than me, and a shepherd."

"Are you going to cut off my head?" Vulcan asked.

Thomas sat back down on his pallet. "I don't have a sword."

"You're an impertinent little bastard, aren't you? Just like your mother."

Thomas shot him as fierce a glare as he could muster. "Don't talk about my mom!"

Vulcan turned to the Warden. "This one's got grit."

"He's scared of her," Thomas said, pointing at the Warden.

"That's very perceptive of you. How did you know?" Vulcan asked.

Thomas shrugged. "I can just tell. He doesn't like it when you talk about her."

The Warden interjected, "I'm not sca—"

Vulcan cut him off with a quick gesture.

"Do you know why he fears her, Thomas?"

The boy shook his head.

"This is a wonderful story. Would you like to hear it? Never mind. Of course, you would. You see, the Warden here isn't a very good guy."

"Is he a bad guy?" Thomas asked.

"Well, that's an interesting question. Let me answer it with my own question — do you think I'm a bad guy?"

Thomas rubbed his chin in a dramatic way. "I didn't use to when you were just a statue. But now that I know you, yes, I think you're a bad guy."

"Have you considered this good guy-bad guy thing is not a helpful characterization? And it creates an antagonistic dynamic that we might otherwise avoid?"

"No."

Vulcan asked, "Would you change your mind about who's a good guy and who's a bad guy if I told you that your mom burned down Mr. Warden's office building?"

Thomas mulled over this new information, before stating his position with a concise, "No."

"Care to explain why?" Vulcan asked.

"Well, if he's a bad guy and she burned his building down, she has to be a good guy?"

Vulcan smiled and nodded approvingly. "That logic is pretty hard to argue with. Now back to my story. Mr. Warden here was off doing bad guy things, and your mom didn't like it, so they got in a fight. Like a real knockdown, drag out. And things went pretty poorly for the Warden. Your mom very nearly killed him. Technically, did kill him, in fact."

"Well, if she killed him, how is he still alive?" Thomas argued.

"That is a poignant question, my boy. And it requires a long answer that I don't care to give right now, but the short of it is that the Warden isn't strictly human. Or isn't only human." Vulcan addressed the Warden. "Show him."

"I'd really rather not. It's rather uncomfortable to do," he protested.

"I'm not interested in your preferences. Show him."

"He may recognize me," the Warden complained.

In a tone that was as much a threat as a command, Vulcan said again, "Show him."

The Warden transformed himself, taking the form of a chimera. He was entirely black — parts lion, goat, and serpent.

Thomas screamed and covered his eyes.

Vulcan said loudly over the screaming, "Looks like you were right. He does recognize you."

Thomas stopped screaming, but he still had his hands over his face and was sobbing. His entire body was quivering.

"Alright, scamper off now, kitty. I need to talk to the boy."

The chimera roared and its tail snapped in Vulcan's direction.

Vulcan said coldly, "It would be better that you were never born than what will happen if you suddenly grow a backbone and turn on me. Scat!"

The Warden slunk off with his hackles raised.

Vulcan said to Thomas, "Walk with me. I want to show you something."

Thomas wiped his face as he came alongside Vulcan. He didn't even come to Vulcan's hip. As Vulcan walked, Thomas nearly had to run to keep up.

"Can you slow down? You walk too fast," the boy complained.

Vulcan slowed his pace.

"Do you know why you are here, Thomas?"

The boy shook his head.

"I am looking for something important. And I think you can help me find it. I think *you* are important." Vulcan stopped and squatted down so he could get as close as possible to eye level with Thomas. But he still towered over the boy. The stark light of the bare bulb from the mine shaft's ceiling cast sharp shadows over his face.

Thomas needed to tread carefully, but he didn't know what the safest route was.

"I don't know anything important," he said.

Vulcan tapped on the side of Thomas' head. "It's not what you know." Then tapping the boy's chest, he said, "It's who you are."

Vulcan stood up again and began walking. "We are almost to our destination. Your mother is very powerful. And I think you are too. Do you believe me?"

Thomas shrugged.

"Noncommittal. That is fine for now. But there will come a time when you must choose."

A room opened to the right. Vulcan pointed for Thomas to turn into it. As they entered, Thomas saw a hill toward the back of the room. But it was uneven and oddly shaped. There were sticks poking out of it at odd angles. He tried to stop to figure out what he was seeing, but Vulcan put a hand on the back of his head and propelled him forward. Once they closed in on he foot of the hill, Vulcan allowed them to stop.

Thomas began whimpering and tried to cover his eyes.

"Do not," Vulcan said. "See it. And understand. I once thought they were important too. But they are not. And now they are here."

The hill was a pile of bodies. Not just humans, but other creatures as well, the likes of which he had not seen and could not describe. Fear pulled at his chest. He took a big breath, but that was when he realized the stench. The carcasses at the top of the pile were fairly new, but those at the bottom were long past bloating and were putrefying. He gagged and became sick.

"Titus," Vulcan called.

A man, clad all in black, emerged from the shadow-filled corner of the room.

"Take our young friend here back to his cage. And let's see if he's ready to eat something."

Titus nodded and began walking toward the boy.

Vulcan had one final word before he left. "Thomas, look at me."

The boy looked up.

"Do not disappoint me."

CHAPTER 21

AGATHA

THE SUN WAS low in the sky when Joseph parked the car and asked, "You're sure this is the place?"

Agatha nodded.

They got out and began climbing the rocky hill. Joseph discovered a footpath that they followed to an opening in the rock about four feet high and three feet wide.

Agatha brushed past Joseph, ducked, and entered the mouth of the cave. Joseph followed her in. The darkness crowded them quickly.

Agatha raised her hand and an orb of light formed above her palm, sending bats flitting about.

"That's a real handy skill you've got there," Joseph said.

They followed the cave downward and straight back. It widened as they walked, and the ceiling continued to increase its distance from the floor until it became something of a cavern. They crossed a shallow stream that cut perpendicular to their path. The dim light was enough for Joseph to see that in it were crawdads the size of small lobsters.

Agatha pushed forward. Despite the confidence she was projecting to Joseph, she wasn't entirely sure where she was going at this point. But unless the cave split into other channels, she figured to keep following it down into the earth.

The cavern took a left turn and led them to a chasm about eight feet across. They stopped at its edge. Agatha sent her orb along the length of the chasm, trying to find a way across. It illuminated a plank that lay across the gap. They walked over to it. Agatha brought the orb down close to inspect it, although plank may have been an overly generous term. It was a twelve-foot-long 2x6. But it looked sturdy enough.

Joseph extended a hand and smiled with one side of his mouth. "Ladies first?"

"How chivalrous of you."

Joseph squatted down and picked up a rock. He pitched it into the chasm. It took a couple of seconds before they heard it clank off other rocks and eventually become still. Joseph shivered.

"I don't suppose you can fly too and were just waiting until a really opportune moment to spring that on me?"

"Nope."

"Then I guess we're going to do this."

Agatha offered, "Let me go first."

"No, no. I'll go first. If anything happens, you're a little more indispensable than me."

"Okay."

"Okay? You're not supposed to agree that you're more important than me."

Agatha pointed, "Quit dicking around and get to it."

Joseph sat down on the board. He leaned forward and started pulling himself across.

"What the heck are you doing?" Agatha asked.

"Distributing my weight."

"Oh, because it looks like you're just being chicken."

He looked around himself. "I see how you would come to that conclusion."

When Joseph was about halfway across and the board was sufficiently bowing and creaking to give her pause, Agatha backed up from the chasm about twenty feet. She took off running as hard as she could and leapt. She landed on the other side with a roll and popped back up.

Joseph scooted himself to the end of the board and had placed his hands onto the edge of the cave floor to transfer his weight.

"Show off," he grunted at her.

"Those Spartan races really paid off."

"As did my early years as a toddler. Where do you think I got those scooting skills?"

"Oh, for sure. It was very inspiring."

She appreciated that even when everything around them seemed to be coming apart, they had both been through such hell in their lives before this that they could still find some levity to make it a bit more bearable. They'd talked before about him getting in trouble as a kid for humor that was inappropriate for the situation, but it had been paying dividends lately.

"Where to now?" he asked.

Agatha sent the orb ahead of them. They saw that the only apparent exit was a crawl space.

"Oh, good. Tight spaces are my favorite," he said. "Are we sure this is the right way?"

Agatha leveled with him. "Honestly, I don't know. I'm just kind of winging it."

He considered it. "Fair enough. Let's go then."

They army-crawled through the aperture, which opened up after a short time to allow them to stand again.

"Kill the light for a second," Joseph said.

Agatha did. After their eyes adjusted, they saw there was the smallest amount of light reflecting off the wet cave walls ahead of them. A bend in the corridor kept them from being able to see too far ahead. So Agatha gave them light again.

Joseph looked at her with his eyebrows raised in a question. She shrugged. She didn't know what it was either.

He started walking, and she followed. As they rounded the bend, the light increased in the barest of increments. The cave opened up into another room. It had occupants.

Agatha immediately recognized Theiona and nodded to her in deference. The pegasus greeted them. "I am pleased you could join us."

Joseph pointed to the source of the diffuse orange light. "What's that?"

Without looking, Theiona said, "The east entrance."

"So just right down that corridor is outside?"

"Yes."

When Agatha received Joseph's accusing glare, she looked back at him indifferently. Then to Theiona, "We appreciate the invitation. Can you make introductions?"

The others stood in a semi-circle to Theiona's left. She started with the creature beside her.

"For Joseph's benefit, I will give both names and the type of being we are."

Agatha sensed that he had blushed in embarrassment.

"Jahaeris is a phoenix. Hydra is collectively known as Rhianu, though she has other names for herselves." While the phoenix was about the size of a big turkey — which is what Joseph would have expected had he ever given it any prior thought — the hydra was smaller than he would have guessed. A hydra was supposed to be imposing and terrifying, not something you could send skittering across the floor with a quick hip check.

"Ophinicus is a griffin. Ekhidna is an orthrus." Now these were what you wanted out of mythical creatures, Joseph thought. A half eagle-half lion and a two-headed Rottweiler. They were still lab experiments gone wrong. What Jeff Goldblum would've said, that their creators were so busy figuring whether they could that they didn't stop to ask whether they should. But at least if you went into battle with them, the enemy would be afraid, not trying to decide whether he could make them into pets.

Theiona turned her attention to Agatha and Joseph. "This is Agatha. She is a zauberin and fought with the Gevalti. Beside her is her husband, Joseph. He is ... a man."

Joseph opened his mouth to say something. Agatha caught his eye and almost imperceptibly shook her head. She stepped forward to close the gap. Joseph followed. The others met them as they advanced and closed the circle.

"I have asked you here because Vulcan has taken children from each of us. There are others as well," Theiona said. "But if something is to be done, we seven must be the ones to do it."

"Why has he done this?" Ophinicus asked.

"Vulcan has reason to believe there is or will be a child who has power like nothing we have ever seen."

"What reason is that?" Rhianu's heads asked in unison.

The sound made Joseph's skin crawl.

"A prophecy," said the griffin. "It is the reason that Vulcan claimed this region for himself so long ago. The prophecy brought him here. And now he believes its time for fulfillment is nigh."

"What is the prophecy?" Agatha asked rather abruptly.

Jahaeris stepped toward the center of the circle, fluttered its feathers, and recited:

In the foothills of the mountains
Whose blood runs red,
Where men have removed the mountain's heart,
One will be born with the power
Over the living and the dead.

Agatha had never been more grateful for the bleak light in the cave. She further dimmed the orb that levitated above them so it would hide her face. A flush of fear ran from her heart down through her legs. Thomas was a schopfer, a creator. She had seen him bring things to life. Did he also have the ability to snuff it out? It stood to reason that he could.

Joseph said, "Well, that's a heck of a poem, but what reason do we have to think it's true?"

Theiona answered, "The oracle prophesied it in the shadow of the Naxian sphinx."

Joseph looked around. "I don't know what any of that means, but y'all seem to be impressed by it. So I guess we'll just run with it."

Agatha grabbed his wrist and applied some light pressure. This wasn't the time for him to start carrying on.

Jahaeris proposed, "Should we identify the abilities of our young who have been taken?"

The griffin answered, "I do not know whether that—"

But Joseph cut him off, "We can start. Our boy Thomas can talk to animals. Regular animals, not like you lot."

Agatha wanted to crawl under one of the boulders, and Joseph seemed to immediately recognize his mistake as the demeanor of the others became less friendly. "Wait. I see now how that was insensitive or racist or something. My apologies. But you know what I mean."

By this point, Agatha was digging her nails into Joseph's arm, but he seemed impervious to her signals. She tugged him toward her and whispered, "Please. Stop."

He nodded.

"Agatha?" Theiona prompted.

"Yes?"

"Do you have anything to add?"

She wavered, weighing the risk of sharing her knowledge versus the ... what? Was there anything useful that might come of telling them? She didn't know.

"He hasn't displayed any of the extraordinary abilities that might be expected of him based on his lineage," she said.

Theiona regarded her for a while, then nodded. She turned her attention to the group.

"Have any of you observed anything extraordinary in your young?"

One at a time, going clockwise around the circle, Theiona made eye contact with them. First, the phoenix. Then the griffin, hydra, and orthrus. Each confessed nothing substantive. Until she was back around to Agatha. They held each other's gaze for a long time. Agatha finally flinched and looked away.

Theiona knew something. Agatha wasn't sure how. But it also seemed that she wouldn't expose the secret ... for now. Maybe she too had her doubts about what might get back to Vulcan.

"So what's the plan?" Joseph asked.

"This is where your expertise is paramount. Both of you," Theiona said. "We do not know what to do or how it must be done. But we are willing to do whatever it is, whatever the cost. This cannot continue."

Agatha nodded. "We will need some time."

"As well as any of us, you know what is at stake."

Ophinicus added, "We will await your instructions."

CHAPTER 22

AGATHA

THE GROUP ERUPTED from their Jeep like a small explosion. The trailhead had been tranquil, serene. But no longer. The five teenagers had been cooped up for the better part of two hours. As they popped out, the remnants of their lunch poured out with them.

"Y'all, you gotta pick up your trash," Guillermo instructed. "And don't put it back in the Jeep either. It'll reek of stale burgers. Use those trash cans over there. Although, the Jeep already smells like Wesley, so fast food may be an improvement."

"At least I don't ..."

The group waited.

"What? At least you don't what?" asked Guillermo.

"I don't know. Nothing came to me."

Another round of laughter.

"Come on, guys," Agatha prompted. "We've only got like four hours of daylight before we have to be back."

"And everybody grab your coats too. It gets cold in them there hollers." Will added.

Guillermo grabbed Lauren by the hand and headed toward the trailhead. "Alright, folk, let's giddy-up."

The other three followed up behind the occasionally insufferable couple. Agatha snagged a look at the map of the Sipsey Wilderness's broad expanse. She found "You Are Here" pin and noted that nothing was around for miles in any direction.

They hustled down the first quarter-mile of trail where they confronted a decision.

"Right or left?" Wesley asked.

Guillermo said, "Left is FT 201. It's a pretty part of the river, but nothing special along the way. To the right is FT 202, which offers bluffs and a path to the river. But most important are the cemeteries, which FT 201 does not have."

"Well, that settles that. 202 it is," Will decided.

"I don't know. That sounds kind of scary," whined Lauren.

Guillermo winked at her. "Don't worry. I got you, babe."

"Oh, gag a maggot," said Wesley before pretending to throw up.

While the others lingered at the fork, Agatha took off down the trail to the right.

"Where are you going?" Will hollered after her.

She yelled over her shoulder, "Hiking."

The rest of the group fell in line, as she knew they would.

After the split, the trail narrowed sufficiently that they couldn't walk three across any longer. Even two put both hikers at risk of being snagged by overextended branches. Ten minutes into the new trail, Agatha braked hard enough that Wesley ran into the back of her.

"Sorry, I was—"

"Shh," she ordered.

The rest of the crew saw what Agatha had already spied. A man walking toward them from up the trail. He had a rifle slung over his right shoulder and a knife on his left hip that Rambo would have envied. The pile of teenagers filtered themselves into a single-file line to give him room to pass.

Agatha found herself still at the front of the line. She pulled her sleeves up to her forearms.

She made eye contact with the hunter as he approached the group. He touched the tip of his baseball cap. "Ladies. Fellas."

No one returned the greeting.

Agatha started walking again.

After there was sufficient distance, Wesley said, "Well, that was weird."

Will said, "He's probably going to circle back around, hunt us down, and bury us in the cemetery. Who would ever find us?"

"Stop it. I'm scared. Can we go back?" Lauren pleaded, tugging on Guillermo's arm.

He grabbed her hand again. "Come on. Deer season opened up a couple weeks ago. He's just hunting."

"Yeah, hunting people," Will persisted. "Didn't y'all read 'The Most Dangerous Game' in Mrs. Miller's class?"

"Knock it off, Will. And no, no one read it except you."

Another twenty minutes of hiking brought them to the cemetery that spanned both sides of the trail.

"I present you Johnson Cemetery. It dates back to the early 1800s."

"Cool." Wesley bounced off to the left, and Agatha with him. The other three veered to the right.

Some of the grave markers were mere remnants the elements had worn away. Others remained almost untouched. Agatha minded her cemetery etiquette and made sure not to walk over the places where the bodies would lay, assuming anything was even left at this point.

She touched one of the markers as she walked past and a shiver crawled up her spine.

Wesley asked, "Possum walk over your grave?"

"What?"

"I said, did a possum walk over your grave?"

"I mean, I heard your words, but what the heck does that even mean?"

He shrugged. "Dunno. It's just what you say when somebody shivers. Heard it my whole life."

"Exactly how country are you?"

"Country enough, I reckon. And it's a good thing for y'all too."

"Why's that?"

"Because like Hank Jr. says, 'Country boy can survive.'"

"Oh brother," Agatha rolled her eyes.

Wesley laughed. "Come on. Let's catch up to those guys."

By the time they got to the river, it was mid-afternoon. The two-and-a-half miles ought not to have taken them that long. But they had to account for the time the boys took trying to scale cliff walls, hurling rocks downhill, and whatever other feats they could think of that were supposed to impress Agatha. And absolutely did impress Lauren, at least where it concerned Guillermo.

Agatha wanted to join them. To do those things. But how many times had her mother told her, "Agatha, you must not show up the boys. Their egos are fragile, and they will resent you for it."

But the river erased whatever feelings she had about inequality. It was extraordinary. The water was a blue she had never seen. Carrying downriver thousands of leaves of all colors that the forest was shedding. She watched the water and leaves navigating around boulders the size of buildings. They looked like gods had thrown them down, playing the same game as her friends, but on a much grander scale.

The other four pulled alongside her, just taking it in. The crystalline water. The canopy of leaves that cascaded down with the breeze. A warm autumn had delayed the seasonal cues.

Agatha broke the spell. "Looks like the trail ends at the river."

"It does," Guillermo said. "We have to go upriver a bit. There's a place to cross over to 209."

"Do we have time?" Will asked.

"Yeah, it won't take us as long to get back."

They walked along the bank for a couple hundred yards, looking for a place to cross.

"How about there?" Lauren suggested, pointing at a shoal that also had several larger rocks spaced far enough apart to step across without anyone having to get their feet wet.

"That's the place," Guillermo confirmed.

A gust of wind blew over the river, bringing with it a scattering of leaves.

Wesley said, "Boy howdy, that was cold. Ags, you got my coat in your backpack? I don't think this is going to be enough." He was pulling at the arm of his long-sleeve shirt.

"No. Why would I have your coat?"

"Well, I just thought you might have grabbed it."

"Literally, the last thing Will said before we closed up the car was for everyone to get their coats."

"Okay. Okay. You sound like my mom. Geez. I'll be fine. That's why I keep myself surrounded in this extra layer of insulation. I'm like a bear."

"Yeah, I don't think that's how that works," Agatha said.

After they crossed, they saw the sign that said FT 209.

"Guess we could have just been looking for the trail marker instead of trying to find some random crossing, huh, Guillermo?" Will suggested.

"I mean, yeah, we could have. But I kind of forgot about it."

"Nice."

They followed 209 downriver until a host of yellow jackets on the trail made them check up.

"What time is it?" Lauren asked.

"Judging by the shadows—" Wesley started.

"Oh, shut up, Jeremiah Johnson," said Will. He consulted his watch. "It's 3:30."

Guillermo did some mental math. "We'd better turn around. We've gone about five miles, and the sun'll set around 5:00."

Agatha said, "Dude, it's gonna be dark by the time we get back to the car."

Guillermo shrugged. "Maybe. It'll be fine."

While they had stopped, most of the group put on their coats. The sweat they'd worked up was cooling on them, and the temperature was dropping with the sun.

"Must be nice," Wesley griped.

"About face," Guillermo said, and started heading back from the direction they'd come.

In the twenty minutes it took them to get back to the river, the ambient light was noticeably dimmer. Agatha realized that when they had talked about what time sunset was, they hadn't accounted for how much less light there was in the holler and under a canopy of trees. They were going to be hiking in the dark sooner than expected.

"Did anyone bring flashlights?" she asked.

Everyone just kind of looked around at each other, hoping the next person would have something in their bag.

"What about a lighter?"

Still nothing.

This might be a problem.

"We need to get a move on," Will said.

Each of them had identified the urgency of the situation and quickened the pace. They crossed at the same shoal as they had before, retraced their steps, and took the first trail on the right. Guillermo took the point and led the climb back up the ravine.

Within a few minutes, Lauren asked, "Is this the right trail?"

Wesley piped up, "Yeah, I don't remember the little crick on the right when we were coming down."

"It's the right trail. Y'all just weren't paying attention

before." Guillermo defended himself and kept going. A dozen steps later, he looked over his shoulder and saw that the group wasn't following.

"Hey, man, this isn't a time to pretend like you know what you're doing. It's okay if you don't," Will said.

Guillermo came back to them.

"Hang on. I'll look at the map." He pulled his trail map out of his back pocket. All five of them leaned in. "Guys, y'all gotta back up. I don't have enough light as it is."

Guillermo studied it.

"Well?" Lauren prodded.

"So I don't know what we're on. I don't think it's one of the marked trails. But it'll probably get us where we need to go."

"No," said Agatha. "We're not doing 'probably.' We need to turn around and go downriver to the trail we came in on."

"We don't have time to backtrack. We're losing light fast," said Guillermo, knowing it was a losing argument.

"We don't have time to get lost in the woods either."

For the second time that day, Agatha started walking, knowing they'd follow.

Single file, with less fervor than before, they made their way back to the river. They made a right at the water and set about finding FT 202. After a few minutes, Agatha slapped the trail sign.

"Man, I didn't see that one either," Will said.

"Me either," admitted Guillermo. "It's already dusky, so we need to stay close together. No straggling. I'll take the front. Who wants to bring up the rear?"

Nobody volunteered to be the last one in line. The one who could be the person to most easily disappear into the Sipsey Wilderness without notice, never to be seen or heard from again.

"Will?"

"Yeah, I guess."

Wesley had taken the opportunity to climb onto a boulder that was sitting in the river. "There's something I need to tell y'all." He paused for dramatic effect. "I'm much too young to feel this damn old." And he launched into his best Garth Brooks impression.

It broke the tension, but not for long. Agatha's imagination was already running away with her. She really regretted that she'd read *The Girl Who Loved Tom Gordon* earlier in the year. She brought her hands to her mouth, blowing into them for warmth. Gloves would've been nice. She watched as the vapor from her breath escaped from between her fingers and dissipated into the darkening air around her.

Guillermo said, "Come on, man. Get down. We gotta go."

"Alright. Hold your horses."

Agatha watched Wesley consider his options. She would have just jumped clear to the bank, but Wesley had a bit more mass and clearly wasn't going with that approach. He sat on the edge of the boulder and began sliding himself down, pointing with his toes, trying to gain a purchase. He found rock about the same time that his triceps could no longer sustain his bulk, shifting all his weight to his feet.

But the rock he found was wet and covered in a thin layer of slime. Wesley's feet flew out from under him, tossing him flat on his back into the cold waters of the Sipsey River, fully submerged.

Lauren shrieked.

CHAPTER 23

AGATHA

WESLEY POPPED UP IMMEDIATELY, spewing water and gasping in surprise. He trudged out of the water and over to his pod of friends. He shivered and his teeth had begun chattering.

"So cold. So cold," he said.

Will offered his coat. It was a couple sizes too small, but it would have to do.

"Are you okay?" Lauren asked.

Wesley took a minute. "I don't know."

"Is anything hurt?"

"Dunno."

"Let's start walking. Maybe that'll help warm you up," Guillermo suggested.

Wesley nodded.

Before immersing herself into the forest, Agatha looked at the sky. The sun had dropped below the hills. The few clouds were the embers of a dying fire.

"Wesley, go between me and Lauren," she said.

He complied without a word.

All levity had been quenched.

They fell in behind Guillermo as he led them along FT 202 back to the trailhead. Their only sounds were footfalls, the rustling of clothing, and breathing. Agatha was listening for Wesley's breathing, which came fast and shallow. Different from her own and Will's behind her, whose breath sounds changed with their exertion levels. He may be in trouble, and they had miles yet to go.

The undergrowth was thick with dormant brush and thorn-laden ivy constantly slapping at their legs. The unmaintained trail was heavy with exposed roots and rocks that grabbed at their toes.

When Wesley kicked a particularly obstinate rock and lost his balance, Agatha reached forward to right him, but was too late. He landed hard. Will and Agatha immediately stopped. It took Guillermo and Lauren a second longer to register what had happened.

Nocturnal forest awakening and Wesley's chattering teeth made the only sounds.

"Come on, Wes." Will leaned down. "Give me your hands."

With some effort, Wesley lifted his arms and allowed Will to pull him to a sitting position, then to his feet.

Will was still looking down when Agatha asked him, "What are you looking at?"

He raised his head in Guillermo's direction. "Are we not on the trail anymore?"

No response.

Lauren said, "Guillermo?"

"I ... I think I lost it."

"How long ago?" Will asked.

Guillermo didn't meet their eyes. "I don't know."

Lauren started whimpering.

Will seethed. It was just like Guillermo to forge ahead into the darkness without having told them he'd lost the trail. How long would they have gone on like that if Wesley hadn't fallen?

"What do we do now?" she asked. "Wesley might be in trouble."

Will said, "We're all in trouble now."

"Well, we can't stop here," Guillermo suggested. "If we keep going, we should come to those bluffs before long. From there, maybe we can pick up the trail again."

Agatha wasn't enthusiastic about the plan, but it was clear they couldn't stop where they were. Although she couldn't make out much, she saw every breath as she expelled it. In the quiet, she heard drops of water hitting the ground as they let go of Wesley's clothes.

"Okay," Agatha said. "Let's get to the bluffs and reassess."

They resumed their uphill climb until the terrain leveled out somewhat. Agatha appreciated the change in grade and paused to rub her quads, trying to ease the burning.

"You good?" Will asked.

"Yeah."

She quickened her pace to catch up to the pack, but realized she had lost little ground. Wesley was slowing down.

"Wes, you okay?" she called.

He didn't respond. But he kept putting one foot in front of the other.

Guillermo yelled from up ahead, "I think I see the bluffs."

When Agatha looked up, a looming shape pushed upward somewhere ahead. She found it difficult to determine a distance since everything was varying shades of gray.

They reached the bluffs within a few more minutes of some combination of walking and stumbling.

Wesley reached the stone wall, put his back to it, and slumped to the ground.

"He can't go any further," Agatha said to the other three as they clustered a ways from Wesley.

"I don't think any of us can. We're lost and can't see anything." Will said.

"We're not lost," Guillermo protested. "We just have to find the trail again. I think—"

Lauren tugged at his sleeve. "Stop. We're lost. And when's the last time anyone ate anything?"

Lunch, which suddenly felt to Agatha like a long time ago.

As if it had been waiting for a cue, Will's belly growled. He put his hands to his stomach. "We have more pressing problems. We have to get Wesley warmed up. He's still got those wet clothes on, and it's cold out here. If we don't ... then ... you know."

Lauren asked, "Anyone have a lighter? Matches?"

Agatha already knew the answer. They had only been coming out for a few hours. No one was prepared for anything, really.

Will walked over to Wesley. "Wes, buddy, do you still smoke?"

The answer was a long time coming, and it he delivered it quietly. "Quit."

That was it, then. That was their last hope. Her last hope.

Several minutes of fear and uncertainty passed without comment.

Will broke the silence. "Agatha."

"No." She knew this was coming.

"Agatha, you can fix this."

"No. You don't understand what you're asking."

"You can save his life."

Guillermo stepped in. "One of you want to fill us in on what you're talking about?"

"We aren't talking about anything."

Even though she couldn't see it, she knew the expression on Will's face. Nothing had been the same since that day at the creek with the bear. They weren't exactly friends anymore. But they weren't not friends. They shared something. A bond. A secret. A trust that he'd never betrayed. Until now.

"Ags, Wesley is going to die. Literally freeze to death. You can keep that from happening."

Lauren asked, "Do you have like matches you didn't tell us about?"

"Not exactly," Will said.

"I don't know what that means." Lauren's confusion showed in the snarkiness of her tone.

Agatha stepped out of the huddle. "Y'all give me a minute."

She walked a few feet into the woods. Behind her, Guillermo asked Will, "What's going on?"

She didn't hear the response. The blood rushing into her ears was too loud. Everything was catching up to her. It was too much. Hot tears welled up and spilled onto her cheeks.

Sticks broke behind her. Will.

"Agatha." It sounded more like a plea than an address.

She wiped her cheeks and rubbed her eyes with the palms of her hands and ran her fingers through her hair.

She turned to face him. "I know."

He had tears too. "I'm sorry."

But even then, he didn't know what he was asking. Couldn't have known.

"I know."

When Agatha and Will returned to Lauren and Guillermo, she instructed them to look around close by to gather some kindling and small branches.

Lauren started, "But how—"

"I'll show you. Just get the wood."

She heard, but could not see, the sigh that followed.

They assembled a small teepee in front of Wesley.

"Now what?" Guillermo asked.

Wesley still sat slumped against the bluff. He either wasn't registering the goings on around him, or just wasn't evidencing it. Guillermo, Lauren, and Will stood together to his right.

On his left, Agatha knelt down. She slid the ponytail holder from around her wrist and pulled her hair up. She extended her arms toward the woodpile and cupped her hands together, right over left. A soft glow emerged from between her fingers. Within seconds the glow hardened, and the light grew harsh. Agatha opened her hands and shoved them under the pyre. The ball of flame rolled off her fingers and burst when it hit the ground, greedily attacking and igniting the wood.

She saw everyone's expressions now. Wesley's had not changed. He was hardly with them. Will emoted wonder. His fear had resolved long ago. Lauren and Guillermo were terrified, awe stricken. They watched the flames and said nothing.

"We're going to need some bigger sticks so this doesn't burn itself out."

Guillermo confronted her first, "What the hell, Agatha? What the hell was that?"

She stared back at him, her jaw clinched. This is the moment she knew would follow. They would want answers, obviously. But there was so little she could say.

"Come on, man. We need to get some wood." Will pulled at his shoulder. But Guillermo jerked away. Agatha saw anger. But it wasn't true anger. It was fear masquerading as anger.

"I want an answer," he said.

They needed to get this resolved so they could tend to Wesley and to the fire.

"I will tell you this one time, and we will never speak of it again. Ever. I can harness energy and create fire."

"So, what — you're like one of the X-Men?"

Will burst out laughing. "I never even thought of that. It's so perfect."

Now it was Lauren's turn to accuse. "And how did you know about this?"

He was still smiling at the revelation. "There was a thing that happened once."

He was going to enjoy being coy about it, to revel in the knowledge gap. But they needed to act quickly. Agatha was done with the conversation. She began searching the area around her for dry wood. It was a little easier with the light of the fire to go by. The idea that she was like Storm or Jubilee had never occurred to her before. She liked it. She might actually have to thank Elle for foisting upon her those endless hours of cartoons she was actually too old to have still been watching.

Agatha returned first with an armful of wood. She stacked it around the existing fire. A dry autumn and several weeks without rain had allowed for dry wood that caught quickly. The others returned and lay their collections in a pile. Will started helping her. Lauren and Guillermo wouldn't come close. Wouldn't look at her.

"Well, I guess that's to be expected," Will said, watching them. "You know, from my own personal experience."

"Yeah."

The exhilaration of the moment had worn off. Sadness started setting in. A longing for normalcy, acceptance.

"Help me with him," she said. She swiveled from the fire so she was directly in front of their still-frozen member. "Wesley, we're going to take off this coat. And we need to get your clothes off of you so you can warm up."

He didn't assist them, but he didn't resist either. After he was down to his underwear, they got him to scoot closer to the fire. As close as they dared.

Will reached out his hand. "Guillermo, give me your coat. Mine's wet, and we need to keep his back covered."

He stepped forward to hand over his coat, while still keeping his distance. But Agatha figured that wouldn't last long. He'd get cold enough soon that he'd have to decide between being warm or staying away from her. She'd make that easier for him.

Agatha stood up and started walking back toward the woods.

"We have enough wood for now," Will called.

"I'll be back."

If she followed the bluff, it should lead her back to the trail. As long as she could find it. As she walked, her eyes re-acclimated to the darkness. She realized that the trees were casting shadows on the bluff walls and forest floor. The moon was rising. In a couple more hours it would be high enough for them to see moderately well.

After several minutes, she looked back over her shoulder. She could still see the fire, so she kept going. Another minute and the ground began rising to meet the top of the bluff. She scrabbled up the incline and stood upright to gather her bearings.

She was standing next to what might be a narrow path. It was hard to be certain in the relative gloom. She needed to know if this was the trail. She shrugged at herself. The secret was dead now. Might as well be able to see.

Agatha stepped onto the path and raised her hands over her head. A flame erupted into her palms. She didn't look up so as not to destroy the low-light vision she'd reacquired. The fire lit the forest floor around her enough to confirm that she was indeed standing on a trail. A left turn should take them to the cemeteries. Then to the fork, and on to the Jeep. She extinguished the fire and made her way back to the group.

The sound of munching greeted her. Even Wesley was eating something. Will reached across and handed her a granola bar. "I had a few in my pack."

She obligingly accepted the offering.

Wesley looked up to her. "Thanks."

"For?"

He gestured at the fire.

She looked over to Will and mouthed, *Does he know?*

Will shook his head.

"Yeah. No problem."

"You gotta teach me how to make a fire like that sometime."

Will covered his mouth and turned his head to hide his grin.

"Sure thing. Girl Scouts really paid off, I guess. Hey, nice duds, by the way."

He looked down at himself. He wore only Guillermo's coat draped over his shoulders and Will's coat turned inside out, covering his lower half.

The other two showed no signs of being amused. They showed no signs at all of recognizing her presence.

"I found the trail," she dropped casually.

Now she had everyone's attention.

"It's back that way." She pointed along the bluff wall where their shadows danced with the undulation of the flames. "Moon's coming up too. It's mostly full. So by the time Wes's clothes dry, we ought to have enough light to make our way back."

"We'll have to go slow," Will said. "But it's better than spending the night out here." He looked at his watch. "We got another ten hours or so until sun-up. Y'all fine with that plan?"

He looked clockwise around the group, getting nods from Agatha, Lauren, and Guillermo.

"Wes, you up for another hike?"

"I guess so. Sure beats sitting in the dirt in my underwear."

Agatha was the second one to be dropped off. Wesley had been first. When the Jeep stopped in front of her house, Lauren got out and tilted the seat forward to let Agatha out. She got back in, but Agatha stood in the opening between the door and the Jeep.

"Listen, what happened tonight ..." The entire way home she'd been thinking about how to have this conversation. She hadn't quite figured it out, so she just kind of petered out mid-sentence.

"Not what happened," Guillermo said. "What you did. There's a difference."

Will came to her defense. "She saved his life. That's what she did."

But it was Lauren who saved her cutting remarks for last. "Don't worry. We won't tell anyone you're a freak. Not that they'd take much convincing."

Agatha took a step back. Lauren slammed the door, and Guillermo pulled off. Will waved at her through the back window. She returned the wave and stood there until they rounded the corner.

When she turned to face the house, she saw that the living room light was still on. Great.

Agatha dug her keys out of the front pouch of her backpack as she walked up to the house. She removed her shoes and took a deep, cold breath, then opened the door, anticipating the barrage.

Her mother rose from her chair. Agatha could tell she was being assessed.

"Where have you been? Do you have any idea what time it is?"

"Yes."

"Well?"

Agatha crossed the room, embraced her mother, and came apart at the seams. All the stress and anxiety of the night bursting from her.

"Baby, what happened?"

Sobbing.

Gertrude grabbed Agatha by the shoulders and pushed her to arm's length. Agatha knew she was a red-faced mess.

"Are you okay?"

She could only nod.

"Okay." Gertrude pulled her back into the embrace.

It took several more minutes for Agatha to collect herself.

"Sit down. But not on my couch. Your clothes are filthy. Let me get you some water."

"Can I have some milk instead? And a peanut butter and honey sandwich?"

Gertrude wore a quizzical expression and shook her head as she entered the kitchen, as if she still hadn't figured out teenage girls, despite having two of them. But she returned with the goods.

She let Agatha eat in peace before the inquisition began. "Tell me what happened."

Agatha recounted her last fourteen hours.

When she finished, her mother sat quietly for a minute. Agatha had watched her demeanor change as she had talked from concerned to ... something much harder.

"This is going to be hard for you to hear and harder still to bear. You may have saved the one, but in doing so, condemned them all."

"What does that mean?"

"Exactly what it sounds like. The Zauberat will decide what happens now."

"Like they're going to kill them?" The hysteria was returning. "Those are my friends. They haven't done anything wrong."

"I don't know what will happen. But you were told long ago that if you used your powers in front of others, the results would be devastating. I don't know what you thought that meant."

"I was a kid. I didn't think of it at all."

"I don't believe that. You are nothing if not considered," Gertrude said. "You made a choice. And I understand why you made it. In some ways, I am proud of you for it. But it was the wrong decision. Maybe you cannot yet comprehend why, but there is just so much at stake."

CHAPTER 24

4 Teens Killed in Sunday Night Rollover Crash in Shelby County

FOUR TEENS DIED Sunday night in a single-vehicle crash in Shelby County.

The crash happened at 9:17pm. on US-31 south of Alabaster, said Alabama State Trooper Charles Walker. The fatality victims were ages 16 and 17, but their identities have not been released.

Walker said the 17-year-old driver, from the Leeds community, was driving a 1992 Jeep Wrangler that left the roadway and overturned multiple times. The driver and all three passengers were ejected from the vehicle and pronounced dead at the scene.

No additional information has been released. Trooper Walker would not comment on whether drugs or alcohol were believed to be involved. Troopers are continuing to investigate the accident.

CHAPTER 25

JOSEPH

JOSEPH WOKE up realizing that the exhaustion had finally granted him almost an entire night of uninterrupted sleep. He immediately thought about Thomas still missing and felt guilty about sleeping while ... who knows what was happening to the boy. But at least it seemed like he'd have some company based on the number of creatures who'd also been taken.

He had to sleep though. He'd gone forty-eight hours without sleep a couple of times before. And things got weird. Hallucinations. Poor judgment. Motor skills deficiencies. None of that would serve him or Thomas well.

When he and Agatha had left the cave the night before, they hadn't talked about next steps. They had hardly spoken at all.

He could tell that she was plotting, strategizing. He had no idea what she'd come up with. He was stumbling around in the dark most of the time. He would be totally blind if Agatha weren't providing some illumination. But he found himself getting frustrated about just how little light she was shedding on things. All he could see was his next step. She was a lantern. What he wanted was a floodlight.

Agatha started moving around beside him.

He thought back to when all this had started, realizing it had been less than two weeks. That struck him hard. It had seemed like months.

He sat up and put his feet on the floor.

"Stay in bed a little longer?" Agatha suggested.

"Can't. Gotta pee."

By the time he came out of the bathroom, Agatha was out of bed too. A pot of coffee percolated in the kitchen. It was the signal his brain needed to shift into second gear. If only coffee tasted as good as it smelled.

"What are you doing about work?" Agatha asked.

"Called in and told them I have the flu. I've got some PTO built up, so it won't be a problem."

"Okay, good. I don't want you getting fired on top of ... you know ... everything else."

"Yeah. Kind of surprised I'd actually thought of it. That's not like me."

"I will decline to comment."

Agatha filled their coffee mugs and placed them on the kitchen table. She sat down in front of hers and gestured for Joseph to do likewise.

"This is ominous," he said.

"Since our meeting last night, I've been thinking about what to do next. And I think I know what it is, but you're not going to like what I'm going to tell you."

Joseph got butterflies in his stomach. He'd been mostly joking when he said it was ominous. But it felt pretty real now.

"I reckon that's about par for the course these days."

Agatha gathered herself to say whatever it was. She was taking her time. Then she just spit it out.

"We have to go visit my mother."

"At the cemetery?"

"No ... at her house in Leeds."

Joseph clenched his jaw. The frustration he'd experienced earlier was boiling up into something else. He slammed his mug onto the table. A wave of coffee sloshed out onto the table and the wall. He pushed up from his chair, knocking it clattering across the floor. Something primal inside him wanted to roar and break things. He stalked to the other side of the kitchen to give himself some space.

He yelled, "Is there anything else?"

Agatha didn't answer.

"Is there any other secret you're carrying around that's going to come rearing its head?"

After a minute, Agatha said, "You don't underst—"

"And why is that?!" Joseph demanded.

She flushed with anger at being yelled at. They'd never done this before. She stood up and approached him. He wasn't sure what was about to happen. The smallest twinge of fear tugged at him.

Agatha hissed, "They would have killed you."

His anger rekindled itself at the implication. "I don't need anyone to protect me."

"Yes, you do! You have no idea what we're up against."

Joseph grabbed her by the upper arms and asked again, "And why is that?"

She reflexively struck him in the chest with the heel of her hand and broke his hold on her arms. Both the suddenness and the force of the blow surprised him, stunning him for a moment and taking some of the anger out of him. Regret immediately filled the void. He had never laid hands on her before. It's not how they did things.

Agatha had turned on her heel and walked back to the other side of the room. Waffles sauntered in to check out the commotion and plopped himself onto the floor with a huff.

Agatha said, "There is one other thing."

"Okay."

"But understand that part of it I knew, and part of it I figured out last night at the meeting."

"Okay."

"The prophecy we heard might be about Thomas."

"What?"

"Do you remember the prophecy?"

"Not really. Something about mountains of blood."

Agatha recited it. *"In the foothills of the mountains, Whose blood runs red, Where men have removed the mountain's heart, One will be born with the power, Over the living and the dead.* I think it's about Thomas."

"But I thought—"

She raised her hand up, cutting him off. "I know. You remember that day we went into the woods and saw the stag? Before we met up with you, Thomas showed me something. He scooped up a handful of dirt and made plants and flowers grow out of it while he was holding it. Then he went over to a dead tree, put his hand on it, and brought it back to life. I've never seen anything like it. He is a schopfer, a creator — it's an ability that is extremely rare and powerful. I don't know when the last schopfer was alive."

Joseph was dumbstruck. But the root of bitterness and anger tugged at him again. "You didn't tell me."

Agatha said, "There was still so much that you didn't know then. You didn't even fully know about me yet."

"That was literally four days ago."

"Yeah, and I think you'd agree with me that quite a lot has happened in that time."

He didn't want to go down this avenue again.

Agatha sat back down at the table, signaling she too was done with confrontation. He was trying to figure out how to reroute when she asked, "You got any more of those cigarettes left?"

"You mean the ones that sent me into a coughing fit and

made me queasy? No. No, I don't. Besides, I don't think they're strong enough to cure what ails you."

She sighed, pushed her hair out of her face, and patted the table beside her. "Come sit down with me, and let's sort this out."

Joseph shuffled across the room and sat down, deflated from the encounter.

"Listen, I'm sorry th—"

Agatha cut him off. "Me too. Forget it. We've got other things to fret over right now."

"Can I just say one thing before we move on?"

She looked at him with a raised eyebrow that always meant *enter at your own risk.*

"That open hand strike really packs some oomph."

"A couple of inches lower and your diaphragm would have been freaking out, and you'd be on the floor trying to figure out how to breathe again." She patted his arm. "But don't worry, I was looking out for you."

A shiver ran up his spine. "You're kind of scary."

"I know. Should we talk about my mother now?"

"Yeah, sure. Tell me about my mother-in-law, who I thought was dead until ten minutes ago."

"Maybe we can talk as we drive? But I'll tell you this. She's had a hard life. She was widowed young. Then my father abandoned her before I was born. She's lost one daughter, and all but lost me because of the choices I made. She's the strongest person I know."

"Well, that's a heck of an endorsement."

Agatha pulled the car to a stop at the curb in front of her mother's house. She sat there with her hands on the steering wheel. Joseph reached for his door handle. Agatha reached her arm out.

"Hang on. I haven't been here since I was pregnant with Thomas. I need a second."

When she looked like she'd collected herself, Joseph asked, "So all those times you wanted to go alone to your mother's grave on Decoration Day?"

"I went to Ruffner Mountain. It was the anniversary of my sister's — what happened to her."

"You've never told me about her."

"Perhaps another time."

Joseph felt like every time he peeled back a layer, it only revealed more layers. There was no end to what he didn't know about the woman he'd lived with, been married to, and raised a child with for the last six years.

"Fair enough," he said. "You ready?"

"Yeah. You?"

"I guess?"

They opened their doors and got out. Agatha met Joseph on the sidewalk.

As they walked to the door, Joseph asked, "I have one more question — what's your mom's name?"

"Ha! That'd probably be helpful. It's Gertrude."

"Gertrude?" He gave her a sideways look. "Isn't that kind of old-fashioned?"

"Says the guy with the four-thousand-year-old name. But also, you should lead with that. I think it'd be a good opener."

He grinned. "Pass. I'll just start with the standard fare. Did you tell her we're coming?"

Agatha shook her head.

Joseph tried to hide his surprise. "Alright. This should be interesting."

Agatha took the three steps up onto the front porch, and Joseph fell in behind her. She knocked on the door. He got knots in his stomach and couldn't imagine what Agatha must be feeling.

The door opened, revealing a woman in her early sixties. It was like looking at Agatha twenty-five years in the future. Her hands went immediately to her face and tears filled her eyes.

"Momma," Agatha said.

Gertrude grabbed her and wrapped her in a hug that lasted several minutes. Joseph stood where he was, feeling every bit the intruder. He tried to avoid making any sound or doing anything that would draw attention to himself.

Gertrude released the hug and held Agatha at arm's length. "You look tired, sister." Then she looked past Agatha to Joseph. "So you're the one who took my baby girl away from me?"

Joseph blushed and found himself without a response.

"I'm just teasing you. Come here. You get a hug too."

And even though he was all but a stranger to her, she embraced him like a son. When she let him go, she said, "Y'all come inside. I assume you're not here on a social call."

They congregated in the living room. Joseph and Agatha on the couch and Gertrude in her favorite wingback chair.

Gertrude led off with, "How is little Thomas? And why didn't you bring him with you to see me? If I'm finally going to meet the family, I might as well meet all of you." As she finished her sentence, she saw their fallen expressions. "Is he ... oh my ... tell me what's happened."

Joseph's heart broke all over again.

Agatha wouldn't or couldn't say anything, so he told the story. About the kidnapping, the burning of the Pythian Temple. He explained Thomas' powers as best he understood them. The meeting with the Mythicals, as Agatha called them. And the prophecy.

"And all of that has brought you back home," Gertrude concluded. "I am so sorry for what you're going through. But I am also so happy that you're here. And Joseph, I am proud that you're adjusting to everything so quickly. I'm sure it's been ... a lot."

"Oh, I'm definitely going to need counseling after this," Joseph said.

"Agatha, dear, what is it you need from me? Because you're a much more accomplished zauberin than I, and if this is beyond you, I'm not sure what I can do."

Agatha pulled out of her daze and joined the conversation. "I need to summon the Zauberat."

"Ah. I see. Diplomacy has never been your strength. And Oberhaupt, have you reached out to him?"

"The Gevalti is not in a position to help."

Gertrude nodded. "There is a darkness looming. Vulcan's influence has been growing. It has been subtle, so far, but the shift in power is evident to those who know to watch for it. Those who have seen it before."

"Before?" Joseph asked.

"You are both too young to remember Birmingham in the Fifties and Sixties. Neither of you was even alive."

"I mean, I know about 16th Street Baptist Church and Bull Connor and all. But what does that have to do with Vulcan?"

"It's not the acts themselves. But the hate and venom. The struggle for power. This is where you can see him. Whenever humanity is at its worst, there are always other forces behind it."

"But what does he get out of that?"

"The same as any autocrat with a lust for power and dominion. The consolidation of power to himself. The oppression or extermination of those who oppose him — us. Unstoppable influence."

"Okay. Even if all that is right, people have been pretty capable of destroying each other for a long time now — what does that have to do with us now?"

"What was the last part of that prophecy? There will be someone who has power over life and death. What greater power is there? He may not have that power himself, but if he can control the one who does, it amounts to the same thing."

"And y'all think that's Thomas?"

Agatha said, "It *could be* Thomas. At minimum, you could interpret his ability that way."

Gertrude added, "Prophecies have a way of writing things into existence that might not otherwise have been. Prophets and prophecies should be considered with a good deal of skepticism."

Joseph looked at Agatha beside him. "But you think Vulcan's bought into this one?"

She shrugged. "The Mythicals do. At least, the ones we met with. And they may be right. It's certainly something he would want to be true and want for himself. So … maybe."

Gertrude said, "That brings us back to summoning the Zauberat for a session."

"What can they do?" Joseph asked.

"Well, if they agree to get involved, they will allocate resources and make this much easier. But from what y'all have told me about the Warden and the Gevalti, I have my concerns."

"So if they don't help?"

Gertrude sighed. "Your task becomes much more difficult."

Joseph put his hands on his knees and pushed himself up from the couch. "Well, let's go find out."

Gertrude shook her head. "It's not quite so immediate as that."

"And you don't get to go," Agatha said.

"What?"

"You're not zauberi. You can't attend."

Joseph looked from Agatha to Gertrude, who nodded.

"What the heck am I supposed to do?"

"I don't know. Sit at home and watch TV, I guess. But we're getting ahead of ourselves. They haven't even agreed to convene yet."

Gertrude stood as well. "You let me handle that. They will convene. I will let you know when. You know the place?"

"I do," Agatha said.

"Alright, you two. Give me a hug. And maybe the next time we're all together, it will be a happier occasion."

CHAPTER 26
THOMAS

THOMAS SAT in his cell shaking. He hadn't been able to rid himself of the image of the pile of bodies that Vulcan had threatened him with. He had no idea how much time had passed since then, but they'd brought him six meals.

He tried to talk to the baby pegasus, but it wouldn't respond to him. Wouldn't respond to anything. It just lay in its cell, eating and drinking as little as it could get by with.

"Ning," Thomas called quietly. He didn't know why he bothered to be quiet about it. There was no one around. And when someone was approaching, he could hear them coming for miles.

He waited for the panda until, with the tiniest pop, it appeared within his cell, holding a fistful of bamboo.

"Top o' the morning to you, Thomas."

"Why did you talk like that when you said that?"

"Just trying a new greeting out. You didn't like it?"

Thomas shook his head.

"Fair enough."

"Is it morning?" Thomas asked.

"Closing in on mid-afternoon now."

There was a long period of silence between them. Each was

comfortable with the arrangement. Thomas glad for the company and Ning munching on his snack. He had good manners enough to offer some to Thomas, who declined.

Thomas eventually broke in with a question. "Ning, can you help me escape?"

Ning considered it before answering, "Yes and no."

Thomas just stared at him.

"Allow me to elaborate then. I cannot physically affect your environment. So I couldn't just, say, open this door for you. But more pertinently, I must do what is in your best interest. And I am not convinced that escaping and wandering around some old mines is in your best interest."

"Please, Ning," Thomas whined.

"I have made my decision, and you will not dissuade me."

Another silence, but this one less comfortable.

A tearful Thomas said, "I guess you want me dead then."

Ning looked taken aback. "Quite not. What a terrible thing to say."

"That's what they do with us."

"Surely not," Ning contested.

Thomas pointed. "Go down the hall and see for yourself."

Ning disappeared with a pop. A minute later, he re-apparated within the cell.

"Do you have a plan?"

"I was right, wasn't I?"

"Most certainly. Now, remember, we are operating within certain constraints of what I can and cannot, or sometimes will not, do. But it seems to me that this," gesturing around the room, "environment is not best."

"Can you get me out?"

"I cannot."

Thomas didn't know what to do or even where to start. Ning toddled through the cell bars to get a look at the lock. "Just your standard padlock. Didn't leave you with a key, did they?" Ning asked, leaning to his left to see around the lock.

Thomas crossed his arms and glared at the panda.

"I thought not."

Ning looked around the room.

"No keys hanging on the wall either. Drat. Let's see here. What are our options? What can you do, Thomas?"

"I can talk to animals," he offered in a helpful tone.

Ning shook his head. "While that is a valuable skill, I don't think it does much for us here. Do you have any other abilities?"

The boy didn't answer.

"Thomas?"

He shook his head.

Ning said, "I cannot aid you without information."

"I can't tell you. My mom said not to tell anyone."

"I see. Let me ponder this for a minute." Ning looked off in the distance, adopting his most earnest expression. "Did she tell you not to *show* anyone?"

Thomas thought about it. The answer was no, but it still seemed like that was breaking the rule.

"No."

"There you have it. You can show me your ability. You don't have to say a word."

"But I don't think—"

"This is not the time for thinking," Ning said. "If you want out of this place, now is the time for action."

Thomas knew in his heart that he was disobeying. Even if it wasn't exactly what she'd said. But he'd seen what could happen to him. He tried not to think about the mound of bodies. About the Warden turning into the thing that had tried to grab him. He shuddered involuntarily and said to Ning, "I guess a possum walked over my grave."

Ning looked taken aback, "Excuse me?"

"That's what you say when you shiver — a possum walked over my grave."

"First, I have never heard of such a thing. And second, possums are a disgusting nuisance and we shall not talk about them. Have you decided whether you will show me?"

Thomas sighed and nodded his head.

"Very well. Please proceed."

Thomas leaned forward on his pallet, placing his hands on the ground like a dome. He concentrated not on his hands, but on what was below them. Soon, something soft pressed lightly against his palms and the bases of his fingers. He raised his hands up to reveal a small village of toadstools, where there had only been a stone floor. He smiled reflexively at his work, then looked up to Ning. He saw awe and wonder in the panda's face.

Ning walked back through the bars to inspect the boy's work. He sat down in front of the toadstools. He reached down to touch them, making sure they weren't an illusion. Then he plucked one up off the ground and popped it into his mouth.

Thomas started to protest, but wasn't sure why.

Ning held up a finger. "That was truly delightful."

"I thought you couldn't ... I don't remember what you called it."

"Your physical environment, yes. Well. Cannot, will not. Who's to say? But more importantly, can you destroy them?"

Thomas thought about it. "I don't know. I've never tried that. Mommy says I'm a shopper. That means a creator."

"Schopfer. A schop-fer."

"Okay."

"Now, I want you to kill them."

"I don't want to," Thomas whined.

"Thomas, look at me. Do you trust me?"

The boy considered the question and shrugged.

"Have I ever given you a reason not to trust me?"

"Well, you're not very helpful sometimes."

"That is a fair assessment. But we must know what you can do. You must know. I can turn my back, if you like."

"Okay. No peeking."

Ning stood up and turned his back to Thomas and the toadstools. Thomas placed his hands over the cluster and focused on them again. They ceased to touch his hands. He kept his attention on them until he knew instinctively that he was done. When he lifted his hands, his earlier joy at his creation was stolen from him. All that remained was a putrefying, black mass. The rotting smell reminded him again of the pile of bodies down the hall. Tears came to his eyes and his nose ran.

Ning turned around when he heard the boy sniffle. "Well done, Thomas."

"I didn't like it. It felt bad."

"Nevertheless, now we know. Are you ready to leave? I have an idea."

"I want to lay down."

"No. Now is the time to go. Cover the toad stools with your pallet."

"Eww. No."

"We cannot leave it where it will be seen."

"Fine." Thomas slid off his pallet, grabbing the nearest edge and pulling it over the remains.

"Now, come to the door," Ning instructed. "Stick your hands through the bars and take a hold of the padlock. Do to it what you did to those delicious toadstools."

"But it's not alive. I don't know if it will work."

"True. But you don't know that it won't."

Thomas did as he was told. When he released the lock a minute later, it was a rusted hull.

"Splendid!" said Ning. "So just reach up there again and pull down. Perhaps it will unlock."

Thomas raised up his arm and grabbed the padlock, pulling down. With some effort and jostling, it unlatched. He turned it sideways and slid it out of the loops, then pulled his arm in and looked at the lock. It looked ready to crumble in his hands. It had aged a hundred years. He showed it to Ning.

"Excellent work. Now you will need to undo the damage."

"Undo it?"

"Yes. You will need to restore it to its previous condition. Otherwise, there will be some reason for suspicion."

Thomas frowned. "I don't know if I can."

"Thomas, listen here. We have a finite window in which to get you out of here. You can either argue with me about what you are or are not capable of when you have not yet tried to do the thing you are telling me you are incapable of doing. Or not. Because sooner than later, someone is going to come check on you or feed you or whatever other reason they may have to come in here, and they going to notice the ruined lock and the missing boy and have questions about how those things happened. I'd rather us not give ourselves away. And I'd rather us be down the road when they find you missing. So restore the lock."

Thomas closed his hands around the lock. When he reopened them a minute later, he had eliminated most of the rust, and it was in fair condition.

Thomas showed Ning. "That's as good as I could do. I'm tired."

"That will do nicely. Now why don't you open that door and we will skedaddle."

The boy stepped to the door and pushed it open. He had taken several steps toward the corridor when he stopped abruptly. "We have to get Kleron."

Ning was confused. "Who is Kleron?"

Thomas pointed at the pegasus.

"We really haven't the time…"

Thomas crossed his arms and stared at Ning with insolence.

The panda threw his paws up. "Fine. Fine. Do what you must."

Thomas went to Kleron's cell and found that they hadn't latched his lock. He removed it and opened the door. "Come on, Kleron, we gotta go."

Kleron got to his feet but seemed uncertain about following.

"Come on. We're getting out of here. We're going home."

Thomas opened the door wide and stood to the side, giving Kleron plenty of room. He stepped forward timidly, stopping in front of Thomas. They were nearly nose to nose. Thomas leaned in and placed his forehead on Kleron's.

He whispered, "It's gonna be okay."

The foal whickered softly.

They walked to where Ning was waiting. Thomas asked, "Do you know the way out?"

Ning waddled away from the cells. "More or less. Well, no, not really. But we can figure it out."

The small party turned left into the corridor and approached a metal door. As Thomas reached for the handle, it turned down and the door opened. He jumped in surprise and backpedaled. Vulcan emerged first, ducking through the door frame that he entirely filled. A cadre of cronies followed him.

"Thomas," he said as he appraised the situation. "Imagine my surprise in seeing you here. Outside of your cell. Where are you going?"

Thomas looked around himself and discovered that only Kleron was still with him. Ning had disappeared. He didn't answer the question.

The rest of Vulcan's crew had come through the door and fell in behind him.

"You will answer my question, and truthfully."

Thomas was scared. Not yet as scared as when the Warden had become that thing, but close.

"We were leaving. Going home."

"And how did you get out?"

The truth was not an option. Or at least not the entire truth.

"The locks weren't ... clicked."

"Is that so?" Thomas saw something change in Vulcan's demeanor. His words sounded different now. "Who was the last person to open your door?"

Thomas pointed to the man who had brought him food and changed out his pee bucket.

Vulcan called him forward. "Miles."

Miles immediately began protesting. "I locked the cell back. I do every time."

Vulcan gestured to Thomas and Kleron. "Would you care to explain their presence if you locked up after yourself?"

His protesting became more of a whine. "I locked it. I promise I did. I don't know. But I did."

With a swift movement that defied his size, Vulcan grabbed Miles by the throat and raised him up off the ground. Miles emitted croaking sounds, struggling to breathe. His hands clutched at Vulcan's wrists but to no avail.

"There is no room for incompetence here."

The muscles in Vulcan's forearms flexed as he squeezed. Miles thrashed until there was a muted crunching sound from the front of his throat, followed by the sound of bones giving way at the back of his neck. Vulcan dropped him in a heap.

Fear and adrenaline flushed through Thomas. His legs turned to jelly. Kleron whimpered beside him. He put a hand on the pegasus's neck.

"That lesson was for them. They must understand the stakes here. As must you. For every failure there is a consequence. You have failed to escape, and now there is a toll to pay."

Vulcan grabbed the hammer that hung from his belt. He raised it high over his head and delivering a thunderous blow to Kleron's head, crushing his skull. The pegasus remained on his feet a moment longer before collapsing to the floor.

Thomas wailed, "No!"

He fell to the floor and buried himself in Kleron's wing.

Vulcan allowed him to carry on for a minute before instructing, "Pick him up."

Two men stepped forward and pulled Thomas to his feet. Thomas sagged between them. He discovered that he had wet himself. But he was too terrified to be ashamed.

Vulcan addressed him. "Not two days ago, I warned you not to disappoint me."

Then he spoke to the men that held Thomas upright. "Get him cleaned up and back into his cell. And lock it this time."

To the rest he said, "Get rid of these two. Put them with the rest."

CHAPTER 27
AGATHA

AGATHA SAT on the steps in front of Quinlan Castle, waiting on her mother. It had always struck her as peculiar that the Zauberat met here. It seemed entirely too on the nose. But nobody had bothered asking her.

She had bigger things to worry about anyway. There would be plenty of opposition to her on the council. The Warden would do nothing to aid her cause. And if she was right about him, he would affirmatively blockade it. Even if he did it discretely. Oberhaupt. Who knew what his official position would be? His visit hadn't provided a great deal of clarity. Then there were the rest, whoever sat in those seats now. But she had her own reasons to distrust them. All these years later, she'd neither forgiven nor forgotten.

Agatha watched as Gertrude rounded the corner. She stood up, meeting her at the gate.

"I'm like the White Rabbit," Gertrude said.

Agatha had no idea what she was talking about. "What?"

"Late for a very important date. You know, from *Alice in Wonderland*?"

"You're so weird."

Gertrude shrugged it off.

Agatha grabbed the sleeve of her jacket. "Any words of wisdom before we go in?"

"A few. Since you asked. Just tell them what you know. Don't embellish anything. Tell them what the Mythicals told you. And we'll see what happens. While they have a vested interest in protecting the community, they do not always attend to things as we might expect."

"Okay."

"Oh, and don't let the Warden provoke you. You may be aware of this about yourself, but you're a bit of a hothead."

Agatha rolled her eyes. "Thanks, Mom."

The conversation and setting combined to make her feel like a teenager again. She needed to get into a different mental space, become more in control than the last time she'd been here, when she was the one being summonsed. There was too much at stake for her to be timid, uncertain. She had to be the irreverent Agatha that didn't allow rank or hierarchy to deter her. But not overtly so. She had a fine line to walk.

"How do we get in?"

Gertrude pulled a key out of her pocket and held it up.

"Oh. Well, that's kind of disappointing, actually. I thought you were going to use your hexerin skills or something."

Gertrude smiled, unlocked the gate, and returned the key to her pocket.

When they entered the Zauberat's chamber, the Warden did not conceal his resentment toward Agatha. "It's quite bold of you to be here tonight, all things considered."

That helped snap her into the right frame of mind. "I believe I could say the same of you," Agatha countered.

"I should have you arrested for what you did."

Agatha's mouth turned up at the corner. "You're welcome to try."

"Folks, before we get too far into the weeds with ... uh ... personal quarrels, we ought to first address the issue that we've been summoned for," Nancy proposed.

In a fit of anger, the Warden slammed his hand down on the desk, "Personal quarrels? Is that what we're calling what she did? She burned a building to the ground. She put us all at risk."

Nancy adjusted the nameplate that the Warden's tantrum had knocked askew. Stadtratin for Apprenticeships. "What you *think* she did," she corrected, every bit the pedantic teacher. "Besides, it's my understanding that anything disconcerting was destroyed or would have been indecipherable to the person who found it."

Agatha was pleased that Nancy was taking her side. She'd always had the impression that her mentor was at best indifferent about her. Maybe she just disliked the Warden more. Or perhaps it was something else entirely. She'd been gone for a while. But the reason didn't matter. It was helpful for now.

"That is decidedly not the point," the Warden said, adjusting his jacket and attempting to look dignified again after his tantrum. "Well, let's just get to it then, if we're going to entertain this—"

"Careful now, Warden," the Stadtrat for Treasury chimed in. "Let's not be improprietous."

Oberhaupt too addressed his fellow stadtrat. "She has more to answer for than just your allegations. But I am willing to set that aside for now." Then turning to Agatha, "Why have you summoned us here today?"

Agatha understood how this was going to go. They hadn't had two interactions in the last couple of days. And he was still bitter about her abandoning the Gevalti. That part likely was true, anyway.

Gertrude stood up from where she sat at the table beside Agatha. "I am the one who summoned you. My grandson has been taken. And because he is zauber, the matter falls within the jurisdiction of this council."

Nancy said, "We do not have any record of him being zauber. What evidence is there of this?"

Gertrude looked to Agatha.

"He can speak with animals. He has spoken with our dog, and I witnessed him communicating with a wild stag in the woods."

"Does he possess other abilities?" she asked. She had the hungry eyes of a teacher searching for her next star pupil.

The Warden attempted to conceal his lust for information, but he was entirely too interested in the answer to do it well. Information was his currency, the means by which he brokered power.

"We have not discerned any," Agatha answered.

"I'm sure that is a disappointment to the family," Nancy said.

Agatha seethed. Gertrude placed a hand on her forearm. Do not be provoked. Something suddenly struck her that she would tease Thomas with when he got mad, *You just gotta be like Elsa and let it go.* She tried to soften her demeanor and unbristle herself. Agatha took a deep breath and did not respond.

Oberhaupt asked of Gertrude, "You summoned the Zauberat. What would you have us do?"

"Vulcan kidnapped Thomas," Agatha answered frankly. "We would have you aid us in getting him back."

"This is preposterous," said the Enforcement Stadtrat. "We have seen no evidence that he is active again."

Even Gertrude was becoming ruffled. "I always find it difficult to see when I keep my eyes screwed so tightly shut that no light can penetrate them."

"Enough," Oberhaupt asserted, bringing them back to Agatha's request. "First, the Zauberat will not *aid* you. Either we will choose to do it, or it will not be done."

Agatha maintained eye contact with Oberhaupt from across the room. He had grown accustomed to people crumbling under the pressure that his size and intensity could apply. But she knew him. She had battled beside him. Once upon a time, they had been all but siblings. Surely, he knew that with her, his usual intimidation tactics were like water to a duck.

"You have leveled quite an allegation, Agatha," said Nancy. "Can you support it?"

"Titus attacked my husband and son. And while Joseph was unconscious, he abducted Thomas. No one has seen him since?"

"Did you see this happen?"

"No. Joseph described to me what he saw when I got to the scene. But I would recognize Titus's work anywhere."

"Is your husband zauber?" Nancy asked.

"No."

Nancy looked at the other stadtrat. "Yet he has witnessed these things. That is something we will have to consider separately."

Agatha's blood ran cold with the implication and the memory of her friends. She stood up and placed her hands flat on the table in front of her. She made sure to make eye contact with each of the five of them. "Let me be clear with you. Anyone who touches my husband will burn slowly and from the inside."

Nancy reacted with shock. "Are you threatening the Zauberat?"

"I am providing fair warning to whoever needs to hear it."

"This is all absurd," the Warden interjected. "No one took her son. Or at least there's no reason to think Vulcan did. Her husband ran into a sinkhole, and the boy wandered off. This other version is just fanciful fabrication."

"There is more," Agatha said, forcing herself not to respond directly to the Warden. "Twice before Thomas was taken, there was what he described as a chimera in our home. On one occasion, it attacked him and sent him to the hospital."

Enforcement looked across Nancy to the Warden. "This is new information. Warden, the chimera is within your domain. How do you respond?"

"Nonsense. That's how I respond. No one has seen the chimera in ages."

"It is yours to constrain, is it not?" asked Enforcement.

"Yes, of course. I do not deny that," he said. "And there is no reason to think that is not being done."

Agatha stepped in, "It attacking my son is at least some reason to think it's not being constrained."

"She has a fair point there, Warden," said Oberhaupt.

Agatha watched as the Warden lost his patience with being questioned. This was a good turn. She planned to stoke the fire rather than let it fizzle out.

The Warden answered, "I don't know what to tell you other than that the beast is behind lock and key. You are free to schedule an inspection of the premises if you like. But this tangent seems to be entirely beside the point of this meeting."

Agatha said, "I appreciate you bringing it back to that, because you couldn't be more wrong. It is exactly the point. You are caught up in this. And no one who's willing to look at the situation with open eyes could see it otherwise."

The Warden's face reddened.

Nancy objected, "Agatha, really, that is a bridge too far. Everyone on this bench has fought to keep Vulcan and those of his ilk at bay."

Gertrude stood up again. "We are not here to dispute the contributions that each of you has made to maintaining peace and order for our people. Nor to downplay the sacrifices you have made. But relying on past accomplishments as evidence of current loyalties is a practice that is fraught with peril. We must be vigilant and constantly on watch for indications that allegiances have shifted. We cannot ignore what is there to be seen merely because it is uncomfortable."

"If you have something to say," the Warden said as he stood up, "let's hear it."

Gertrude put her hand to her chest as if she couldn't believe that anyone would draw any direct inferences from what she was saying. "What I was sayi—"

"What she's saying," Agatha jumped in, seizing the opportunity to fully catalyze the situation, "is that you're a lying liar who lies. And anyone who chooses not to see that is reckless or foolish."

"I wasn't saying that *exactly* ... but I don't disagree with it either."

The Warden looked at the other members of the Zauberat, none of whom seemed prepared to rebut what Agatha had said.

"Unbelievable," he spat. "I will not stand here and be accused of this kind of treachery."

He stormed out of the doors at the back of the chamber.

There were several minutes of peculiar silence as those still in attendance tried to figure out what decorum dictated must come next.

Finally, Nancy reached a decision, "We will advise you of our decision once we ... uhh ... reconvene."

"We appreciate your time and consideration," Gertrude said formally, as if all present hadn't known each other for most of their lives.

Agatha still stood where she had been for the last several minutes.

"Let's go," Gertrude whispered, giving her the cue she seemed to be awaiting that nothing would be resolved in this moment.

When they got back out to the sidewalk, Agatha asked with a half grin, "How do you think that went?"

Gertrude shook her head. "You have all the diplomacy of a water moccasin. Strike first, question second."

Agatha's half grin became full. Until her mother spoke again.

"They will not go with you on this. There is too much at stake."

Agatha nodded. "After what Oberhaupt told me when he came to the house, I didn't think they probably would, but I had to give them the chance. Considering our past ..."

"They don't think they owe you anything. They decide based on what they think is best for all the zauberi. There is no second guessing, no remorse. Your personal loss is inconsequential to the greater good. I'm surprised you still haven't come to terms with that."

"There is right and wrong, and no room for dabbling in the murky gray area between the two."

Gertrude placed her hands on the side of her daughter's face and pulled her forward, placing a kiss on her forehead. "I have always loved that world is so clear to you. For most of us, it is so much more opaque than that." Gertrude zipped her coat. "Now, walk me to my car before we catch our deaths in this cold."

"Mom, it's like forty degrees."

"Like I said, cold."

Before they rounded the corner onto Richard Arrington Boulevard, Agatha looked over her left shoulder, glimpsing Vulcan's giant iron statue that overlooked the city, and thought, *I'm coming for you.*

CHAPTER 28

JOSEPH

JOSEPH SAT BACK on the grass with his arms braced behind him, looking at the cartoonish iron statue of Vulcan. Keeping watch over Birmingham. A beacon atop Red Mountain.

"Why are we here?" Joseph asked.

"Because whatever happens next is going to involve him. So I want to sit here in his shadow doing some mental visualization exercises about how it's going to go and what I'm going to do to him." Agatha added, "And to make sure we're on the same page about what's at stake."

"That sounds kind of dramatic. He has our son. I pretty well understand what's at risk."

"Not the risk to Thomas, but to us."

He sat forward, looking her directly in the face. "Agatha, this is starting to feel insulting. I have made sacrifices for causes much more abstract than this. But you bring me here to Vulcan Park and question my courage. Again."

Agatha looked down. She was not expressing herself well. "I'm questioning none of those things. I have no doubts about you. I want you to fully understand what you're getting into. You've flown through the last two weeks mostly blindfolded."

Joseph let out a harsh, barking laugh. "That's a fairly accurate description."

The stress was getting to them both. "Joseph, dying isn't the worst thing that can happen to us."

"You mean like, if something happened to Thomas?"

"That's not what I mean. Listen—"

"Agatha, no. Everything except the boy is inconsequential. I don't even want to hear the possibilities, because they don't matter. They won't change anything."

"Well, in that case," Agatha pulled herself up off the ground, and reached down to pull Joseph up, "there's something I want you to see."

He reached up and grabbed her hands.

They walked over to the back side of Vulcan's pedestal. Agatha pointed at an oversized storm grate. "If it comes to it, that's our insurgency point."

"Here at the park? It's a little obvious, don't you think?"

"I do," she answered, "But he can't help himself."

"So what now?" Joseph asked.

"Now we wait."

"On the Zauberat?"

"Yes," she said.

"I don't much care for waiting."

Agatha didn't particularly care for that option either. "I don't think we'll have to wait long."

"Will they help?"

"I am hopeful. But if not, it'll tell us what we need to know about which way the power is ebbing."

Joseph looked down at the storm drain. "So he's down there right now?"

"Somewhere in that labyrinth of tunnels, yes."

"And Thomas?"

"I expect so. He will keep them close. He thinks Thomas and the others are the key to his rise to power."

"Fine. We wait. But can we at least wait inside somewhere? It's darn cold out here."

"Yes," she grabbed his hand in hers. "I forget my big, strong man is so sensitive about the cold."

Agatha's phone rang. She had a terse conversation that was monosyllabic on her end.

When she hung up the phone, she said. "That was my mom. Looks like we're about to get our answer. The Zauberat has reached a decision."

"And?" Joseph asked with a knot in his stomach. To be exact, the knot had mostly been there since he'd regained consciousness at Oak Mountain. Just in varying degrees of acuteness.

"She doesn't know. They're sending a council member to her house to deliver the decision."

"Why her house?"

"She's the one who summoned them. Do you want to be there when they tell her?"

"Does a bear—"

"Don't."

"Fine. But if you ask rhetorical questions, you get rhetorical answers."

"Let's go before I decide to uninvite you."

As they drove, Joseph found it hard to say which trip seemed longer, the one where he was going to meet the mother-in-law he'd thought was dead for the past six years, or the one where he was going to find out whether the magical government — is that what it is? — was going to help him rescue his son from a Roman god. No, not a god. A supervillain.

Maybe someday they could just get together for a nice meal. Maybe a minor holiday. Anything approaching the normal end of the life spectrum seemed entirely too much to ask right now.

That led Joseph down a rabbit hole. When he emerged on the other side, he asked, "Before me and before we had Thomas, did you celebrate Christmas?"

"You mean because I'm a Germanic pagan witch?"

Joseph took his hands off the steering wheel and raised them to his shoulders. "Whoa. I'm not into using labels but … yes?"

"No. That wasn't a thing for us. I adopted it with Thomas, hoping to give him a normal childhood."

"I guess that's out the window."

"Yeah," Agatha agreed solemnly.

Everything came back to Thomas right now. It was inescapable. Every conversation. Every stray thought. All took a path back to him. Some winding. Others direct.

Joseph was glad to pull onto Gertrude's street. Now they'd get some clarity about how this was going to go. He looked for unfamiliar vehicles, but as this was only his second time here, any of them could be out of place. He'd have no way of knowing.

As he parked and unbuckled himself, Joseph saw that Agatha began pulling her hair into a ponytail. She too was preparing. Her entire demeanor changed. It was something he recognized from his own deployments. All manner of shenanigans and absurd conversation might occur in the convoy on the way to an assignment, but as soon as they encountered the first sign of trouble or it came time to disembark the vehicles, there was a palpable shift.

She was singularly focused. It's not even like she was being a mama bear. She was so much more disciplined and concentrated than that. This was the Kommandantin.

Joseph fell in behind her as they walked to the front door. Agatha didn't knock this time. She turned the handle and entered. From the entryway, they walked into the living room, where Gertrude was already hosting Nancy. They sat in the pair of wingback chairs that sat angled toward the sofa.

Joseph saw that both women sat so upright that it defied comfort. Even the air in the room was oppressive. This would not be a good meeting.

Once they were seated and still, Nancy delivered the message.

"The Zauberat having been summoned by Gertrude Strom, it held a hearing on Decemb—"

Agatha interrupted. "Just cut to it."

"Agatha, please," her mother prompted.

She did not break eye contact with her mentor. "Say what you're here to say. Don't cover it up in formalities."

"The Zauberat will not provide you assistance in recovering your son. It has determined that there is not enough evidence that Vulcan is directly involved in the alleged abductions to warrant taking any action against him."

"Alleged?" Agatha said in as cold a tone as Joseph had ever heard. Just knowing what lay behind it was enough to make him shiver.

Nancy raised a hand in apology. "I misspoke. No one disputes that your son—"

"Thomas."

"—that Thomas is missing. Or even that he was taken. But there is nothing concrete tying it back to Vulcan. And we are not equipped to police every wrong that is perpetrated."

"It sure didn't take you long to conclude your investigation."

"The Warden and Stadtrat for Enforcement conducted the necessary investigation."

"Convenient that the Warden didn't turn anything up."

"If you have other allegations to make, you may summon the Zauberat and present your case," Nancy offered.

Agatha dismissed it. "You're not going to look too closely into one of your own."

The volleys mesmerized Joseph. Neither woman conceded an inch.

"No, Agatha, you haven't heard *me*. You have not yet begun to hear me. You have heard only the message from the Zauberat that they sent me to deliver."

Agatha flinched.

"Now, would you like to know what I think?"

Agatha nodded.

"Something is happening. I don't know what exactly or how far it goes. And you may be right that it's Vulcan. If so, that would be ... disconcerting. But for now, there's nothing anyone can do in their official capacity. We can't usurp protocol without something more."

It took Agatha a minute to decide her approach. "While I am trying to appreciate what you're saying, how does that help us?" She asked, glancing over to Joseph.

"I understand that it may not carry much weight, but on a personal level, we are not abandoning you. We just didn't have the vote," Nancy said.

"Who's we?"

"Oberhaupt and myself."

Joseph tried to read Agatha's reaction, but she was doing her darnedest to be stoic about things. Regardless, it meant something to him. Not in practical terms. They'd still have to figure out on their own how to get Thomas back. And fight Vulcan and his minions to do it. That still didn't sound right to him.

Joseph realized that in his musing he had missed something.

"—now I am too old to be of any use to you as you make your plans to recover Thomas. But Oberhaupt is not. He was very insistent that I ask you to include him."

"He didn't seem too keen to support me at the council meeting."

"We are in a precarious position right now, Agatha," Nancy said. "Of all people, you know that the political side of Oberhaupt's position is not where he excels. But if you are planning to get the boy back from whoever has him, you would be working to your detriment not to involve him."

Agatha was non-committal. "We'll see. Is there anything else?"

"Agatha," her mother chastised, "manners."

"No, there is nothing else. I will see myself out."

Gertrude started to rise to walk her to the door.

"No need, Gerty," Nancy reassured her. Then to Agatha and Joseph, "I truly wish you the best. And Agatha, if I may step into my former role, and offer one piece of advice — whatever you do, mind your temper. Do not let the kettle boil over."

They watched as she left the room. The door opened and closed. The three of them remained unmoved and considering for several minutes.

Gertrude popped up. "I'm going to make us a pot of coffee."

She headed to the kitchen that was next to the living room.

Agatha sat leaning forward, the heals of her hands on her face and her fingers shoved into her hair.

"So what now?" Joseph asked.

When she didn't answer or acknowledge the question, Joseph prompted her, "Agatha?"

She slowly sat forward. Her face was red and tears stained her cheeks.

"I can't do this. If we screw it up, they'll kill him."

Joseph opened his mouth, then closed it. What did you say to a mother in this position?

Gertrude came back in the room. She squatted down in front of Agatha and grabbed her daughter's hands.

"Listen to me, baby girl. You must do this. A fate worse than death awaits that boy if you fail."

Joseph had the same doubts. But it was time to set them aside and act. Their other options had been removed.

Agatha nodded.

She stood up and rubbed her eyes with the palms of her hands. "Give me a minute," she said, and walked to the bathroom.

When she opened the door, she looked almost a different woman. Her normal pallor had replaced the splotchiness in her face. She stood upright. He didn't know whether it was confidence or determination. But either would do.

"We need to tell Theiona that we're on our own here. She can tell the other Mythicals."

"And then?" Joseph asked.

"We make a plan to get them back."

"Oberhaupt?"

Agatha nodded. "I will include him. We need all the help we can muster."

Joseph wondered at something. "You really thought they were going to help, didn't you?"

"Of course, I did," she said. "Maybe I shouldn't have if I'd been thinking about it more objectively. But whatever."

Gertrude added, "The Zauberat's sense of self-preservation in the face of change and adversity may be stronger than its obligation to the people it serves."

Agatha was ready to move on from it. "It doesn't matter now. We're done with them. Let's have a meal together with the Mythicals and Oberhaupt, where we can develop our plan."

"Let's do it here," Gertrude proposed. "I will prepare food for everyone. Tomorrow night."

Joseph thought of a question. "Can they all get here, you know … without being seen."

"There are many ways in and out of a place."

Joseph tilted his head to the side, trying to sort out what he'd just heard. "I don't know what that means."

Both women smiled at him.

Gertrude said, "I know."

CHAPTER 29
THOMAS

THOMAS SAT on his pallet with his blanket draped over his shoulders and his back against the bars of his cell. With his right hand, he pitched pebbles into the pee bucket that he kept pushed to the furthest corner of the cell from his bed. With his left hand, he was using a rock to keep tally on the floor of how many times in a row he splashed a rock into the bucket without missing. His record so far was seventeen.

He alternated between activities as he grew bored with them. He'd figured out that in the corners of his cell, if he put his hands and feet on the perpendicular bars, he could shimmy up to the top of the cell and use it like monkey bars. Sometimes he shuffled back and forth along the bars. Other times, he'd just hang until his hands and shoulders started hurting.

There were also some *Sports Illustrated* magazines for him to flip through. Most of the words were too big for him to work out, but he liked the pictures of the players. He'd even tried drawing some of them with rocks on the stone floor. It hadn't been very successful, but at least it had occupied some time.

The door opened and closed in the corridor. There were two voices, so he immediately laid down and pretended to be asleep. This had become his default mechanism until he figured out who it was. Some guards were friendly and would talk to him. But others were just mean and harassed him, though they'd mostly leave him alone if they thought he was asleep. Thomas fantasized about what he could do to the mean guards if he wanted to. But to do so would give himself away. So he just told Ning about it whenever he'd pop in.

As soon as he made out the speakers, he continued feigning sleep. Their talking got closer, but he could tell they hadn't crossed the opening to his room, as he'd come to think of it.

The Warden announced, "The Zauberat will not interfere."

"Very well. You have delivered on the laissez-faire administration that we negotiated when I consented to your ascension to the role."

The voices got somewhat closer and with less reverberation. Thomas squinted while trying to be still. He saw that they had paused, facing each other in front of his opening.

The Warden grinned like a child being praised by his teacher.

"And it is a good thing too," Vulcan said, "because you have few other qualities that befit you to the role."

His smiled was smeared away.

"What about the giant?" Vulcan asked.

"He is with us."

"You are certain of that? He has many reasons not to be."

"We have reached an understanding," the Warden assured.

"Which is?"

The Warden waved him off. "Do not bother yourself over the minutiae. What will you do about Agatha? She will not go quietly into the night, as they say."

"She may not go quietly," Vulcan answered, "but she will go. As they all do."

"She is quite powerful."

Vulcan cocked his head to the side and with a smirk asked, "Are you scared of her?"

The Warden didn't hesitate. "Yes. Of course, I am."

"Good. You would be a fool to be otherwise," Vulcan said.

"And what of the boy?"

"What of him?"

"Is he the subject of the prophecy?" the Warden inquired.

"It seems not. Or at least, he has not yet been willing to show me any extraordinary abilities. But prophecies are fickle creatures, always looking to be fulfilled. Makes you wonder what would come of things if the prophecy had not been made."

"Would you like me to, you know...?"

Vulcan cast a disgusted look at the Warden. "We have slain dozens of them, and you are still too squeamish to say it aloud. Now it is my turn to ask you a question that has been percolating for a while."

"Okay?"

"Why did you adopt the title Warden, rather than Direktor, like all your predecessors have borne?"

The Warden shrugged, "I liked the way it sounded better."

"You have always been about flourish. Form over function. It is a weakness, you know."

"It has gotten me this far," countered the Warden.

"Yes, but how much further will it carry you? Or is this the extent of your ambition?"

To deviate from the subject, the Warden asked again, "So what will you do with Agatha?"

"If she makes it necessary, I will do with her as I have done with all of my adversaries for ... well, a long time now. I will dispose of her."

Thomas had heard as much as he could take. He jumped to his feet and ran to the front of his cell, banging into the door. "Don't talk about my mom like that!"

Vulcan turned to him with an amused expression. "Well, look who's awake now."

Vulcan approached the cage and looked down at Thomas through the top. "Would you like to be turned out for a while?"

Thomas determined not to answer.

"Still angry about your horse friend?"

"He was a pegasus," Thomas corrected. Then he covered his hands over his mouth, realizing he'd spoken, despite his intentions.

Vulcan smirked and held his arms out beside him, claiming his minor victory over the boy.

"Now that we're on speaking terms, I'll ask again — would you like to be let out of your cell for a bit?"

Thomas resumed his protest.

Vulcan slammed his hand down on top of the cell with such force that the bars bent in response. Thomas fell to the floor, cowering and covering his ears. The noise was thunderous in the cavernous room. He watched Vulcan's neck and face redden in anger.

"Do not think, boy," Vulcan growled down at him, "that because I admire your temerity, I will tolerate your disrespect."

Thomas was too scared to respond now.

"Do you hear me?"

He nodded, wiping away tears while he did so.

"Good. Now, you've spoiled my good mood. But I'll let you out anyway." He looked back to the entryway where the Warden still stood. "Unlock his cell."

The Warden patted his waistcoat and suit jacket. "I don't have any keys to the lock."

"No keys?" Vulcan coughed out a mirthless laugh. "The Warden doesn't have keys to the jail. What did I say earlier? All form and no function."

He turned back to Thomas, who had pulled himself back into a sitting position.

"No field trip today, then. Stand up and come here."

Vulcan squatted on his haunches. Thomas approached the front of his cell cautiously.

"I want to make sure you hear me well."

Thomas felt Vulcan's warm breath falling on him.

"You have a finite time to prove your utility to me. If you cannot do so, I will move on. And there is no coming back from that. Do you understand what I'm saying to you?"

Thomas considered it and shook his head.

"Let's try this a different way." Vulcan pointed to his left, and Thomas followed his giant hand. "Remember that pile of creatures at the other end of the corridor?"

Thomas' voice quavered as he said, "Yes."

"They outlived their usefulness. Now, you told me before that your only ability is speaking with animals." Vulcan tapped the lightly rusted padlock. "But I don't believe you."

"I—"

With the same hand, Vulcan lightly smacked the door of the cell. The effect was still jarring. "I am not asking you to answer right now. But when I do, be careful of your response. I will not ask a third time."

Vulcan placed his hands on his knees and pushed himself into a standing position.

"The Warden and I have other business to attend to now. I'll send Titus around to check on this," gesturing at the cell that stood somewhat askew, "since you have a propensity to wander."

CHAPTER 30
JOSEPH

JOSEPH WAS certain this was the most bizarre thing he'd ever seen. He couldn't imagine that there would be anything he'd ever see that would top this dinner on the weirdness scale. Of course, he'd learned in the last two weeks that his imagination may have been underdeveloped all these years.

But a dinner party with a pegasus, hydra, griffin, orthrus, phoenix, giant, two witches — nope, zauberin — and himself was ... a lot. And then there was the variety of food. He had no idea how Gertrude scraped all this together in the last thirty hours.

The enclosed back porch was cramped, with Theiona and Oberhaupt taking a considerable amount of space. But it was the biggest space available to house them all. Joseph was glad that the combination of Gertrude's privacy fence and the cold weather would keep any neighbors from having some questions that might be difficult to answer.

He looked around the table slowly, wanting to soak it all up. Agatha sat to his left, eating the same thing he was, roast and potatoes and carrots. If this dinner represented the possibility of some last meal before a great battle, he couldn't have had a better send off. Despite the peculiar company.

Just the aroma took him back to Sunday afternoon lunches in his childhood. The roast would go into the oven early in the morning and cook for hours, the smell of it wafting through the house making him ravenously hungry. By the time lunch was ready, his mother would already have kicked him out of the kitchen a dozen times, asking if it was ready yet.

That was the real magic, that his olfactory sense was a time machine catapulting him thirty years into his past with such vivid recollection. He wondered about Agatha's childhood, whether she had the same associations. It's another of those things they'd never really talked about. Which kind of made him wonder what they *had* talked about all these years. Mostly the boy. The boy. *We're coming for you, Thomas. You just hang tight.*

He needed to focus on the present before he started getting all misty-eyed at the table. The orthrus had a dish of chicken and rice that Joseph thought, with some gravy and a dinner roll, he'd have been happy to eat as well. Ekhidna's heads took turns eating, with only an occasional growl from one to the other when the order got out of sorts. Joseph got curious about its digestive tract and where everything came together, but shook his head lightly to bring himself out of that rabbit hole.

Theiona, at the foot of the table, stood with her bowl of barley and oat mash and a tidy assortment of apples. She seemed self-conscious about eating in front of the others. Because of her regal station, he expected she perceived herself as superior to all the rest of them. Maybe it was undignified for her to be eating with them.

Noticing that her ribs had been healed, he wondered at what kind of power it took to heal the damage that he had seen.

The phoenix ate only herbs and spices — frankincense, myrrh, and cinnamon. Gertrude had explained to him when he'd asked about the collection in the kitchen, "This is Jahaeris's death meal. It is symbolic of his funeral pyre as he prepares this life cycle to end and a new one to emerge."

The griffin's meal was truly enviable, or at least, would have been if his own weren't so good. Gertrude had taken a monstrous ribeye, sliced it thinly, and put it on a plate. Raw was a bit underdone for Joseph, but not by much. The marbling on it was perfect, and he had no trouble imagining the almost melty goodness that a light sear on both sides would give it.

Then there was the hydra's meal, which was revolting. He regretted choosing a seat directly across from her. Insect larva, worms, and snails — it was too much. Gertrude must have just gone out to her shrubbery and plated whatever she dug up. But each of the heads seemed to be content with the offering. So that's what really mattered, right?

Oberhaupt, at the table's head, had an entire roasted turkey to himself, filled to bursting with stuffing. He eyed it like a child might do his presents at Christmas, and tore into it with the same enthusiasm.

Gertrude refused to sit and eat with them. She kept herself busy serving everyone, clearing or replacing dishes as they emptied. She was as gracious and thoughtful a host as anyone could want. Especially considering the darkness and sense of foreboding that overlay the evening.

Their little fellowship was bound together by their losses. Once they finished with their meals, it would be time to plan their invasion. He wondered if this is what it had felt like at Yalta when Churchill, Roosevelt, and Stalin planned the liberation of Europe. Or at least, that had been Roosevelt and Churchill's plan. Such different worldviews unified by a singular cause.

After he finished his second plate of food, Joseph helped Gertrude clear the dishes rather than risk saying something regrettable. Again.

When they were in the kitchen after the last load of plates, Gertrude asked, "Do you have a plan?"

"I suspect we're about to find out what the plan is. Agatha

and Oberhaupt were hashing it out before everybody else got here."

"When?"

"Tomorrow evening, I think. Give everybody time to catch some shuteye and get in place."

Her demeanor changed from inquisitive to reflective. "I'd sure like to meet Thomas."

Joseph agreed, "I intend for that to happen." Then he realized, "He doesn't even know you're alive. He'll be so excited."

She smiled back at him.

Joseph looked toward the back porch, where there was a lull in the conversations.

"Looks like it's about time."

He started that way when Gertrude grabbed him by the wrist. "Bring my baby girl back to me. She's all I've got left." Her eyes shone.

Joseph got a knot in his throat and didn't trust himself to speak. He nodded his head and rejoined the group on the back porch.

As he sat beside Agatha, she reached back against the half-wall and grabbed a rolled-up map. She slid the rubber band off and unfurled the map, laying it flat on the table. She had kept a couple of pieces of silverware to put on the map's ends so it wouldn't roll back up.

It was a topographic map of Red Mountain, showing a part of the ridge that ran from Red Mountain Expressway on the east side to Bessemer on the west. She placed her finger on the far right side of the map.

"This is Vulcan Park. Joseph and I will access the mines from here. There is a storm drain in the park that has access to an old shaft. From there, we will make our way west."

She ran her finger along the mountain's ridgeline and stopped about halfway to Bessemer.

"Red Mountain Park is here. The rest of you will meet Oberhaupt at the trailhead. The park closes at 5:00. It will already be getting dark, so be ready to go as soon as the last car leaves after sunset. From there, you'll take the Eureka Mines Trail about a half mile to the BMRR South Trail, which you will follow all the way to Ishkooda #15 Mine. That's probably another three quarters of a mile."

She looked over to Oberhaupt. "You may have to get creative to access it. This isn't one that they've unsealed yet."

"I think I can manage it."

"Efficiency is more important than whatever noise you need to make. There shouldn't be anyone else around at that time."

"From Red Mountain Park to Vulcan Park is about five miles as the crow flies. Over the years, Vulcan has connected the mine shafts and tunnels for the entire distance between our two drop-in points. We have a lot of ground to cover, and I expect there will be resistance."

Theiona asked, "Where will they be?"

Joseph thought at first that she was asking where Vulcan's men would be. But when Agatha gave her answer, he realized she had inferred incorrectly who *they* referenced.

Agatha said, "Well, that's the $64,000 question. We could come in right on top of them. Or they could be anywhere in between." She looked back to Oberhaupt for affirmation. "We just don't know."

He agreed, "Vulcan has burrowed there many years now. There is no way to know. But he is comfortable there. Not threatened. I hope that we will find it not as tightly guarded as you might expect. But we are preparing for all reasonable eventualities."

There were a lot more questions than answers in this plan, Joseph realized. But with the short timeframe and lack of resources, there weren't any better alternatives.

"Questions?" Agatha offered.

No one raised any.

Joseph looked around the table again. The eight of them were about to invade a god's stronghold. Whatever the betting odds were for their success — heck, even their survival — he wouldn't have taken them.

CHAPTER 31

AGATHA

AGATHA READ the message on her phone. "They're all there. The last car is packing up, so they'll get started shortly. Ready?"

"Ready. But I was wondering, how does he type on a phone with those massive paws of his?"

"He uses a tablet. Now are you ready to focus?" Agatha didn't bother to hide the annoyance in her voice.

"Yeah. My brain just flings out these random things sometimes. I'm good."

"One last thing," she said as she grabbed the door handle, "these jumpsuits were a good idea."

"Thank you, ma'am. I figured we needed a way not to look like a couple of random folks entering a storm drain at night. Kristen and Dave with their jumpsuits and toolbags should be less conspicuous."

They opened their doors and went around to the trunk. When the lid popped open, Joseph reached in and handed a toolbag to Agatha.

"We don't actually need tools," she said.

"We do if one of the park folks stops us. You can ditch it as soon as we're down there."

Next came the headlamps. Then Thomas reached for his arsenal in a bag.

"You know, the last time I got this bag out, you burned down a building."

"I'm gonna burn a hell of a lot more than that tonight. Let's go."

Joseph closed the trunk.

They made their way through the parking lot, along the sidewalk, and up the cascade of steps, toward the base of Vulcan's pedestal. Agatha could see her breath as they walked. The cold temperature seemed to have kept most of the would-be visitors away.

She stopped as they topped the hill. The city of Birmingham lay below them, lights twinkling and cars traveling soundlessly from one place to another. Joseph paused beside her, and she slid her hand into his. One last moment of peace before the war. The sun had dipped below the horizon and set off a display of colors in the sky that was now trending from yellows and oranges to reds and purples.

"Alright," she said, grabbing the hair tie off her left wrist and pulling her hair up.

They took a right and walked toward the back side of the elevator tower. Joseph reached down to pull up the storm drain cover and slide it across the grass.

Joseph asked, "Has no one ever thought it's curious that there's a storm drain at the top of the hill when all the water is just going to run down the sides anyway?"

"I assure you, no one has put that much thought into it."

Agatha shoved the handles of her toolbag up over the biceps of her left arm, then clicked on her headlamp and started down the ladder. Over the jangling of tools, she heard water running beneath her. The cold, damp ladder had her wishing for gloves, but she needed her hands uncovered. As she neared the bottom, she could tell that the water was little more than a trickle. Just enough to make the surface mossy and slick. Her first step off the ladder was tentative, but she quickly stepped to the curbed edge that met the wall.

Agatha whistled up to Joseph, who began his descent. She set her bag down, glad to rid herself of it and have her hands and arms free. She heard him slide the grate back over the hole.

While she waited, Agatha peered in either direction as far as her headlamp would carry. She clicked it to the high beam. The east end appeared to be walled off about fifty yards down, which made sense — go much further and you'd pop out the side of Red Mountain at the cut-through for the expressway. She switched her light back to the red beams.

When Joseph got to the bottom, he stepped to the curb on the opposite wall. He shrugged off his giant duffle bag, which he'd been wearing like a backpack. He set the bag down in front of him, unzipped it, and pulled out a waistbelt with a holster attached. He handed it to Agatha.

"I'm good," she said, showing him her hands.

"Just humor me. Slide the holster around to your back and you'll forget it's even there." Next he handed her a Smith & Wesson Sigma series 9mm. "Remember, there's no safety on this one. So it's loaded and ready to go."

Agatha conceded and strapped it on.

"Which way?" he asked, picking up the bag and throwing it on with the shoulder strap.

"West."

The tunnel was tall enough that even Joseph didn't have to hunch.

What light came in from the entry point didn't permeate very far. It wasn't long before their lamps were the sole sources of light. But their path was straight and at a steady downhill grade.

Agatha suspected they had a ways to go.

Vulcan would have made his home right in the mountain's heart. Wherever that was is where they would find him.

Joseph whispered, "Will there be cameras down here?"

"Doubt it. He won't want anyone to monitor his coming and going. He's paranoid like that."

They hadn't gone more than a couple hundred yards, when she caught movement at the edge of her light. Joseph was slightly behind her so he could catch her signals. She held up a fist, and they stopped. She pointed ahead of them. Joseph nodded and reached to his belt for a flashlight that had a more intense beam than their headlamps. He pointed it in the movement's direction and hit the strobe button that should disorient the person on the receiving end.

It was hard to say whether it worked. The two rats that were quarreling over a snake froze, which is about what you'd expect, whether the light was flashing or constant. As soon as they regained their composure, the rats scurried back into the darkness. But only one of them had the presence of mind to hold on to dinner.

"Two rats and a snake," Joseph said. "Is it going to get better or worse from here?"

Agatha was still bringing her heart rate back down. It had been a while since she'd been in a combat situation. She needed to rein herself in. She was no good to Thomas if her heart was redlining and she was making poor decisions. Agatha took several slow, deep breaths before realizing that she was long overdue to answer Joseph's question.

"What? Oh. Hard to say. They'll be getting bigger and better armed though,"

"You alright?"

"Yeah. Just, you know, rats. Let's go."

They walked several hundred more yards without incident. The grade was steadily downhill. Agatha saw that the trough in the middle of the tunnel was diverting to the sides. Something was changing. She followed the new path to where the water on the left was funneling into a small hole in a wall. A wall blocked off the tunnel about twenty yards ahead of them.

The beams from Joseph's headlamp were giving him the same revelation. Their lights met in the middle of the wall where there was a door. It looked like an industrial vault door, the kind with a spoked wheel in the middle.

They approached with increasing caution.

But there were no indications of life, or that anyone had been here in years.

Agatha gestured to the vault's wheel. "Wanna give it a spin?"

Joseph stepped up, grabbed the spokes, and tried to turn it counterclockwise. Nothing. He strained but achieved not the smallest budge. He adjusted his hands, trying different holds to see if he could get a better grip. Nothing. He got to the side to attempt a combination of pushing and pulling. Still nothing.

Joseph stepped back, huffing from the exertion.

"Mind if I try?"

"Have at it."

She tried different variations of all the same techniques and achieved similar results.

"It's all seized up in there like the Tin Man," Joseph said.

"You didn't bring an oil can in that bag, did you?"

"Afraid not."

They inspected the wall in front of them for anything that might belie another entrance. But they found nothing and met back in front of the door.

Agatha said, "If we're going in, it'll have to be here."

In the coarse light, she saw Joseph have an idea.

He asked, "Did you ever watch the X-Men?"

This wasn't what she'd expected. "What?"

"X-Men? Did you watch it?"

She wore a skeptical look and started to protest the line of questioning.

"Just follow me for a second," he said.

"Yes, I've seen the first couple of movies and the cartoon that was on when we were kids."

"Good. You know how Cyclops had to wear glasses because he shot lasers out of his eyes?"

"Okay?"

"Well, can you do that with your hands? Like, a concentrated beam of heat that can cut through metal?"

A jolt of uncertainty swept through her. "I—I don't know. Never tried it before."

"Well, unless you can think of something else ... there's no time like the present."

"Okay, I'll give it a go."

"Just start at the bottom so you only have to do three sides, and make the smallest rectangle that we and our gear can fit through."

Agatha nodded.

She squatted down with her arms extended in front of her. Her hands about eighteen inches from the door. She placed the heels of her hands together with her palms and fingers cupped so that a softball could have fit into the pocket it formed. A glow emerged.

Agatha broke her hands apart. "What if somebody's on the other side?"

"Then I reckon they're about to find out we're here."

"That's not helpful," she said.

"I've got some concussion grenades and a set of thermal goggles we can use to check before we crawl through."

"How much stuff did you steal when you retired?"

"The word you're looking for is re-appropriate. And the answer is — a lot. Now quit dillydallying and get to it."

She simultaneously glared and smirked at him. There may have been a lot of things about her he hadn't known, but she recognized in this moment that despite it, he knew the real her as well as anyone.

Agatha put her hands in position again. She focused on a spot on the wall. A beam of fire several inches wide emerged and splashed against the door. Agatha adjusted her hands, narrowing the gap between them. The beam emitting from the glow between them grew more concentrated.

The metal that she assaulted began to glow. Then a cut appeared. She noticed Joseph make a small fist pump, but she tried to push everything out except the door. Slowly, she made an arc across its face.

As she reached the arc's apex, she wondered how long this was taking. Minutes? Hours? Were they losing ground to the other team? It didn't matter. It took how long it took.

When she was about ninety percent through, there was a thud as the left part of the cut fell to the floor. She felt the impact in her feet. A few minutes later, a second thud as she cut through the last of the door.

Joseph said, "I thought we agreed on a rectangle."

"Shut up."

She wiped the sweat off her forehead.

"You may want to give that a minute to cool before you drag it out of the way," she suggested.

Joseph tapped the side of his head. Good thinking.

After a few minutes, Joseph slid his gloved fingers into the gap between the arc and the door it had been attached to. "Here goes."

With a good deal of lower back straining, he dragged the left-most corner until it had swung a full ninety degrees and sat perpendicular to the rest of the door.

"Ladies first?"

"How chivalrous of you, sir. But I'll make an exception."

CHAPTER 32

AGATHA

JOSEPH GRABBED his phone out of his pocket, turned the camera on, and held it down to where it peaked into the cutout.

"What are you doing?"

"Seeing what there is to see before I poke my head down there and get it shot off."

"Good call."

The camera screen was black. It was pitch dark on the other side of the wall.

"That's a good sign, right?" he whispered.

Agatha leaned in to where she could see it too.

"I guess? Either nobody's there or they had the presence of mind to turn out the lights while you made all that ruckus, dragging the thing across the floor."

"Me? What about the light show you put on?"

She shrugged. "That could have been anything." When they turned their headlamps back on, Agatha said, "So you had the foresight to grab a thermal imager on the way out but not night vision goggles?"

"Well, I see now how that would have been useful. So if it's any consolation, present-me isn't entirely unhappy with past-me's decision there."

"Alright, hop to it, little guinea pig."

Joseph dug into his duffle bag, grabbing the thermal goggles. He clicked his headlamp and pulled it off his head. He shoved it into his pocket, placed the goggles on his head, and flipped the eyepiece down into place.

"Wow!" he said.

Agatha was immediately concerned. "What?"

"You're really hot."

"Geez. Is there ever a time when you're not ridiculous?"

Joseph paused before answering. "I can't think of any."

He sidled up to the hole Agatha had carved and peeked into the opening. After a few seconds, he said, "It's all blues and purples in here."

"Good. Let's go."

Joseph stood and flipped the goggles up. "Once we get in there, we should keep the headlamps off and use these."

"That'll work fine for you. But I'll be walking through total darkness."

"Hang onto my bag and you'll be fine. It opens up a bit on the other side and the ground is flat. This'll keep us from giving ourselves away."

"I mean, I get it," Agatha said. "I'm just pointing out the shortfall."

"What do you want to do?"

"Let's go with your plan for now. We can adjust it if we need to."

Joseph zipped his bag, moved it in front of the hole, and shoved it through. He got down on his belly, flipped his goggles back down, and started army crawling, pushing the bag ahead of him.

Agatha waited on her side and checked from the direction they'd come. Joseph gave the all-clear, and it was her turn to wriggle through.

Once she came out the other side, she whispered, "Should I pull the door piece back in?"

"Better to leave it as is, in case we need to make a hasty exit."

Agatha stood up and looked Joseph in the face. "We're not leaving without him."

Joseph raised his hands up. "That's not what I meant. In case we need to make a quick exit *after* we get Thomas."

"Okay. Sorry."

Joseph had put his bag back over his shoulder. "Ready?'

She grabbed the shoulder strap with her right hand. With her left, she clicked off her headlamp. "Don't let me trip on anything or run into a wall."

"Ten-four."

The complete darkness was worse than she'd thought. When the shoulder strap pulled forward, she started walking with no idea where or toward what she was going. The blackness was almost palpable. She found herself high-stepping, trying to make sure she didn't trip on anything. With her eyes useless, her other senses tried to fill in the information gap.

With each step, cool drafts brushed the exposed skin at her hands and face. Their steps were extraordinarily loud, but the silence between each footfall was somehow louder. In the void, she heard everything, nothing. And imagined everything in between. Even smell and taste contributed to overstimulating her brain. The water running nearby had the sharpness of iron ore and limestone.

The bag's strap went slack and started pulling her to the left. The mine shaft had changed directions. The grade flattened until it seemed like they were finally on level ground again.

The inability to discern distance distorted her sense of time. Had they gone a hundred yards or a half-mile? She checked in with the muscles in her legs. She was still fresh. Her feet were warm and didn't hurt. They couldn't have gone all that far.

They'd gone west from Vulcan Park, but had they gone as far as The Club? And how far under the surface were they?

She wondered what kept the mines from collapsing. She shivered. How long would abandoned mines stay structurally sound? This was all messing with her head.

"Joseph," she whispered.

He jumped in surprise.

"Sorry. I've got to turn my light on. The darkness is kind of getting to me."

"Okay. 'Bout made me jump out of my skin there."

She clicked her red light on. The amount of relief that accompanied even that small thread of light was indescribable. "Yeah. You good?"

He flipped his goggles up and pinched his nose and rubbed his eyes, which made a squishing noise when he did it. She hated that sound so much.

"Yep. Was just a little hyper-focused there. Any idea what we're expecting?"

"Your guess is as good as mine."

"Alright."

He flipped his thermal imager down and started walking again. She was glad to have both hands free again. She looked down at her watch. A little after six o'clock. The other team should be into the Ishkooda mine now and headed their way. That's assuming they didn't have any problems unsealing it. She trusted Oberhaupt had a plan for that. And whatever it was had probably taken less time than she'd used in cutting that door open.

That had felt really good. She didn't mind admitting that it was nice to be using her abilities again after they had been dormant since ... since she'd gotten pregnant with Thomas.

Joseph threw his left hand out. He grabbed the front of her jumper and pulled her as he scrambled to an inlet on their left.

"Kill your light," he whispered.

They waited.

Up ahead, voices. She made them out, but barely. "Did you hear something?"

"Dunno," a second voice said. "Thought I saw something, though. Just a flicker."

Footsteps.

Total darkness again.

Their steps sounded confident. How could they see?

Joseph tapped her leg twice. There were two of them.

With his left hand, he found her right wrist. She heard metal sliding against leather. Then there was a handle in her hand. She ran her left hand along the blade. It was serrated toward the handle. He'd given her his Ka-bar.

A small click from above and beside her. Joseph had flipped up his goggles.

Her heart sped up. Joseph touched her knee with his flashlight. Once he felt her touch it, he pulled it back. She understood his plan. Stun and attack.

The footsteps brought the guards closer. Is that what they were? It didn't really matter. They were between her and Thomas, and had no innocent reason for being here. She couldn't tell how close they were. She didn't know if Joseph could either. Not unless he peaked around the corner and risked being spotted. But he'd know when they were directly in front of them. No, she reminded herself. He was blind now, too. This was all guesswork based on the sound of moving feet. She just had to be ready to strike.

She slowed her breathing. Rhythmic, steady, quiet. Finally, she slipped into years of training.

Any second now.

She felt a brisk movement. Then a strobe. It was almost as disorienting to her as to the panicked guards. The flickering light set everything into slow motion. The fear on the lower halves of their faces. They had equipment on the top half. Night vision goggles. Their hands went up to their faces. The light blinded them. Joseph shoved past the closest one, like a defensive lineman shedding a blocker.

Agatha pounced. With her left arm, she clutched the closest guard's shirt as he stumbled backwards. As she pulled herself into him, she swung her right arm up. The knife pierced his skin under his jaw, breaking through his upper palate, tearing through his sinus cavities, and severing synapses. She fell in a barrel roll as his body went slack.

As she rolled, she saw Joseph raise a knee to the other man's abdomen. He expelled spit and air as he doubled over. Joseph brought down his knife and lodged it into the base of the other man's skull. He fell with a thud.

She shivered. She'd known that existed within Joseph, but she hadn't seen it before. Hadn't experienced it. He was as much a warrior as she was.

A calm followed as the adrenaline finished its surge.

He turned the strobe to a steady beam and found her. "Ags, you okay?"

"I'm good." She clicked her own light back on.

He moved his beam to the subject of her attack. "Nice work."

"Yeah."

"You know we have to get those out now, right?"

She hadn't thought about that. They didn't know what was ahead, and may need them again.

"Umm ... they're your knives? I'll hold the light for you."

He stepped over the corpse and reached down a hand to help her up. "How generous of you. Here."

He handed her the flashlight and reached down to retrieve the Ka-bar. He gave it a tug, and the head wiggled, but the knife didn't release its hold.

"Dagummit."

Joseph sat down beside the guard, put the sole of his boot

against the bottom of his jaw beside the knife, and yanked. It came clean with a combination of sucking and scratching sounds.

Agatha gagged.

"Weak stomach?" he asked.

"Shut up. That was just a little much."

"Wipe this one down while I get the other one." He handed her the knife, and fetched a bandana out of his back pocket.

The other knife released itself with less fuss.

With a thorough wipe-down, she handed the Ka-bar back and offered the bandana. He accepted the knife but declined the soiled fabric.

Agatha pulled the night vision goggles off the man she'd killed. She tugged off her headlamp and put the goggles onto her head, adjusting the straps so it fit more snugly. She tested them to make sure the fall hadn't broken them. Still good. She flipped them back up and finished patting him down for anything else useful. Wallet, phone, keys. She snagged the keys.

Joseph checked out the other body.

"Do we need their rifles?" she asked.

"No, we're set. But we do need to drag them over to that inset so nobody sees them."

He grabbed his guy under the armpits and started dragging him. Agatha did likewise, but with a little more effort.

Once they had stowed the bodies, Joseph unzipped an outer pocket of his bag and pulled out a bottle of water for each of them.

"Oh, bless you," Agatha said. After a couple of deep pulls, she asked, "How come you can't be this prepared all the time? I don't recall you ever loading a single diaper bag."

He shrugged. "Stakes weren't high enough, I guess. Ready?"

"Sure."

They each flipped down their goggles and stepped back out into the corridor.

CHAPTER 33

AGATHA

THE NIGHT-VISION GOGGLES made all the difference. Agatha's spatial awareness and sense of time were far less distorted now, allowing for a much clearer mental space. She hadn't realized the sense of dread that had fallen over her until it had lifted. Not to mention the helplessness of entirely depending on Joseph.

Agatha was glad to help carry the burden of spotting trouble. Which she did, in relatively short order.

She reached out to her right and touched Joseph's arm.

He whispered, "Got 'em. Looks like a couple dozen or so." He stopped and knelt down on one knee.

She maintained her position. "I can't tell what they are. Just a whole bunch of movement."

"Spiders. But the size of king crabs. About a hundred feet out."

The squadron of spiders approached steadily.

"Seventy feet. Listen, I can take them down, but it's gonna be awfully loud."

Agatha could make out their fangs and their eight eyes, marbles set into sable bodies.

"Fifty feet."

She stepped forward. "I got this."

"Sure? Aren't you scared of spiders."

"I don't usually get to set them on fire."

As they advanced, the arachnids sped up as if greedy for the attack. Agatha clicked her goggles up and listened to the tapping of hundreds of feet on the rock. When they were as close as she could bear, she unleashed a torrent of flame from each hand, carpeting the floor in front of her.

She heard feet skittering and bodies bumping into each other as the spiders tried to stop. There was a smell of burning hair. They squealed as they roasted. The momentum of the first few had carried them to within a few feet of her before they stopped and lay smoldering. She started to hear popping sounds as the spiders' boiling insides burst through charred exoskeletons.

Two toward the back had mostly escaped the inferno and were in the process of retreating to wherever it was they came from.

Joseph raised his MP5 to his shoulder, "Should I?"

"No. They may know we're here. But I'd rather not give away our position."

He lowered the gun.

As the fires mostly burned out, Agatha was once again immersed into darkness that was accented by sunspots where the flames had been. She dropped her goggles back down.

"Pick your way through carefully," Joseph advised. "No sense getting bit by one that's playing possum."

None were. Once they were on the other side of the carnage, they stopped to take in Agatha's handiwork one last time. She smiled. "I gotta say, that was fantastic. Like a therapy session."

"You know you'll burn the house down if you do that at home, right?"

"Shush. Just let me have this."

As they continued their course, it wasn't long before there was light emitting from around a bend in the mine shaft. It soon became bright enough that they removed their headgear. There were bulbs strung along the ceiling as they came through the curve. When the corridor straightened out, everything in front of them was lit and a little more finished and less rough hewn than what they'd been traversing to this point. They were getting somewhere.

But ahead of them, three centaurs stood abreast in the corridor. Behind the centaurs, the path forked.

She stopped, as did Joseph.

Agatha said, "There's something I need to tell you about centaurs — they're total morons. The least intelligent combination of horse and human."

"Okay, so what's that mean for us?"

"Whatever their orders are, they will follow them without question or deviation."

"That sounds useful."

"Yes and no. What was it Mike Tyson said? 'Everybody has a plan until they get punched in the mouth.' Well, they aren't capable of adjusting the plan. They'll march themselves right into a death trap if that's what they've been told to do."

"So what's our plan?"

"Let's see what happens when we get closer. But be ready, because they may be stupid, but they're deadly accurate with those crossbows."

Agatha and Joseph walked forward until the centaurs shifted their positions to a more ready stance. It was subtle but unmistakable.

"Slowly," she breathed.

One more step and the middle centaur ordered, "You shall not pass."

"Who are you — Gandalf?" Joseph responded. "That line's taken."

Agatha scowled at him. "Maybe let's not provoke them with your witticisms that are entirely lost on them anyway."

"I thought you said I couldn't provoke them."

"What if their instructions were to shoot the next smart-ass that comes along?"

"Well … I hadn't considered that."

Agatha didn't tell Joseph what she was about to do next.

She took another step forward to address the middle centaur. As soon as she did, he raised his crossbow and fired with such speed that it barely registered. Time seemed to slow as the bolt grew larger and closer. She jerked to the right, but not fast enough. The bolt tore through her, above the collarbone.

As she fell to the floor, having lost her balance, Joseph let loose a spray of fire from his MP5. He swept the corridor from left to right. By the time she hit the floor, a line of bullet holes ran across the chests of the three sentries, tailing slightly upward from the recoil, like matching scarlet tattoos.

From the floor, Agatha watched Joseph recenter his weapon. But the centaurs hadn't had time to react. The blood was pouring out of them too quickly. They faltered and collapsed in quick succession, with the outer two never even having gotten their weapons raised.

Joseph turned to her, "Did it hit you?"

She had her hand up to the wound. Blood was leaking out from between her fingers.

"Let me see it," he said.

She pulled her red hand away. Joseph looked at the hole in the front of her jumpsuit, then leaned over her to see the back. She tried to look down at it, but the muscle movement was excruciating.

"Looks like it's through and through, but I need to see your shoulder."

She reached up with her right hand to unzip it, but Joseph stopped her.

"Sit still. I got it. You just keep looking at those tunnels up ahead. They know we're here now."

She'd been so focused on her shoulder, she hadn't thought of that. The rattle of a submachine gun would carry a long way in this rocky subterranean landscape.

He unzipped her jumpsuit down to her stomach and slid the shoulder down to check out the damage.

"Looks like it went in above your clavicle and came right out the other side. You're lucky. Closer to your neck and … well, you know."

She nodded. Even that hurt.

"Can you move your arm?"

She winced, trying to raise it.

"Can you heal it yourself?"

"It's not ideal," Agatha answered.

He gestured at her shoulder. "Yeah. Neither is this. Can you do enough to stop the bleeding?"

"I think so. Help me get my left hand onto the back of my shoulder."

He took her hand. "This is going to hurt," he warned.

"Yep."

She groaned as he moved it into place. It was wet and sticky. She could feel that the hole was about the size of a dime. She placed her right hand over the wound in front. Agatha closed her eyes and began the work of making the blood coagulate and stayed long enough to repair some muscle fibers. Even this small amount of work provided a great deal of relief. She thought her left arm would be fully functional. That was really the most important part. She could contend with the pain. When she opened her eyes, Joseph was holding out Tylenol and her water bottle.

"It's not much, but it'll help."

"Thank you," she said, taking them. Yes, that arm movement was much better. Still painful, but tolerable.

"We'd better skedaddle," Joseph suggested. "Somebody's bound to check out all that racket before long."

Joseph put Agatha's water back in the bag and zipped it up. He threw it over his shoulder, then reached down, offering Agatha his right hand. She grabbed it and pulled herself to her feet.

"Ready," she said.

They walked to the fork in the corridor. Agatha listened for any sounds of approach. When they got to the split, they peered down each. There wasn't an obviously right or wrong choice.

"What now?" Joseph asked.

"Just pick one, I guess."

"Or — tell me what you think — we each take a path, go down it for a bit, and meet back here in ten minutes."

"Let's check the phones for service down here. Or maybe there's Wi-Fi."

They both pulled out their devices and discovered no signal of any kind.

Agatha asked, "You didn't bring any radios in your bag?"

"No. I don't like the idea of splitting up either, but it gives us our best chance to find Thomas."

"I don't know." This was their best option, but she hated the idea of it. "What if one of us gets in trouble?"

"Listen, I'm not going to force the issue. If you want to pick one and go together, we will."

"No, you're right. It's just ... I don't like it."

"Yeah. I'll make it easier for you. You go left, I'll go right. Out seven minutes and back in three. And hopefully, we'll have a better idea of the best way forward."

"Okay."

"Set your timer on your phone. See you in ten."

"Be careful," she told him.

He nodded. She lingered for a second as he started down his path. Then she started down hers, every sensory receptor and nerve end on high alert.

CHAPTER 34

THOMAS

AFTER CATCHING pieces of several hushed conversations, Thomas summoned Ning, who appeared within his cell. The panda immediately settled in on Thomas' pallet and reclined against the bars.

"What's happening, Ning?"

"I have gorged myself on overly much bamboo, and I will take a nap fairly soon."

"No. What's going on here? Something's happening."

"Oh, I see. I thought you were asking more casually. I don't know what's happening here. Does it seem to be good or bad?"

"I don't know. I don't want to hurt your feelings, Ning, but you're not very helpful."

"First of all, I do find that hurtful. And second ... secondarily? ... secondly? I understand why you might say that. My specialty is comforting children from bad dreams, night terrors, and the like. There are other companions more competent in," he waved his paw around, "this line of work. But they had already assigned me to you. And it is a good deal of hassle and paperwork to amend assignments. So here we are. All making do rather well under the circumstances, I'd say."

"They said they're going to kill me like the others."

"Well, yes, there's that. But beyond that, your more imme-diate needs are being met. Plenty of food and water and a bed to sleep on."

Thomas said, "I think I want you to leave, Ning. You're making everything worse."

"I may not be tip-top right now, but I hardly think—"

"Just go, Ning," Thomas ordered.

Ning huffed and disapparated without so much as a goodbye.

Thomas didn't like hurting Ning's feelings. But he really was better off alone. It's just that it was so boring.

The door outside opened and closed again. He could tell from the sound of the footsteps that it was Vulcan.

"Thomas, my boy," he greeted Thomas in a cheerful tone.

Thomas jumped right in with his question. "What's happening out there?"

"I'll tell you exactly what's happening — they're coming for you, Thomas."

"Who is? The police?"

"No, no. Your parents are fighting like hell to get here."

Thomas found this confusing. "Then why are you so happy?"

"Chaos and disorder are in my blood. They get me out of bed in the morning. And things have been entirely too quiet. I am the god of fire and destruction. But ever since Mt. Pinatubo, there has been a moratorium on volcanoes. And I am bored to death. Do you know how long it's been since I have had a worthy adversary, Thomas?"

The boy shook his head. Vulcan's enthusiasm for the moment diminished, almost into a pout.

"Me either. A long time anyway."

Thomas said, "My dad is going to kill you."

"Oh, that's doubtful. He's an unterlegen. But—"

"What's that? What you just said?"

"Do not interrupt me, Thomas. But I will tell you anyway. Because what else am I going to do? He's a commoner. He has no magic. But your mother, on the other hand," here hope and cheer crept into Vulcan's demeanor again, "there's a real chance with her. She is special. And angry. And I have her young. That is all the motivation a mother needs."

"What will you do until she gets here?"

Vulcan looked as if he hadn't considered what to do with himself. Thomas sensed the nervous, excited energy that radiated off of him. It all but crackled.

Vulcan opened a portal in front of himself and pulled out a massive throne made from igneous rock. It was black and rough. He set it down with a thud.

Thomas said, "Your chair doesn't look very comfy."

"Oh, it absolutely isn't."

"You should go to the furniture store. There's one in Chelsea that we go to. Where did the chair come from?"

"Home."

"I thought you lived here?"

"Yes and no. I am not welcome at home. My mother tried to kill me, so I made a trap for her and held her captive for a bit. And my wife ... perhaps, you are still too young for that story. So I am a nomad. I wander."

The outer door opened and closed.

"Sir, Oberhaupt is here to see you."

"Good."

Vulcan stood up. "I'll be back, Thomas. Don't you go anywhere."

CHAPTER 35
JOSEPH

JOSEPH LOOKED AT HIS PHONE. Four and a half minutes of nothing but a long, dank mine shaft, with the same wire-caged bulb strung every thirty feet.

Finally, he spotted something different ahead. A concrete wall and a metal door framed within it. The door stood open.

He picked up his pace, but not too fast, or the contents of his bag would start clanging against him. What he saw through the open doorway looked to be wider than the corridor he was in. Maybe a room.

The closer he got, the clearer it was that this was a room. On the far side of the room was another open door; the mine shift continued beyond it.

As quietly as he could, Joseph lifted the strap of his bag up over his head. He set the bag down against the wall. The gear inside jostled and shifted as it settled. Joseph fussed at himself for the noise he made.

He scanned the third of the room that he could see from his position opposite the door. It was entirely empty. He checked his phone again. Six minutes. He'd check the rest of the room out and head back. With his left shoulder against the wall, he snugged the MP5 to his right. He was glad to have the 30-round magazine, but wished he would have changed it out for a full one.

With a deep breath, Joseph spun into the room.

A man leaned against the far wall. Early sixties, well dressed. The man pushed himself upright.

"Welcome, Joseph. We've been expecting you. Not you necessarily, but either you or her. Or perhaps both."

The man couldn't have been more contemptuous at the mention of Agatha if he'd spit afterward. One corner of Joseph's mouth turned up in a smirk. He appreciated her ability to have that kind of effect on someone.

"Do you know who I am?" the man asked.

"I reckon I can sort it out. Agatha once described to me a spineless, weak-eyed old man who preyed on others and ridiculously called himself the Warden. That seems to fit you."

"You should be careful who you address with such irreverence."

"I'll take my chances, I guess. Can't go changing my stripes now."

The Warden stood quietly, taking him in.

Joseph asked, "Do you have Thomas?"

"We do."

"Is he alright?"

"He is."

Joseph offered, "If you'll give him to us, we can avoid any further ... unpleasantness."

The Warden tutted at him. "That's simply not true. You know as well as I do that she won't let this go that easily."

"Well, you made that bed, so I guess you get to lie in it."

Joseph nodded toward the door to his right. "Is he through there?"

"He is."

"Then I think I'll just see myself out."

"That's not going to happen."

"Then let's get—"

The timer on Joseph's phone chirped, interrupting him. He held up a finger with his left hand and pulled the phone out of his pocket.

"I'm late to meet Agatha," he said, waggling his phone toward the Warden. "She'll wait on me for a minute. Then she'll come looking. And I don't think you'll want to be here then."

"Oh, I don't plan to be."

As he finished his sentence, the Warden transformed into a monstrous creature. Joseph didn't know what to call the thing, but it was definitely a problem. Half lion, half goat. A tail that was a snake. The shape of its head suggested it was some sort of viper, and almost certainly venomous. The entire creature was dark as night. Fear crawled up his spine.

"Agatha forgot to mention that," he muttered.

The creature paced for a minute before squaring up with him. It crouched. Joseph readied himself for the attack.

The creature pounced faster and more overwhelmingly than he had expected. By the time he reacted and brought up his weapon to fire, its enormous paw struck his arm. The burst went wide. The bullets splintered into fragments as they struck the stone. The force of the collision knocked Joseph backwards and sent the gun skittering across the floor and out of reach.

He rolled onto all fours and pushed himself up. His opponent paced again. It had positioned itself between Joseph and his gun.

He took a second to self-assess. There was an extraordinary pain running up his left leg. He saw two small puncture holes in his pants. While the lion had pounced, the serpent hadn't been dormant. His right arm was mangled with claw marks. But there was something else going on too.

He pulled up the sleeve of his jumpsuit. Around the claw

marks were blisters. He'd fared worse in this initial exchange than he'd thought.

Joseph realized where he'd seen those marks before.

He looked up at the Warden in his beast form. "You. You're the one who attacked Thomas."

He felt a renewed energy to avenge his son.

The chimera roared. A deafening sound.

It attacked again, taking a swipe at Joseph's head, which he protected with his left arm. It knocked him to the ground. The creature backed away again. It was toying with him, allowing him to get up a second time.

Besides the damage to his left arm, which showed ribbons of flesh and fabric from his forearm to shoulder, there was another bite mark on his left leg. The swelling was significant, and the leg was already stiffening.

As swiftly as he could, Joseph whipped his knife out of its sheath on his belt and sprung at the creature as it walked away from him, hoping to land a blow. It kicked him in the chest with both hind legs, knocking the breath out of him. He landed on his back and tried to gasp for air, panicking.

While he was immobilized, the creature approached. It looked at his hands. Joseph realized they were empty. He had dropped his knife. If a lion could grin, this one did. It walked up and stood over the top of him. It ripped his chest open with a casual ferocity. Joseph yelled.

He instinctively arched his back in response to the pain. The Warden used his paw to pin Joseph to the ground. He grit his teeth at the pressure being applied to his newly opened wounds. As he was being pushed back down, Joseph felt something under the small of his back. He slid his hand down and wrapped it around the handle of his knife. He had one chance.

He struck quickly, lodging the knife in the soft joint between its shoulder and ribs. The knife's edge scraped bone. He had missed. The blade hadn't penetrated the ribs.

The Warden roared in pain and rage.

Joseph was helpless now. The chimera looked down at him. The indifference gone, replaced by contempt. It opened its jaws and clamped down on his throat. Joseph yelled until he could not.

CHAPTER 36
AGATHA

AGATHA WASN'T QUITE BACK to the rendezvous point when her timer started fussing at her. "He's going to kill me," she muttered as she picked up her pace and jogged back to the fork.

When she got there, she found that she was alone. Joseph was only thirty seconds overdue, but still. "Now who can't manage their time?" After years of always being the person who was running late, she was finally the one on time. Well, not quite on time. But not as late as Joseph.

Her scouting trip had been a total waste, leading eventually to a wall of rock that had holes drilled but had never been blasted.

Agatha heard the sound of ... what? An animal roaring? Then the rattle of a submachine gun. Distorted, but still distinct. She took off at a run. She couldn't fully sprint. She still had to be cautious. If Joseph had reason to use his gun, there might be something between them.

As she ran, she formed a ball of fire in each hand. Ready for whatever she might encounter. But it was only an empty mine shaft.

Joseph yelled again. She wasn't all that far away, by the sound of it. Seconds later, there was a roar that sounded like a lion, followed by Joseph yelling again. But this time, it was contracted, cut short.

Still, all she saw ahead of her was the corridor, although it bent to the left up ahead. When she rounded the curve, she saw an open door set into a concrete wall. Joseph's bag was on the floor beside the door. She sprinted the rest of the way. Agatha burst into the room with her right arm cocked and ready to pitch her molten orb.

Joseph's mauled body lay on the floor to her right. The room was otherwise empty aside from his MP5 that lay across the room.

She ran to him and threw herself on her knees at his side. The rivers of blood that had been pouring out of his chest still pulsed, but almost imperceptibly. Agatha grabbed his left hand and called his name. She thought he squeezed her hand, but it was so brief and weak that she couldn't be sure. A rattle emerged from his throat as his chest spasmed. Agatha realized the teeth marks on his neck. His larynx had been crushed. He couldn't breathe.

Joseph became still. The streams running out of him became pools.

Agatha wailed, "No! Joseph, no!"

All the strength ran out of her. She buried her face in his stomach and sobbed. She lost sense of everything else. Time lost its meaning. First the boy, now Joseph. Everything was losing its meaning.

Until she heard footsteps.

Agatha bounded to her feet. Her eyes bleary from tears. She pressed the heels of her hands to her eyes to clear them. Her palms came away streaked with the blood that covered her face. She looked down to see that she was adorned in crimson. The blood that hadn't soaked into the fabric or coagulated dripped to the floor.

The footsteps grew imminent. They came from the far doorway. She put the heels of her hands together in anticipation. She hadn't realized until now that the flames she'd walked in with had dissipated.

Titus entered the room. The hair on the back of her neck raised. He was the one who took her boy, who brought this on them. A fire coursed through her. Mourning replaced with fury.

But when Oberhaupt walked in behind him, Agatha almost collapsed to the floor. Her legs had all the rigidity of a jellyfish. A weak, "No," escaped her lips, and her hands fell to her side. The giant took his place beside Titus.

Titus laughed. Oberhaupt wouldn't look her in the eye. He looked to the wall beyond her.

Titus nodded at Joseph, "This unterlegen was no match for the chimera. And of course, your animal friends were no contest for the giant here."

The provocations and insults helped Agatha regain her focus. Her fury returned. But she looked questioningly at Oberhaupt.

"Tell her," Titus commanded.

She saw Oberhaupt bristle at taking orders. He had never cared for them.

He answered, "They are gone."

Her sadness grew, but this time, it did not quench her rage.

Titus laughed again. "Only you are left, Agatha. And even that is only a matter of time. Of course, it was always going to go this way. You have merely helped us eliminate the resistance by congregating so much of it here for us. Now, it's just a matter of the boy. Is he what the prophecy suggests? Or will he be discarded like the rest?"

Agatha summoned energy to her hands, and balls of flame erupted within her grasp. The ground quaked under her feet.

"Play nice, Agatha. Vulcan would have you for himself, but he won't be overly angry if I bring your crushed corpse to him. Or maybe he will. He's ... particular about things. You know how petty his kind can be."

She extinguished the flame. The floor became still again.

"That's a good girl."

Agatha gave no response.

Titus filled the gap, "I remember you always being so much more mouthy, so — what's the word I'm looking for? — smarmy. It's a shame to see what you've become."

"It's a shame what *I've* become? That's rich coming from you. Judas would have blushed at your betrayal."

She had to check herself. He was trying to tempt her into something rash. She wouldn't give him the satisfaction of it. She was in a bad spot and needed to think her way through it. Even if she could take down Titus, and she didn't know if she could before he crushed her, she would have to contend with Oberhaupt. He had skin as thick and coarse as an elephant. Her fire would be less effective against him.

One thing at a time.

"Come with me, and perhaps Vulcan will allow you to see the boy before he ends your miserable existence. Can you do that?"

She nodded, not trusting herself to speak.

"Very well. I knew I could trust you to make a good decision." Titus directed a thumb at Oberhaupt. "He was less certain that you'd come willingly, all things considered."

Oberhaupt still wouldn't look at her.

"But first, we're going to have to do something about that." Titus flung a hand in the direction of her blood-soaked jumpsuit. "I assume you have something on underneath?"

She nodded.

"Well, then." Titus said, becoming impatient.

Agatha unclasped the belt holding her 9mm. She lowered it to the floor carefully. She unzipped the jumpsuit down to her stomach, revealing a black tank top. She shrugged it off her shoulders, wincing at the movement of her left shoulder, and helped it down off her waist. Black pants covered her legs. She sat down to remove her boots, slide the jumpsuit over her feet, and retie the footwear.

When she stood again, Titus moved toward her, stepping in front of Oberhaupt. As he did, Oberhaupt raised his arms high over his head. He clasped his hands together and brought them down in a hammerfist. The amount of force he generated was exaggerated by being several feet taller than Titus.

Agatha's eyes widened in confusion and surprise.

Titus started to turn his head, but it was too late. The impact collapsed the dome of skull and drove him to his knees. He thudded to the floor and didn't move again.

Agatha took a step backwards and readied her hands. She didn't understand what was happening.

With his boot, Oberhaupt nudged the corpse that was Titus. He was pretty clearly dead. The giant stepped over the body in Agatha's direction. She braced herself. With her speed and agility, she may be able to get to a weapon.

Oberhaupt held out his hands. "Wait, Agatha."

With his left hand, he reached slowly around and pulled something out of his belt. He presented it to her with an open palm. Joseph's Ka-bar.

"Pulled this out of the chimera. Passed him limping away on our way here. Joseph got a good lick in before..." He didn't finish. Didn't need to.

She nodded, still uncertain what to make of this turn. Her world had been turned upside down. But it had partly righted itself again, apparently.

"Agatha," Oberhaupt called her out of her daze. "The Mythicals are okay."

"What? How?"

"After I unsealed the mine entrance, we came to a vault door."

"How did you open it?"

"The hydra spit venom at the hinges until they all but dissolved, so I applied some force to get it opened. I needed to get here without them to figure out where things stood. So I went through the vault door first and pulled it back into place behind me. They howled and pitched a fit on the other side."

"So they're alright?"

"They're fine. They'll get through there, eventually. Probably have by now. I dispatched with the resistance they would have encountered."

"And this — you being with them — is what? A charade?"

"I did what needed doing. You were going to need someone with information from inside."

"Like?"

"Like Thomas is okay."

Agatha's hand went to her heart. Her chest heaved in a sob both of joy and sadness. She couldn't help but look at Joseph's mangled body. What he had given up to get Thomas back. She couldn't allow it to be for nothing.

"Can we finish this conversation elsewhere?" she asked.

"Of course." He reached out. The knife still lay in his open palm. "Take this."

She did. Oberhaupt turned on his heel and walked toward the door he had entered through. Agatha picked up the gun belt and holster that lay beside her discarded jumpsuit. After strapping it back on, she walked over and knelt at Joseph's side. She kissed him on the forehead. "Goodbye, Joseph. I'm going to get our boy back. But first, I will avenge you."

Agatha wiped the last of her tears as she unbuckled the belt that held the Ka-bar's sheath. She slid it off and fitted it onto her own belt. Before heading toward the door to meet Oberhaupt, she covered Joseph's body as best she could with her discarded jumpsuit.

They began walking once she was in the corridor. "Shall I

take you to Thomas? I expect Vulcan is with him. I think it will take both of us to deal with him. Perhaps even that will not be enough."

"Not yet. I have a chimera to deal with first."

CHAPTER 37
AGATHA

"WHERE IS IT?" Agatha asked.

"I don't know now, but it won't have gotten far. There is an intersection ahead. You will go to the right. It will be there, somewhere."

She nodded. "And Thomas?"

"Down the same corridor. Everything you are looking for lies that way."

"How did you convince Vulcan that you were with him?" Agatha asked.

"It took some doing. But he is prideful. He *wants* to believe that people adore him and can't help but side with him."

Agatha looked up into his face. "Did he ask about her?"

Oberhaupt shook his head. "I think he was afraid to."

"But why does he think you will have forgiven it?"

"He's probably suspicious. But he has to balance being suspicious against his needs. And he needed what I could deliver. Like you. You are still suspicious of me. But hopeful that I am on your side."

"What did you have to deliver?" Agatha asked.

"Information. Votes in favor of the Warden's agenda. Vulcan's agenda."

"The offspring?"

"No. He had others for that."

"I would find that unforgivable," she warned.

"As would I. Some things are beyond redemption."

This satisfied Agatha. "What are you planning to do?"

"I'm going to intercept the Mythicals. Kill as many of his minions as I can find along the way." He answered her question before instructing, "There won't be that many. Wait until I get back to make the attack on Vulcan. He is too much for you alone."

She nodded again.

"Agatha, I'm serious."

"Okay. I hear you."

At the intersection, Oberhaupt said, "Be careful. The chimera may be even more treacherous because it is injured."

"Will do."

She took off at a light run. With no gear, she covered ground fairly quietly. Before long, she made out a shape between the shadows up ahead. She heard the clop of hooves. She did not slow her pace.

The serpent tattled on her as the creature approached a closed door set in a wall like the others. She had cornered it. Hurt and cornered. She would have to be careful.

The chimera paced with a significant limp as she closed on it. Agatha brought herself to a halt when she was twenty feet away. That should give her enough room to react if it charged.

The chimera stopped and faced her, closing some distance between them. It stared. Perhaps weighing its options, measuring its opponent.

Agatha had something to say.

"The Warden should have never let you off your leash. You came into my house and terrorized my boy. You killed my husband. And now you will atone for it."

The creature roared with all the thunder of waves crashing

against stone. It was truly terrifying. For the first time, Agatha considered and began to doubt the outcome of this encounter. Its hot breath wafted past her, smelling of blood. She realized that it was Joseph's blood and strengthened her resolve.

Perhaps the sable monster sensed the change. It crouched. She didn't doubt now that even injured, it could spring across the gap. Her flames would not stop it in time once it had launched.

In a swift, fluid motion she pulled the 9mm from its holster, brought it level, and fired two rounds into its right shoulder. She had intended the center of its chest but gone wide in her haste. The creature's forelegs faltered. Devastating injuries to both shoulders made for too much damage to support its weight in that moment.

As it hit the floor, it transformed. Instead of a chimera, there was a naked man on the ground in front of her. His legs pulled under him. It struck her that he was positioned like the Great Sphinx. But instead of a head raised proudly, his face bowed to the floor. Blood still oozed from under his arm on the left side — Joseph's knife wound. Two steady streams poured to the floor from his upper right chest. No exit wounds. The hollow-points must have hit the scapula and shattered.

"Stand up and show yourself."

"Agatha, please," he whined without looking up.

She knew the voice immediately.

She gritted her teeth. "You bastard."

Agatha stalked over to the man and putting the sole of her boot into his ribs, shoved him onto his side.

The Warden drew up his legs and pulled his arms in with a whimper.

"Mercy. Please. I beg."

"Mercy?" Agatha scoffed. "You'll get as good as you gave."

Another whimper.

"And here I thought I was coming to put down a cat. But this is so much better."

Something occurred to Agatha.

"You're a cat. That's how you did it the last time I killed you. I thought maybe you'd sold yourself to Vulcan to bring you back. But you didn't have to. Besides, that shriveled up shell of a soul wouldn't have been worth the price of admission."

With a great deal of fussing, the Warden raised himself upright. "Agatha, it's my last one."

Agatha laughed. "You should have been more careful with it then. But you weren't. You invaded my home. Twice. I was out, done, but you brought me back. I even warned you. Still you did not desist. And now you have killed Joseph and taken my son and brought us to this."

"I didn't take the boy," the Warden protested.

"Only because you failed."

Agatha knew what was coming. There was a part of her that dreaded it. A part of her that was conflicted. But only a small part, and it was becoming increasingly quiet.

She said, "I would ask if you have any last words, but there is no one who cares to hear them. So let's forego the formality. There's just one last thing."

"Yes?"

He still had the smallest ray of hope in his voice. He shouldn't, though. He was just so accustomed to worming his way into and out of situations. She figured he couldn't help himself but to be looking for an angle.

"Do you recall the night the Zauberat heard my petition for its assistance?"

"Of course. It was only a few days ago."

"Do you remember it well?"

Uncertainty clouded his face. "I believe I do."

"Good. I warned of what would happen to anyone who touched Joseph. What were my words?"

Fear showed on his face, replacing the uncertainty. "I ... I don't know."

Agatha nodded. "I thought maybe you didn't. What I said was 'Anyone who touches my husband will burn slowly and from the inside.' And it's time for the reckoning."

Agatha holstered the handgun she was still holding. Then she placed both hands in front of her. She summoned vast amounts of energy and focused it toward the Warden. There was no visible flame, but the effect was immediate.

The Warden yelled, "No! Stop! Please stop!" His words devolved into screams. Piercing, primal, and unforgettable. He slumped backward to the ground, his legs still contorting under him. Still, he cried out in an unhuman sound.

She already regretted this course. But it would be worse to stop now. She must finish what she had begun.

The blood that had collected at his wounds bubbled and boiled. No more noise came from the Warden. The room smelled of cooking meat. It was almost unbearable. Bile rose in her throat. She had to get out of here. She stepped over the Warden and spit on his naked torso as she reached out for the door handle in front of her. The spit sizzled where it landed. She shuddered and pulled the door open.

A voice on the other side beckoned with a taunting lilt, "Agatha. Oh, Agatha."

CHAPTER 38

AGATHA

AGATHA FOLLOWED the sound of the voice. It came from a room that opened up to the right of the corridor. Her heartbeat accelerated. She paused to take a few deep breaths and collect herself. She pulled out her ponytail holder, shook out her hair, and put it back up.

Rounding the corner, Agatha took in the room all at once. To her right, Vulcan sat in a throne made of volcanic rock. Looking as smug as ever. To the left of him sat a prison cell with a boy in it. Thomas.

Her breath caught in her throat.

Thomas. He was okay.

"Mommy!" He jumped to the front of the cell.

"Hey, baby boy. How are you?"

"Okay. Did you come to get me?"

"I sure did, baby. But I'm gonna have to talk to Vulcan about that. He may not be ready to let you come with me yet."

"Are you going to kill him? I told him you were."

Agatha looked to Vulcan, who took in the interaction with a most amused expression.

"That's not a very nice thing to say. And it's a little more complicated than that."

"He wasn't being very nice to me either. He broke my room because he got mad." Thomas pointed to the top bars of this cell that were still somewhat concave. Thomas turned to his captor. "Tell her what you did."

Vulcan shrugged. "He was trying my patience. I may have lost my temper."

"He's six. He spends two-thirds of his life testing people's patience. What did you think would happen when you kept him penned up for a week?"

Thomas continued his tattling. "And he said he would kill me like he killed my friend."

"What friend?" Agatha asked.

"Kleron. He's a pegasus. He hit him with a hammer."

Vulcan's jaw set. Agatha suspected he was tiring of this. Good. It's time that he was uncomfortable.

"Are they all dead?" Agatha asked him.

"All of them," Vulcan answered without remorse. "They were useless. Just as he seems to be." Vulcan tilted his head to the side and raised an eyebrow. "Maybe we can make this a family affair? Get rid of you all and save myself some trouble."

Agatha stepped further into the room. "You're welcome to try. But I think you'll find me a bit more troublesome than most of your victims."

Vulcan stood up at the challenge. "I'm counting on it. But I'd be remiss if I didn't first offer to allow you to join me. If you're here, I suspect I need a new right hand. Care to tell me what happened to Titus?"

"Oberhaupt happened to him. I expect his vertebrae are mostly a powder now after the blow he took."

"Oberhaupt." Vulcan shook his head. "I should have known better than to trust the Warden on that front. I will have a word with him about that."

"Not unless you're planning to visit your pal Orcus, you're not." Agatha gestured with her head in the direction that she'd come from. "What's left of the Warden is a smoking heap on the other side of that door."

"I wondered at who was making those awful noises. It's just as well. He was rather tiresome. Now back to my offer."

"Oh, I just assumed you were intuitive enough to infer my response."

"I'd rather hear it from the horse's mouth."

Agatha drew, aimed, and fired her pistol, putting three rounds in the center of Vulcan's chest. Thomas' eyes grew wide. But Agatha knew this was an entirely fruitless exercise, however cathartic it was in the moment.

Vulcan looked down in annoyance. "So what's your plan, Agatha?"

"Inflict as much pain as I can before ..."

Vulcan taunted her. "Before what, Agatha?"

"I know how this ends. My only chance was to find Thomas when you weren't here. That didn't happen. So I'll prolong the inevitable as long as possible and deal you as much pain as I can manage in the meantime."

"You can't imagine my disappointment. I had just been telling Thomas here how I was hoping you'd be a worthy opponent. But it turns out, you're just a pest. No more harmful than a mosquito."

"I don't know. Malaria has killed a lot of folks."

"I don't think you have that kind of time."

Agatha again raised the 9mm and methodically unloaded the six remaining rounds into Vulcan's torso. Every shot made him visibly more angry and did about as much damage as a pellet gun might to a human — penetrated the skin and drew blood, but little else. She had been hoping for more of an effect, but she'd drawn blood. That wasn't nothing.

"My turn," said Vulcan. He took the forging hammer from his belt and began his approach.

Agatha circled in a wide arc to her left. She knew she was

backing herself into a corner. But she was also taking Thomas out of the line of fire. Once Vulcan had followed her arc and come between her and the exit, she put the heels of her hands together in front of her and pummeled Vulcan with a stream of fire.

The force of it caused him to take a step backward, but he recovered his balance. Vulcan mocked, "You can't fight fire with fire, Agatha. Volcanoes follow my commands. Conflagrations are my calling card."

There was a stench of burned hair. His beard was scorched. There were char marks on his skin. She was doing something, just not enough. He was trying to shake her confidence.

Vulcan shoved the haft of his hammer back into his belt. "On second thought, I want this to last. I want you to feel every blow. And I want your son to see it so he understands what true power is. So that he understands that your abilities are pittances. A gesture of power. They should serve only to remind you of the great forces that are beyond your capacity. Beyond your reach."

Agatha ran at him and jumped, carrying fire in her fists. She planned to shove the flame into the wounds she had created.

Vulcan intercepted her, landing a brutal punch to her torso that sent her flying backwards and sliding into the back wall. While she lay there stunned, Vulcan said, "I've had a change of heart. That's quite enough of this."

He retrieved his hammer again and stalked toward her.

Thomas was yelling, "Mommy! Get up, Mommy!"

Agatha pulled herself up off the floor, but she was wobbly and swaying. Seeing bursts of light between her and Vulcan. She watched almost as if from outside of herself as Vulcan raised his hammer high over his head. He grinned at her.

Thomas was rattling the bars of his cell when he screamed, "No!" It was not only fear, but a command. The cell burst apart, shrouding the room in bits of metal.

Vulcan covered his face to protect it from the debris. Then he looked down to see what had become of the steel cage. It had aged a thousand years. The remnants ground to dust when he stepped on them.

"Well, that was unexpected," he said.

"Run, Thomas! Run!"

Thomas ran to the room's entryway, where he stopped.

"Go, baby boy," Agatha urged.

She used the confusion of the moment to launch another attack. She ran forward and sprang upward as high as she could, turning her hands to flames. She would burn out his eyes. Vulcan closed them in time to avoid being blinded, but her hands burned into his eyelids.

As Agatha fell away, Vulcan struck her aside with his forearm. She spun while falling and landed on all fours.

She still had no hope of victory, but she would leave him tarnished before he killed her. And give Thomas time enough to get away.

CHAPTER 39
THOMAS

W HEN T HOMAS SAW Agatha land in a crouch, he thought she looked like Spider-Man. The girl Spider-Man from the new one. Gwen Stacy.

He understood that she could not kill Vulcan like he'd said she would. She had told him to run, but he wouldn't leave her.

Ning appeared beside him. "It's time to go, Thomas. I can show you the way."

"No. I'm not leaving."

Vulcan roared in frustration at Agatha's spryness.

Ning suggested, "I thought that might be your response. So in that case, let us get some help. Follow me, Thomas."

The boy watched as Ning loped down the corridor. He had never seen Ning hurry about anything before. He had to choose.

As Thomas ran to catch up to Ning, Vulcan laughed. "Even the boy has abandoned you now ..."

Thomas couldn't make out any words after that. He caught up to the panda before it entered the room at the end of the corridor.

"I don't want to go in there," Thomas said.

"You must."

Thomas whimpered.

Ning repeated himself, "If you want to save your mother, you must go in there. No time to waste."

The heap of bodies was still piled in the center of the room, moldering and reeking of decay. Thomas saw Kleron atop the mound. And Miles, the guard Vulcan had killed first, beside him.

"Raise them up, Thomas."

"I don't know how."

"It is just as you did with the mushrooms."

"I can't do it," Thomas said.

"You must. This is our only hope. Besides, you have not yet tried," Ning countered.

"There are too many."

"You needn't do them all at once. Start with the least dead one."

"They are all the same amount of dead, Ning."

"Then it does not matter where you start. But I cannot stress enough the urgency of the situation."

As if to emphasize the point, they heard Agatha yell out in pain from the other room.

Thomas positioned himself in front of the body of a small child. It was laying to the side of the mound, rather than on top of it. Thomas squatted down and held out his hands, as if warming them by a fire. After several seconds, the body moved. It pushed itself onto its hands and knees. And finally, upright. Only after it turned around could Thomas and Ning see the state of decay. The skin was gray and, in many places, torn. Its eyes were shriveled and having trouble staying in their sockets.

"Ning," Thomas whispered

"I'm sorry, Thomas. I didn't know. But we must finish."

Thomas nodded. He pointed to the animated corpse, then directed his finger to the room's entryway. It followed the signal and walked where instructed.

Thomas returned his attention to the heap. He started with

his hands in the same position as before. There was a movement of bodies atop the pile. Climbing down. Slithering. Taking flight. Slowly, Thomas raised his arms upward, palms toward the ceiling. He kept them raised there as if he were Moses, until his horde of corpses collected at the corridor and awaited his command.

Ning said, "This is quite the grim little army you've assembled."

"I just did what you said."

"Indeed."

They heard a thud and a roar from Vulcan.

"Hurry, Ning. Let's go."

Thomas took off running back to his mother. Ning and the corpses followed. When he careened around the corner, Agatha was on her back, crawling in his direction with her forearms and the heels of her feet. Vulcan was pursuing her with his hammer raised. He stopped short when he saw Thomas.

"Foolish boy. You shouldn't have come b—"

He never finished his sentence.

Agatha took the beat to roll onto her stomach. She pushed herself up and started toward the boy, but she too stopped.

The horde had gathered behind him.

"It is you," Vulcan said in wonder. "You are the fulfillment of the prophecy."

"What have you done?" Agatha asked.

"We came back for you, Mommy."

Thomas pointed toward Vulcan. The griffin, phoenix, and pegasus swarmed toward him. They struck at his face. The griffin tore at him with its beak and raked with its foreclaws, while the pegasus thrashed with its hooves. Vulcan swatted at them, knocking them back. Parts of their bodies tore away and shattered. But still they persisted.

At Thomas' signal, the children, Miles, and other mythical creatures launched their ground attacks. They amassed at

Vulcan's legs, amd began clawing, biting, and tearing. The hydra coiled around his left leg, striking with an endless barrage of fangs. Vulcan tore her off his leg and flung her at the wall. She struck it with an awful smacking sound, but as soon as she hit the ground she began crawling back toward the titanic foe.

It wasn't clear how much damage they were inflicting. Vulcan's defenses were taking a toll on the corpses, which were becoming increasingly disabled.

Agatha rejoined the fray, streaming fire at Vulcan. In a spark of inspiration, Agatha launched a flaming orb into the collection of bodies. It burst against the floor, lighting everything in its vicinity. Fire spread quickly among the corpses, who continued their assault.

The door clanged open behind Thomas. He turned to find a dark-skinned giant emerge through the doorway. The Mythicals followed on his heels. Thomas was amazed by what he was seeing. The grown-up forms of the monsters he was controlling. Their parents, he realized.

With a sweeping arc of his hammer, Vulcan cleared space around himself by sending his attackers sprawling across the room. With his left hand, he opened a portal.

Thomas raised up a hand to pause the attack. The fires had gone out among the corpses, whatever clothing or fur had adorned them having burned away. A dank smoke clouded the room.

"This is not finished, Thomas. You are the key to my ascension. And I will have you."

"Then why are you leaving? Are you chicken?"

Agatha said, "Thomas. No."

Thomas glanced quickly to Agatha, who's face was ashen. He looked back to Vulcan, who was scanning the room.

Vulcan scoffed, "You do not lack for courage, boy. We will do great things together. I shall return for you."

Vulcan strode through the portal and closed it.

The room was silent for a time. Thomas' army remained where he had suspended them. Agatha walked over to him and whispered in his ear, "Let them rest now, Thomas."

Thomas raised his arms above his shoulders with his palms toward the ground. He slowly lowered his arms to his side. As he did so, the children, Miles, and mythical creatures he commanded lay gently on the ground, as if preparing for a nap.

Thomas turned to his mother, who had squatted down behind him. He broke down into tears and buried his face in her shoulder. She wrapped her arms tightly around him.

"It's okay, baby. I'm here."

Thomas raised his head up to ask, "Where's Daddy?"

Tears sprung into her eyes. She squeezed him tighter, "Oh, baby boy."

CHAPTER 40
AGATHA

AGATHA COULD SEE in his eyes he knew the answer to his question. But he still needed to hear it. She had to say it.

"He's gone, baby."

He steeled himself, trying to be brave. Or what he thought was being brave. No boy should have to face what he had seen the last few days. Was still seeing.

"What happened to him?"

"He was trying to find you, but the chimera got him."

"The Warden," Thomas said.

"You know?"

The boy nodded.

"Yes, the Warden."

"Where is he?"

"I ... handled him," Agatha answered.

"Did you kill him?" Thomas asked.

"Yes."

"Okay."

"Give me a hug, buddy. I've missed you so much."

Agatha wrapped her arms around him and squeezed. While she hugged him, she noticed what else was happening around them.

Sounds of wailing arose throughout the room. The Mythicals located and began the process of mourning their young.

One by one, Oberhaupt delicately picked up the bodies of the twenty or so children and creatures whose parents were not present. He lined them up on the floor in the middle of the room. Then he set about identifying them against the offspring the Zauberat knew to be missing. He noted it on a pad that had been in his pocket.

Theiona nuzzled Kleron, then lay beside him and covered his body with one of her wings.

The hydra, Rhianu, slid two of its heads under the body of her young and carried it on her necks to the line that Oberhaupt had assembled. Gently, she lowered the body to the floor and took turns touching each of her noses to those of her dead child.

Agatha watched with amazement at the tenderness and affection the hydra displayed. She had innately assumed it to be more like the serpent it resembled, whose care for its offspring ceased after it hatched, a moment as touching as anything else she saw.

Ekhidna the orthrus found his pup and began bathing her, licking the wounds and scorch marks. The pup had the gangly legs and oversized feet of an animal who would have outgrown her parents. When the task was complete, Ekhidna picked up his pup by the nape and the tail, and placed her alongside the hydra. He then stepped back and stood shoulder to shoulder with Rhianu as the others tended to their young.

When Theiona stood, she summoned Oberhaupt to assist her. He knelt down and scooped up the foal with both arms, delivering it to its place beside the orthrus.

It took Agatha back to the night this all began. At least, the night it began for her family. Until Joseph had encountered the pegasus being kidnapped in their driveway, she had protected him from all of this. Just a regular family living a normal life in

Birmingham. And now? Joseph was gone, and Vulcan was going to pursue them to the ends of the earth.

Thomas no longer had the luxury of living a normal life. She had to prepare him for what was coming. But there would be time for that. For now, she needed to stay here, in this moment.

Jahaeris carried itself with a different demeanor than the others. Agatha didn't know how old the phoenix was, but if they lived a thousand years as believed, it would have seen many atrocities in its lifetime. Agatha took Thomas by the hand and walked over to Jahaeris, who was preening the feathers of its murdered offspring.

"May I?"

Jahaeris nodded.

Agatha squatted down to pick up the magnificent creature with its scarlet and gold wings. She laid it beside Kleron. With this done, Jahaeris retreated to the assembly of Mythicals.

Only the griffin remained. Its young had fared worse than the others in the conflict. Its savage attacks against Vulcan had resulted in its mutilation. Oberhaupt assembled the remains in his enormous hands and delivered them to the end of the line.

Oberhaupt walked over to stand beside Agatha. When she called his name, he looked down to her.

"Joseph."

He nodded.

Agatha knelt down to Thomas. "Buddy, we need to go get your daddy. Either you and I can stay here, or we can go with Oberhaupt to bring him back here."

"I want to go."

She grabbed the boy's hand. "Okay, come on."

They followed Oberhaupt into the corridor and to the doorway to their left. He pushed the door open. It bumped against and concealed most of the Warden's corpse. From there, they entered the labyrinth.

Agatha and Oberhaupt retraced their steps back to the room

in which Joseph and Titus lay where they had fallen. Agatha was glad she had covered Joseph. She wouldn't have wanted Thomas to see the mangled body.

Thomas laid down against Joseph and wept. It was a bitter sight for Agatha. She turned away, wishing she could do something. This was a wound that could only heal in time and was certain to leave terrible scars.

After a few minutes, Thomas sat up. He said to Agatha, "I could bring him back." It was more a question than a statement.

Agatha sat down, pulled him into her lap, and wrapped her arms around the boy. She rested her face on his head. "No, baby, you can't. What you can do is amazing. But his spirit has left. What makes him your daddy is gone now. We just have to remember him in our hearts."

"Okay." Thomas pulled out of the embrace and stood up. "I'm ready now."

Agatha stood beside him and asked Oberhaupt, "Can you get Joseph?"

The giant had been standing across the room, giving them space. He passed the body of Titus and asked, "What about him?"

"Leave him. Let him rot."

Oberhaupt nodded and sidled up to Joseph. He squatted down and cradled the body. Agatha took Thomas by the hand, and they walked out of the room ahead of him. Agatha slowed her pace so that the giant walked beside her.

"I thought there would be more — I don't know — resistance," she said.

"Oh, there was plenty. Many fled. Many others, I..." he glanced toward Thomas, who looked back at him, "dispatched with."

"I see."

"Those who ran will get their comeuppance. I expect we'll

have an easier time now getting the Gevalti back in order. And it seems we have an open seat on the Zauberat as well."

They retraced their steps back to the great room where everyone was congregated. The room was quiet and solemn. Oberhaupt deposited Joseph beside the others and returned to where Agatha was standing.

Theiona approached and said, "We will need wood for the pyres."

"Y'all are okay with that?" Agatha asked.

"It is what we must do."

"I agree. I think it's the best option."

"I'll be right back," Oberhaupt said. "There is some wood we can use."

In three trips, Oberhaupt returned with a half dozen desks and tables. He arranged them side-by-side. Then he and Agatha took the dead from the floor and placed them alongside each other on the desks and tables. After they'd placed the last lone child on a desk, they returned to the entryway, where the rest of the group had assembled and watched the transfer.

Agatha knew what must come next. She was both ready to be done with it and in no hurry to do it.

"This does seem rather unceremonious," the griffin observed.

There was a muttering of agreement. But no one introduced any ideas to resolve it.

Thomas stepped forward and walked up to the last of the bodies that Agatha and the giant had laid in their final resting places. He stood at the child's head as if deciding what to do.

Thomas cupped his hands together, and when he opened them a plant was sprouting from his palms. Leaves unfolded themselves from the stalks. Buds appeared and bloomed into lavender-colored sweet alyssum flowers that cascaded over his hands.

There was a murmur of wonder from the congregants. He

reached up and placed the flowers on the child's chest. Then moved to the next one. Thomas did the same miracle for a dozen bodies, alternating among lavender, pink, and white, before coming to Kleron. He touched his forehead to the pegasus and rubbed his muzzle.

Agatha's eyes glistened. She looked to Theiona, who looked back at her and held her gaze. Agatha moved over to stand close beside her. The chief steward of the forest leaned against her in a manner that Theiona would have been too proud to have tolerated before. Whatever bond of kindness and compassion had developed between their children had extended to themselves.

Thomas moved on to the hydra and down the line until he reached his father. The boy's shoulders had already begun to sag from the effort of what he was doing now, in combination with what he had already done.

As he stood beside Joseph, Thomas dropped his head and sobbed. He did not hide it. The unfettered mourning of a child whose loss was unbearable. For Agatha, watching this was more intolerable than her own loss.

She started toward the boy, but Theiona called her name softly, "Agatha. The boy needs room to grieve. Allow him to have it. We are in no hurry here."

Agatha's heart broke more with every tear he shed.

Thomas gathered himself after several minutes of weeping. He kissed his daddy on the side of the face, then stepped back and cupped his hands together. He opened them to reveal a dozen stalks springing up and transforming into white trillium flowers. He placed them gently on the jumpsuit that covered Joseph's chest and returned to Agatha's side.

She knelt down and hugged him tight. "It's perfect, baby. Thank you. Do you understand what I have to do next?"

"I think so."

"It's how we care for those who have passed on."

The boy nodded.

Agatha stepped forward and took a deep breath. She directed her hands toward the desk and table immediately in front of her, pouring a conflagration at their bases. She spread her arms outward to light the rest of the furniture. She focused her energy on making the inferno as hot as possible so it would incinerate everything. Once the pyres were well and truly burning of their own accord, she stepped back beside Thomas and draped her arm over him. He reached up to hold on to her hand.

The remaining clothing, fur, and feathers burned away. The flowers singed, curled up, and turned to ash. Smoke rose upward and crawled along the ceiling toward the ventilation shafts.

Once the fire burned down, the group began shuffling their feet, preparing to leave. Jahaeris said, "It is not yet time."

The group stilled itself again and waited.

A shape emerged from the embers. A head and wings made of flame burst upward. As the phoenix distanced itself from the fire and cooled, the flames morphed into feathers and solidified into a body.

Agatha's breath caught in her throat. The transformation was extraordinary.

The risen phoenix landed in front of Jahaeris, who placed her head on that of her offspring. "Now it is time for us to depart."

CHAPTER 41
AGATHA

AGATHA LOOKED TO HER MOTHER, seated on her left. "I can't believe you already had a bag packed when we got there."

Gertrude nodded. "When I considered all the potential outcomes, there were very few that would have had me staying in Birmingham. And with you and Thomas leaving, there's nothing there for me anymore."

Nothing but memories, Agatha thought. And so many of them were heartbreaking.

"Do you know what to do when we get there?" Agatha asked.

"Once we land, we'll get a car and drive south to Hornberg. We have people there."

"But I mean, do you know specifically?"

Gertrude looked at her with a smirk. "Agatha, this is going to be one of those figure-it-out-as-we-go things. I know you like to have a plan. But this is not that. So you're just going to have to get as comfortable as you can with that."

"Mother knows best and all that?"

"More like — you're right that it's safer for y'all to leave for a time. But that means you can't tell anyone where you're going or that you're coming. So there is going to be a fair bit of fluidity in our arrangements. We know what our next twelve hours look like, and that has to be good enough for now."

Agatha knew the truth of what she was hearing. But she didn't care for the uncertainty.

"He's such a sweet boy, Agatha. I'm so happy to finally know him."

"He's just seen so much. And *done* so much. You've never seen anything like the things he can do."

Gertrude nodded.

"I don't know if he can be the same after that."

"We will see. Children retake their natural shape pretty well. They're like rubber that way."

Agatha looked out the window and listened to the din of the crowds in the terminal. Planes on the tarmac taking people to and from family. She was with all that remained of her family. All but Elle, anyway. Their plane would take her to ... uncertainty. The unknown and unfamiliar. But also hope. If she dared have any.

Thomas popped his head up. "Have I ever been on an airplane before?"

"No. This is your first time. Are you scared?"

"Huh-uh. Should I be?"

Agatha shook her head. "There's no reason to be. But if you are, it's okay."

"What's it like?"

"It's loud at first when they rev the engines up for takeoff. Then the plane goes really fast on the runway and lifts up into the sky."

"That's cool," he said.

Agatha leaned in closer to him. "Can I tell you a secret?"

He covered his smile with his hand and tilted his head toward her.

"I'm scared of flying."

He turned to look directly at her. His eyes showing his

surprise at the revelation. "I didn't think you were scared of anything."

Agatha reached and tousled his hair. "Everybody is scared of something, buddy."

He took a minute to process this before asking, "Where are we going?"

"Home, baby. We're going home."

Thomas looked confused. "We just were home before we picked up…"

"No, we left the house. This was never home. We were always strangers here. You've just never known anything different."

He didn't look any less confused now, but he had another question. "What should I call her?"

Agatha smiled. The boy had never had a grandparent before. "Does anything came to mind that you want to call her? Like something you've heard your friends call their grandparents?"

Thomas shook his head.

"Can I give you an idea?"

"Okay, I guess so."

"Where we are going, many kids will call their grandmother Oma. What do you think of that?"

"Sounds kind of funny. But I like it." With that decided, he put his headphones back on and re-immersed himself in his tablet.

She looked from the boy to the monitor at the gate.

Frankfurt. 11:30. On time.

AUTHOR'S NOTE

This isn't the first novel I thought I would write. It's not the first novel I've tried to write. Nor the second. But sometimes the muse is working behind the scenes, aligning things just right so that you'll be ready when the time comes.

Three of the chapters in this book were inspired by real life situations. And while I wrote them down as they transpired, it didn't occur to me until the third one that I could write a novel that featured these events. That was at the end of August 2020. By early December, I had finished my first draft of *Vulcan Rising*.

In early January 2020 (before the world went sideways here in the United States), my five year old, Jack, started calling for me in the middle of the night. I looked at the clock and saw that it was 3:40am. With only an hour and twenty minutes left until my alarm was set to go off, I knew that my good sleep was pretty much done for.

I went up to his room and tried to coax him back to sleep. But when he told me that he couldn't sleep because he didn't want to be alone anymore, I felt really bad for him and laid down beside him.

But in that little bed with only a minimum of covers made

available to me, my mind started racing. And I came up with the scene where Thomas finds Ning in his bed and dismisses Joseph to return to his own.

A couple of weeks later, I had a really strange dream. As far back as I can remember, I've always been a vivid dreamer. For a time during my 20s, I wrote down my dreams. But that seemed to somehow magnify their intensity and creepiness, so I stopped. Then the dreams returned to their baseline weirdness levels.

More recently, I've started writing down dreams that are particularly interesting and stick with me. I've started letting my dreams fuel my fiction writing, rather than let them dissipate into the ether.

In late January, I had a dream that was graphic and surreal. I remembered every detail — three men were kidnapping a pegasus colt, and I stopped them in my driveway and shot one of them; then I had to return the mythical creature to its mother.

I had an inkling the dream could be the inciting incident for a much bigger story. But what I had in mind then was a much different story than what *Vulcan Rising* became.

Fast forward seven months to August 2020. Sometimes you have weird interactions with your kids. It seems like their brains are working overtime all the time. Not infrequently, those conversations lead to story ideas. So when that happens, I try to run as far and fast as I can with it.

One morning, Jack came down from his room and snuggled up right beside me on the couch. He was unusually somber and his responses to my conversation prompts were monosyllabic and noncommittal. His demeanor caused my mind to wander, thinking about its potential causes. One of which was whether he thought he'd seen something in the stairwell. Perhaps, he had. Whatever it was, it probably wasn't a chimera. But who's to say for sure.

Here's hoping things stay at least moderately weird for the foreseeable future.

January 3, 2021

ABOUT THE AUTHOR

Vulcan Rising is the debut novel for J. W. Judge, who lives in Birmingham, Alabama, also known as The Magic City. In his day job, J. W. is a lawyer, practicing civil defense litigation.

If you enjoyed *Vulcan Rising*, sign up for his newsletter for information about the second book in *The Zauberi Chronicles* trilogy: *Walls Ascending*. You can also follow him on social media for updates, developments, and news about other projects.

And if you'd like to reach out to him by email, please do so at jwj@jwjudge.com

CPSIA information can be obtained
at www.ICGtesting.com
Printed in the USA
LVHW081730110521
687116LV00019B/521/J